BLACK FISH

Sam Llewellyn is one of Britain's favourite sea writers. A native of the Isles of Scilly, he is a lifelong sailor. His columns appear in yachting magazines in Britain and America, and his books have been translated into fifte[illegible]

FIC Llewe

Llewellyn, S.
Black fish.

MAY 11

PRICE: $19.95 (3559/he)

Some other books by the same author

DEAD RECKONING
BLOOD ORANGE
CLAWHAMMER
DEADEYE
DEATH ROLL
THE IRON HOTEL
MAELSTROM
RIPTIDE
THE SHADOW IN THE SANDS
HELL BAY
THE SEA GARDEN
THE MALPAS LEGACY

Non-fiction

THE WORST JOURNEY IN THE MIDLANDS
THE MINIMUM BOAT

For children

EYE OF THE CANNON
PIG IN THE MIDDLE
THE WELL BETWEEN THE WORLDS – LYONESSE 1
DARKSOLSTICE – LYONESSE 2

BLACK FISH

Sam Llewellyn

SHERIDAN
HOUSE

This edition published 2011
by Sheridan House Inc.
145 Palisade Street
Dobbs Ferry, NY 10522
www.sheridanhouse.com

Copyright © 2010 by Sam Llewellyn

All rights reserved. No part of this book may be reproduced, stored in a retrieval system, or transmitted in any form or by any means, electronic, mechanical, photocopying, recording, or otherwise, without the prior permission in writing of Sheridan House.

This is a fictional work and all characters are drawn from the author's imagination. Any resemblances or similarities to persons either living or dead are entirely coincidental.

A CIP catalog record for this book is available from the Library of Congress, Washington, DC.

ISBN 978-1-57409-311-7

Cover design by Garold West
Printed in the United States of America

for Garlinda, Bertie, Dave & Tim

1

It was all going so well.

Solent City lay across the horizon to the north. To the south was the Victorian clutter of Cowes and the pepperpot towers of the Royal Yacht Squadron. When I looked over my shoulder, the army were twenty-five yards of nice blue sea astern. Their foredeck man was standing in the nose of the boat, grasping the pulpit bars like a gorilla in the zoo. A cross gorilla. He was cross because the man by the mast was shouting at him. The man by the mast was cross because he was being shouted at by the man on the helm. The man on the helm was cross because he could not get a sailful of breeze, because the police had put themselves in the way. The police being me, and my mainsheet man, and my tactician, and the other five guys stumping round the deck of the Sigma trying not to smirk.

I saw the army helmsman glance up at his mainsail. I saw him say something to his mainsheet man. I saw him ease the helm down, trying to get out of our wind-shadow so he could sneak away and make a dash for the line, a mere two cables ahead now. He was a nice guy, the army helmsman, a sergeant with a medal. I was a police inspector. He had got his medal by being brave. I had become an inspector by being a nuisance.

'Follow him down to cover,' said the tactician, a detective constable from Poole CID.

I was already following, making a smooth curve in the nice blue sea, echoing the curve the army was making twenty-five yards behind me and on the right. From the corner of my eye I saw the speed pick up.

'He's going to tack,' said the tactician.

The army's boom was well out over the boat's starboard side now. He was edging up on us. 'Never,' I said.

The tactician had been in the navy before he had been a policeman. 'Pongoes,' he said.

'Going,' said the mainsheet man. 'Going, going. Gone. Bastard.'

This cursing was partly down to the fact that I had put the helm up, and we had crash-tacked to cover. But mostly it was because the army man on the weather deck had not got out of the way of the boom. I saw it fly over. I saw it take him in the midriff. I saw him describe an arc in the air and hit the water. And I said, 'Trim!' spinning the wheel through my hands so we went round in a big curve, gybed, came head to wind, and arrived alongside the man in the water, everything flapping, so two beefy constables could put their arms over the side and haul him in through the guardwires.

'Welcome aboard,' I said. He spluttered at me and looked angry. 'We'll put you back if you like,' I said. He grinned then, and shook his head, and thanked us. Meanwhile the mainsheet man had hauled in his mainsheet, and the genoa winch jingled, and we slid up alongside the army and gave them their man back, though judging by the expressions on their faces they were not all that pleased to see him. Then we powered away for the line, which we crossed two full minutes ahead. Goodness, we felt smug.

And we felt smugger later on the lawn sloping down to the water, watching an elderly woman in a hat and white gloves making a speech. 'This year's Alban Cup for match racing goes to the police,' she said. Dazzling smile. I stepped forward and took the cup. 'Good luck in the Olympics,' she said.

I bowed and mumbled something about teamwork and shuffled back into the crowd. Most of whom I did not know; but I did not care, because they knew me, bright hope of detection and sailing. I commiserated sportingly with the army skipper, and drank three glasses of champagne double quick. Then I noticed a tall blonde woman smiling at me over the top of the crowd with more than sociable warmth, and thought, hello, and started towards her.

And it was downhill from there on in.

So when all this really begins, three years later, I am a yacht broker. I know what you are thinking. Yacht. Blue cocktails, white cushions, property developer in saloon. Yacht is a big, important word, and it smells of money. But when we are talking about what I do, the word with the big message is not yacht, but broker, as in broke.

So welcome to my sophisticated hi-tech office in the wheelhouse of my luxury tugboat tied up alongside the Fish Quay at Achnabuie, with its folding chairs nicked from the village hall, its state-of-the-art Murphy ashtray (slightly melted), and its army surplus desk with second-hand Dell. Over there is the desk of my large, loyal and very attractive assistant Maureen Cameron, useful to her on the rare days she turns up to work. As she often points out, the tug is cold and damp, and there is very little work to do, and she gets paid very little for doing it, so she might as well stay in her nice warm house, so she usually does. Sometimes I get the feeling that she would like me in the house with her. I think about it from time to time, but somehow I have not yet found the right moment to ask.

Beyond the wheelhouse windows the glorious Achnabuie Riviera stretches away: a scatter of moorings, thirteen boats covered with Bradshaw tarpaulins sagging under puddles of rain, a couple of derelicts filling with water and midge larvae, and a chalet park visited in high summer by masochists from Leicestershire.

It is not high summer now, or even low summer. Autumn is coming, and this is Scotland, so it is raining. Still, the yard is full of life and movement. That is because it is only small, and Georgie Strother is big enough to fill up a much bigger space than this as he comes stamping through the puddles on the quay. Perhaps he has popped over for a chat about the weather. But the expression on his face suggests otherwise. I experience a slight hollowing of the stomach. There is stuff in my dealings with Georgie that causes me uneasiness. I rise to leave.

Too late.

The door opened. A trawler-galley smell came in, with notes of whisky and grease and a long finish of smuggled Bensons. 'How's tricks?' I said, and waited for him to tell me. But he didn't. Instead, he came over to the table behind which I was sitting, grasped one end of it in each hand, and hurled it through the wheelhouse window and into the sea.

I do not necessarily mind people throwing my desk out of the window. But I think it is nice that if they do wish to express themselves in this manner they open the window first.

I moved away from the blast of rain and midges, and incidentally from Georgie, who was large and violent enough to do my blood pressure no good. I said, 'Am I to assume that you are not here to bring me a nice fish?'

'What do you think?' said Georgie.

We ex-policemen are pretty acute, and a yacht broker is nothing without intuition. 'I think there is a problem,' I said. 'Are you going to tell me what it is?'

'There is no fish,' said Georgie. 'I do not give fish to feckin' arses who steal my boat. Even if I have got fish, which with a stolen boat I will not have, will I? Because how would I get fish without a boat?'

Once Georgie gets going like this he can carry on all day. So I said, 'Get to the point.'

Georgie's eye settled on the computer, and his fingers flexed, and I could see that he planned to send it after the desk. This was not good. In the mind of that computer, Gavin Chance Marine inhabited sunkissed harbours full of glossy fibreglass, not midge-gnawed swamps paved with dry rot. It was important that this idea should exist somewhere, even if it was only on a rusty hard disk. So I was very keen to keep this computer on my desk where it could dream its dreams and help my customers dream theirs.

'You know what the point is,' he said.

'I do not,' I said.

'Someone stole the boat your partner sold me.'

My heart commenced sinking like an express lift.

'And,' said Georgie, ploughing the old furrow, 'I need it back, so I can go fishing in it.'

I could see he was going to start again. 'So tell the police,' I said.

Here Georgie's face became even grimmer. 'I hate the polis,' he said. 'Besides, I haven't the papers for the boat, so they won't believe me. You used to be a polis yourself. You find it.'

There was a pause, during which I stirred bits of broken window with my toe. Georgie was right about my past in law enforcement. But this did not make me want to go looking for his boat, which I had sold him fair and square except for the lack of papers, which were to follow, the boat having arrived in the brokerage through my partner Johnny Bonneville-Clark . . .

Here the sinking of the heart accelerated.

'I will break your fecking arms,' he said.

'The police would not like that,' I said. Georgie was under the impression that I still had a splendid circle of chums in the Service, and I did not really want to tell him that this was not the case.

He stood there breathing like a bull with asthma, and I thought I had fixed him. Then he said, 'Well, what's gone is gone,' and squinted at me out of his little black eyes. 'At least I'm insured, eh?'

My heart slammed into the base of the shaft. 'Yes,' I said, using someone else's lips. 'Certainly.' I wagged the cranium. 'But it won't do your no-claims bonus any good.'

'Or yours,' he said. 'Aye, if you won't help me look, I'll just have to go to the insurance.' His eyes strayed to the computer again, and his salami fingers flexed.

'All right,' I said. 'If I go looking, what's in it for me? Time's money, you know.'

'It takes a good long time for arms to mend,' said Wee Georgie, and left.

I watched his hulking shoulders barge through the rain and midges. I shouted, 'So when did you last see your boat?'

'Monday evening,' he said, not turning round. 'I tied her up by Drummie. I told your partner.' He climbed into the cab of his Dodge Ram, emitted a cloud of black smoke, and was gone.

I sat down and took some deep breaths. On the plus side of the account, it was nice that Georgie had not thrown my computer into the harbour. The minus side was bigger. Georgie had paid a nice big premium for his boat insurance, of which I was entitled as broker to 20 per cent. Unfortunately, the brokerage was not prospering, and this 20 per cent had not been enough to let me fulfil various obligations, in particular certain payments to my ex-wife's father. So I had temporarily borrowed Georgie's premium, without troubling him by letting him know this was the case. As an ex-police officer, I was aware that this was somewhat illegal. And as the possessor of two as yet unbroken arms, I was strongly committed to the notion of keeping them that way.

So I picked up the phone and got the emergency glaziers out from Oban. Then I looked up Drummie on Google Maps, and the computer crashed. So I got out the AA *Book of the Road* for 2004 and rang Maureen. She agreed to take care of the great volume of business that would doubtless transpire in my absence, and reckoned she had never heard of Drummie, and told me to hurry home. I told her I would, and was surprised at the warmth this generated. Then I applied Easy-Start to my N-reg Land Rover Discovery. And away I bounced up the cart track from Achnabuie Yacht Haven, reading the map on my knee.

As I turned on to the main road there was a howl in my ear, and I jammed on the anchors just in time to avoid being creamed by a truckload of langoustines on its way to Marseilles. I sighed a bit, and headed for Lochgilphead, and the winding road south.

The telephone rang.

Quick look in rear-view mirror. Couple of sheep. Pick up. Look at screen. MIRANDA. Press the green button. Say, 'Miranda?'

'Gavin.'

'How lovely to hear you.'

'Liar,' says Miranda. This was not verbal foreplay, or

anything like it. I used to be married to Miranda. It was likely that she would want to talk about the payment due her father after the one I had taken care of with Georgie's funds; but this, too, looked like being unavoidably delayed owing to operational difficulties. 'Now listen to me and don't hang up,' said Miranda. 'It's not about money.'

'All ears,' I said, relieved.

'It's Johnny,' said Miranda. 'Have you seen him?'

'No. Thank goodness.'

'Bastard. He's vanished.'

'He's always vanishing.'

There was a silence. This was undeniable. Eventually she said, 'Don't be unpleasant,' without much conviction. 'If you —'

I did not hear the rest. There was a car in the rear-view mirror, very dressy in a luminous Battenberg chequer and blue lights on the roof. The lights began winking, and the siren started. I turned the phone off and flung it into the far back in one balletic movement. The Disco juddered to a halt. Clump, clump alongside. And there was the face, up against the window, mouthing like a goldfish because the window is electric, broken. Open the door, dealing the constable a sharp blow on the kneecap. 'Sorry,' I said. 'Window's stuck. Just on my way to get it fixed.'

The officer's face did not move. He said, 'Were you using a mobile phone?'

'Me?' I said. 'It's against the law.'

He smiled. He said, 'Licence?'

I showed him. I knew what happened next. He said, 'Mr Chance. Where are you from?'

'Achnabuie.'

'And before that?'

'The South.'

His mouth turned down at the corners. 'Southampton?'

'That's right.'

He went through the licence, the MOT, the insurance. Then he said, 'And now will we look at the phone log?'

'If you want.'

'Or will we just write out the ticket?'

I said, 'Write the ticket.' Sixty quid for phone use while driving. Three points, making nine, leaving three to go before disqualification. But the first lot I had got well after the trouble started. So in only a year I would be back down to six points. By today's standards that was practically a lottery win.

The policeman wrote. He gave me the ticket. He said, 'I hate a bent copper.'

'Me too,' I said.

There are things you should know.

2

My name is Gavin Chance, and I am a son of the south coast.

In the case of many, this means mahogany tan, platinum credit card and powder-blue Mercedes. Not me. Certainly I learned to sail, but in the workaday Sea Scouts, not the glamorous Laser Worlds. This knowledge I used later to take girls to secluded beaches for the purposes of fornication, and still later to be eyed by Olympic selectors.

I learned seamanship by finding anchorages for my dad's Westerly Centaur in exactly the right amount of water to go aground for four torrid hours, walking the fine line between staying afloat and wrecking the boat. A night with a romantic fingernail of moon produced a spring tide that left me aground with Samantha Stead, daughter of Ricky Stead, a prominent figure in fruit machines and violence along the South Coast then and later. Ricky combined the temperament of a wolverine with the morals of an ayatollah. As Samantha lay naked in my arms on the banquette conversion, she said, 'My dad's goin' to kill you,' and wriggled in a not unpleasing manner.

I laughed heartily, and said, 'Only if you tell him.'

'I always tell him,' said Samantha.

'Why?'

'Because he's a bastard,' said Samantha, sucking my lower lip. 'Hey! What's happened to you?'

'Diabetic coma,' I said. But actually what had happened was fear, because I had remembered that Samantha's last boyfriend had turned up at the pub on crutches speaking in a new high voice, which he said he had got by falling off a ladder. And I suddenly suspected that he might not have been telling the whole truth.

Perhaps Samantha was why I joined the army. Or perhaps it was because I could not think of anything else to do. Anyway, I joined. I did some more sailing, which was when there began to be serious talk of the Olympics, though not from me. I had an interesting time creeping around Bosnia and elsewhere, and developed a talent for informally blowing things up, to the point where various people mentioned that I might like to apply for the Special Boat Service. But in the end I found I was not good enough at obeying orders I would not have given myself. So I left and joined the police. I spent the first nine years being very, very patient, and listening to people I worked with talking a language that never ceased to be strange, and acquiring a convenient reputation as a loose but useful cannon. By this time I was an inspector, and big in Solent City Police sailing. And there I was on that lawn in Cowes, being introduced to a tall blonde woman called Miranda Bonneville-Clark.

You did not have to be a great detective to spot Miranda. She was wearing a summer dress, a sapphire choker that went nicely with her eyes, and a pair of lizard-skin cowboy boots. She was talking to a big chap with a cold face and a short haircut, but I did not notice him. I just saw this dazzling woman smiling at me with the full million candlepower as I stood there tanned and victorious in my police fleece. Talking to her was like falling into a vat of champagne, and I loved it. I first guessed that the feeling might be mutual when she suggested we go into the rhododendrons and make love. Through a mist of pain, I heard myself saying that I did not do it on a first date, though what I really meant was, not with all these policemen watching.

The second date was different. And so was life from then on. She was beautiful and funny and warm, as long as she got her own way. We moved in together. My home life became very exciting. But things began to go badly at work. My bright-bad-boy reputation stopped doing me any good. Life got dull. When I was not interviewing mad people in old folks' homes I was sieving ditches for significant condoms. And there was a shortage of promotion. I mentioned this to Miranda. She said, 'Poor you. I was afraid of that.'

'Of what?'

'You know that man I was with the day we met?'

'Would I notice him with you there?'

'*Sweet*,' she said, with the princess smile. 'He was Bruce Wallace.'

'Oh,' I said, vaguely, because I was thinking about her breasts. Then I said, 'Assistant Chief Constable Bruce Wallace?'

'Correct.'

'Oh.' The old folks' homes became clear. So did the fingertip searches of septic tanks. 'You were his girlfriend?'

'Fiancée. I turned the ring round when I saw you. You were *soo* lovely.'

I should say that I am five foot eight, wide enough to look stocky, with big hands and feet. 'Irresistible,' I said.

'I've got this thing about policemen,' she said. 'Particularly you.'

'Hooray.'

She laughed. We laughed a lot. But when we had stopped, I felt the first inkling that things might not be quite right.

And then we decided to get married and she introduced me to her brother.

Enough about that. We are arriving in Drummie.

Drummie turned out to be a clutter of houses along the Clyde Relief Canal. This is a waterway someone built in the nineteenth century in the hope that ships would use it as a short cut to Glasgow. They did not, mainly because it had twelve locks in the space of two miles and ended where the money ran out, halfway up a hill. The canal banks were nose-to-tail with boats. There were a couple of motor-sailers with huge wheelhouses that to the practised eye said HOME COMPLETION – DO NOT INSURE. There were some hulks covered in gull-whitened tarpaulins, and a small fleet of fishing boats in various stages of decomposition. None of them, I noticed, was the boat I had sold Wee Georgie.

I knocked on the door of the first house. A woman opened it. She was wearing pearls and a skirt five years too tight for her, and her nails were polished blood red. 'Yes?' she said. The corners of her lipsticky mouth turned down as she clocked the Disco steaming like a green horse in the drizzle.

'I'm looking for the lock-keeper.'

She made a tutting noise. 'Are you going to tie up your boat here?'

'No.'

She seemed to like me a little better for this. At the bottom of her garden, an ash tree was growing out of the roof of a prawn trawler's wheelhouse. The trawler smelled as if it had been tied up six months ago with a full hold.

'His name's Nairn,' she said. 'If he's not in the house he'll be in the Queen's.' She made the tutting noise again.

The lock-keeper's house had a picket fence. A peeling sign nailed to it said VESSELS PASSING LOCK REPORT TO LOCK-KEEPER – BY ORDER. Nobody answered the door, so I walked up the locks to the Queen's. The beer garden had a fine view of veils of drizzle sweeping up the Clyde. The bar was a cave in whose shadows figures moved like fish. I put my elbow on the counter and said, 'Talisker, please. And a glass of water.'

The barmaid did her stuff. I put my elbows on the bar, sniffed the whisky, put it down and took a sip of the water, not because I am a connoisseur but because if I drink whisky I get pissed. I said, 'I'm looking for Mr Nairn.'

The shadows moved. One of them said, in a thick, schoolmasterly voice, 'I am he.'

I walked towards the voice. My eyes were getting used to the dark. He was hunched over a table with a couple of other men. 'Gavin Chance,' I said. 'I'm looking for a boat.'

'Many are,' said Nairn, and his companions made fatalistic noises. By the yellow glow that seeped through the glass bricks he had a sandy cowlick, a nose with a saddle of broken veins, and watery pale-brown eyes.

'A trawler,' I said. 'The *Sirius Gleaner*.'

The eyes blinked. The back of the hand smeared away the water that squeezed out. 'She's in the canal,' he said.

I sipped more water. 'Where?'

'Above lock two.'

'Show me.'

'It's raining.'

'There's a reward.'

The blink again. He said, 'If I show you, I get the reward?'

'You do.'

'And it is?'

'A percentage of the boat's value.'

He was up now, one arm in his coat, making stabs at the other armhole. We walked into the daylight, blinked, and looked at each other. Neither of us seemed particularly impressed by what he saw. 'Come far?' he said.

'South coast.' Which was true, in a way.

We climbed some stone steps and walked along the side of Lock 2. Water was leaking through the top gate with a steady roar. 'Make your head sore,' said Nairn, spitting into the basin. 'Boat's up there.' He pointed, not looking.

There was no boat. I said, 'Where?'

The freckled face turned. The eyebrows drew together. 'Oh,' said the voice, making a fairish stab at surprise. 'She's gone.'

'Two or three days ago,' I said. 'Apparently. You didn't see her go?'

'No,' said Nairn. A grey tongue went round the lips.

'You're the lock-keeper. How could that be?'

Nairn looked ill. I had seen the look when I had been a policeman. He was not going to talk, not conceivably. He knew he should not have played this the way he had. The drink had fogged his planning. Now he was going to keep his mouth shut. And the reason was that he was frightened. Of what?

Perhaps I could apply a little fear myself. 'Bollocks,' I said.

'What?'

'Nothing gets out of here without you knowing. There's a sign on your house.'

'Nobody reads it. Nothing did.'

I said, 'There are people who want to know where that boat has gone. Serious people.'

The mid-brown eyes settled on me in a way that made me think I was not having much effect. He said, 'Are you trying to threaten me?'

I went and stood a little too close to him. I said, 'Not trying. Doing it. Now stop telling porkies.'

'Oh, aye,' he said. A mobile phone came out of his pocket. He dialled fast: 999 is not a complicated number. Things had gone wrong, and would soon be wronger. I twitched the phone out of his hand and slung it in the basin. 'Hey!' he said. And he was reversing away, heading at a shambling run for the house by the bottom lock.

I watched him go. Excellent, I thought. The only man who could have helped you, and you have drowned his phone. But it is all right. He is a liar, and frightened, and he will not call the police. I turned my back on him and walked across to the house of the lady with the pearls.

She opened the door quickly enough for me to realise she had been watching. Her eyes were beady. 'Was he drunk?' she said.

'Not very,' I said, breathing on her so she could smell my intense sobriety. 'But I'm trying to find a boat, and he wouldn't tell me.'

'Him and his boats,' said the woman. 'He's no right to let out moorings, you know that? But he does, and he takes a fortune, a fortune. And there they are cluttering up the view, nasty rotten things.'

'Horrible,' I said. 'But one of them's gone. The *Sirius Gleaner*.'

'Really?' she said, in a voice that told me she was by no means a subscriber to *Ships Monthly*.

'A green boat,' I said. 'Tied up over there.'

'It went,' she said. 'First thing day before yesterday morning. I couldn't sleep. Worry, you know. I mean house values are not what they were, specially with these awful hulks parked all over the view. And I saw them going down the lock. One less, I thought. But there will always be more . . . '

'How did they get down the locks?'

'In the boat.'

'But did they have help?'

'Oh. Aye. I see. Yes, they had Jocky to, I don't know, make the locks work, whatever they do.'

'Jocky?'

'Lives down in the but-and-bens along the river. Front yard's covered in rubbish. You can't miss it.' She looked me up and down. 'I'm Jean Craigie, by the way. Would you like a cup of tea?'

She was actually quite attractive in a slightly antique way. I opened my mouth to say yes. Then I felt a sudden phantom pain in my arms, as if they were broken, and Wee Georgie's face blotted out hers. And I found myself outside the house, walking down the locks.

This gave me a bird's-eye view of the bottom lock. And there outside the lock-keeper's cottage was the blue-and-luminous chequer of a police car; and Mr Nairn, confiding in the uniformed driver.

I backed out of sight and walked quickly down towards the but-and-bens.

Jocky's rubbish was a useful landmark. I picked my way through the disused bedsteads and televisions to the front door, and banged on it hard until it opened.

Jocky was a seventy-year-old alcoholic of restricted growth. He stood in the doorway blearing at me from a fog of Cyprus sherry. 'Wha?' he said.

'Polis,' I said.

'Ine done nuffin.'

'Then you will be able to help us with our inquiries,' I said.

His eyes went up the street and down again. 'Come intae the hoose,' he said.

'No,' I said, because I could smell the house, and more important, I wanted the kind of quick answer only deep stress to his reputation would provide. 'You helped the *Sirius Gleaner* down the locks, right?'

'And?' he said.

'Who was on board?'

'Couple of boys,' said Jocky, demonstrating teeth yellow and black as a wasp's body.

'Aye,' I said, venturing into the vernacular. 'And where were they heading?'

'They didna exactly confide in me,' said Jocky, and his eyes travelled in a series of loops towards my belt. With extreme reluctance I drew forth a tenner. Jocky stuck out a trembling hand and vanished the banknote. 'I heard someone say Milford,' he said.

'Milford?'

But the door had slammed, and I heard the bolts go, bang, bang. So I pulled my coat collar up round my ears and went back to where I had parked the Disco. The police car was still outside Nairn's house, but there was no sign of the driver. The car started on the third attempt. I drove towards Glasgow until I saw a café, and went and drank a cup of tea and ate something called a bridie, and leafed through the AA *Book of the Road*, the Fugitive's Friend.

There were plenty of Milfords, none of them places you could get to in a fishing boat unless it had wheels on it. So I had another cup of tea and gazed at a map of Britain on the café wall and wondered if the grease would ever come off my teeth. And then thought: Milford Haven, and groaned.

Milford Haven is at the extreme bottom left-hand corner of Wales. It is a broad inlet much used by VLCCs and fishing boats, not to mention yachts. It is bloody miles from Achnabuie, and it would be a practically superhuman task to get the Disco all that way, and it was not definite that I would find the *Gleaner* when I got there, or that I would be able to do anything about it if I did. There was, however, a bright side. If southwest Wales was a long hike from Achnabuie, it was also a long way from Wee Georgie. Also, as far as I knew they did not have bridies in Wales.

So I climbed into the Disco, and left a message on my answering machine to tell Maureen where I was heading. And I drove to Milford Haven.

It took the best part of twelve hours, not counting stoppages for diesel, oil, oil and a bit more oil. But as the sun levered itself over the horizon and into the rain I was following the lane that snakes along the northern side of the inlet, past a grubby-looking oil refinery and into the wet grey streets of Milford Haven.

Milford Docks is a basin, with a lock that opens two hours before high water. It contained half a dozen fishing boats, but none of them was the *Sirius Gleaner*. I parked in the Tesco car park by the harbour and got out and walked twice round to stretch my legs. Then I climbed back into the Disco and settled down to watch. The rain cleared. The lock opened. A couple of yachts came in. I went to sleep.

The phone woke me. I groped around for it and pressed the green button without thinking. 'Well?' said the voice on the other end; a voice that sounded like one of the rock crushers from the Glensanda quarry by Fort William. The voice of Georgie, with a car engine howling behind it.

My arms began to ache like teeth. 'Well what?' I said.

'Have you found my fecking boat?' said Wee Georgie.

I opened my mouth to give vent to the excuses queuing behind my tonsils. The windscreen was foggy with breath. I wiped it away, seeking clarity. And there in front of me was the grey water of the basin, and a tug and a dredger alongside. Tied up alongside the dredger was a green fishing boat with streaks of rust on the white shelter deck. It was too far away for me to read the lettering on the bow. I did not need to. I knew this boat off by heart. It was the *Sirius Gleaner*, large as life. Inside closed lock gates.

'Your boat?' I said, with the quiet confidence of the true professional. 'I'm looking at her now.'

'I'm on my way,' said Wee Georgie, and the phone went *eeee.*

On his way where? I thought.

The phone went again. The voice on the other end was old and cold. It said, 'Chance?'

I let on that this was me.

'Maxwell,' said the voice. 'Have you sold my boat?'

I experienced a weary feeling. Captain Maxwell was a retired merchant skipper who was in the process of swallowing the anchor. I had his antique fibreglass ketch on a mooring at Achnabuie, and nobody had yet been to inspect it. But I said, 'Someone may come and view next week.' Well, it was always possible.

'Hurry it up,' said the Captain. 'I want the money.'

I expect I laughed weakly, because he grunted and rang off, and left me contemplating the *Sirius Gleaner.*

3

The *Sirius Gleaner* was pretty much your average old-school fishing boat. She had a wheelhouse and accommodation aft, and a big hatch forward, and a shelter deck for the protection of unfortunates working up in her nose. As fish became harder to find, someone had adapted her for their transport rather than their catching. She had hydraulic hatch covers, and a nice new derrick, and refrigeration gear to keep her ice cool. The trawl deck by her stern was just about redundant, and seemed to be doing service as a seagoing scrapyard. She was a bit of a mess, in fact. But that did not alter the fact that she was in need of recapture.

This was the time to surge into action. But a sleepless night followed by a three-hour nap in a driver's seat leaves a good deal of fog in the head, and it was not easy to work out exactly what action to surge into. There were difficulties with calling the police – no time to go into them now, but take it from me. On the plus side, the lock gates were shut, so the boat was not going anywhere. Then I saw the minus side walk out of the wheelhouse and go up the side of the dredger, heading for the quay.

There were two of them. One of them was the size of a large saloon car. The other was the size of a small saloon car. They went over the dredger in two strides each. I watched them round the quay and into the bar of the Lord Nelson. I did not recognise either of them. I sat there and wondered what to do.

After a while the fog in my head swirled a little, and I began to see the outlines of some quite unpleasant things. I got out of the Disco to see if air would do any good, and found myself walking towards the lock control box. 'What time's the next exit?' I said.

The man in the box looked down at me, and saw that I was dirty, unshaven, and in other respects similar to his regular customers. He said, 'Half an hour.'

I looked at my watch. It was noon. I said, 'I'll be through.' He nodded and smiled, kindly humouring the inexperienced. I walked back to the Disco and pulled a suit of oilskins out of the back and shoved my feet into the trousers, feeling deeply apprehensive. One step at a time, as they used to say at the Boscombe Chapter of AA.

So step by step I walked round the quay. Step by step I went down the iron ladder on to the dredger's deck, and picked my way round the elevators and mud pumps, and arrived at the rail. Here I paused, contemplating the deck of the *Sirius Gleaner*. It hummed gently. That would be the refrigeration units, which meant there was fish in the hold. This was odd. There had not been much time for fishing if they had worked round from the Clyde. And two men was a small crew.

As I finished this thought, I became aware that I had stepped onto the *Gleaner*'s deck, taking care to keep the wheelhouse between me and the bar windows of the Lord Nelson. I shivered, and felt something in my hand, and noticed it was the handle of the wheelhouse door. The handle turned in my hand. The door swung open. Then I was inside, inhaling the mingled perfumes of burned grease and antique fish. I ran my eye over the instruments. Plenty of diesel: they must have been on the fuel dock while I put in my three hours in the Disco.

The engine key was in its socket. I mean, who was going to steal a fishing boat with a crew of giants tied up inside a closed lock gate?

Me, apparently.

I put out my hand. I shoved the fuel cutoff all the way in. I twisted the key for a bit of preheat. Then I turned it clockwise, my eyes flicking nervously to the Lord Nelson's windows.

The engine turned over. There was a judder in the deck. A bloody great thundercloud of black smoke rolled out of the stack, shouting, *Look at me, I'm nicking your boat*. When I glanced across at the lock I could see that the gate was open. I picked up the VHF. Brazen. 'Milford Lock, *Sirius Gleaner*,' I said. 'I'm coming out.'

The VHF said ready when I was. I hoped they did not have a set in the Lord Nelson. I walked down the deck to the bow. It seemed about a mile long, and the nonchalance wore off halfway. I bent to undo the figure-eights on the cleat. I was unwinding the last one when I heard the clang of boots running on the kind of steel they make dredger's decks out of, and looked up just in time to see the light blotted out by a vast figure plummeting out of the sky, and went down under it with a bang, smacking my forehead against the deck. There were stars, and it hurt like hell. Something went round my throat and started to squeeze, and it became unpleasantly hard to breathe. And as the lights dimmed and the blood thundered in my ears I began to feel very frightened, thinking, goodbye to the people I liked, and Achnabuie and the tug and Maureen. It had not been much of a life —

The pressure on my throat eased, and a voice said, 'It's you?' and the weight came off me. And I knew by the smell of the breath that this was my esteemed client Wee Georgie Strother.

I sat there rubbing my throat. The bow line was off, and the *Gleaner*'s nose was wandering out into the harbour. I croaked, 'Stern line.' He gazed at me for a moment with his mouth hanging open. Then he scuttled aft down the boat, and I hobbled after him, squinting at the Lord Nelson.

No movement.

I engaged SLOW AHEAD. The *Gleaner* crept across the harbour and squeezed into the lock as the gate began to close. 'Cuttin' it a bit fine,' said the lock-keeper.

He had no idea.

Then we sat alongside, motoring gently against a breast spring, while I massaged my neck and watched the Lord Nelson side of the lock and the water drained teaspoonful by teaspoonful out of the sluices.

'What's your problem?' said Georgie. 'You look scared. What of, though? It's my boat. Maureen told me you were coming here. I wanted to take it back myself, is all.' He looked positively exhilarated. I could see that he had already forgotten who had found the boat, and who had got as far as casting off the bow line to bring it back to him. 'And now it's ho for lovely Scotia.'

I wanted to tell him the exact size of the men in the pub, but you need a windpipe to talk, and mine hurt too much, and anyway the gate was opening. I cast off the spring. Water boiled under the transom and we moved slowly ahead. A shadow fell across the lock. Two shadows; big, dark ones. I looked up. The Lord Nelson had lost a couple of its drinkers. They were standing by the lock, interfering with the shot of a tourist who was trying to get a picture of Our Brave Fishermen for his camera club. The big one had a shaved head and a little pointed chin. The smaller one had greasy shoulder-length hair that did not hide the jail-swallows tattooed under his left earlobe, and a face that looked as if it had collided with a truck, and wrecked it.

The wheelhouse window shot up. Georgie's head came out. 'That them?' he said.

'Ss,' I croaked.

'All right!' roared Georgie. 'You wankers! See you! If I clap eyes on anny of youse again you can call to your fecking whore mammies because you will be on the point of fecking death, right?'

The men did not answer; not with their voices, anyway. The big one gave me a smile he had been taught by a shark. The one with the jail tattoos moved his coat aside to scratch his barrel stomach. And my heart or an organ quite near it turned to a chunk of ice. For stuck in his belt was something that a combination of army in Bosnia and police training told me was the butt of a pistol. A target pistol; .22, small, but useful to people other than target shooters.

We were out of the lock and into the channel. I gave the men the finger and walked back to the wheelhouse on weakened knees. 'Well, that's that,' said Georgie, highly genial now. 'We found it, and we got it back.'

I was relieved enough not to argue with the plural. He was right. We had the boat back. Possession was nine points of the law, though nobody said out of how many. The *Gleaner*'s nose pointed at the far shore as she picked her way across the mud flats and into the channel. It was over.

No it wasn't. My car was still in the car park.

I pulled out the phone and the wallet and rang the AA. 'Breakdown,' I said, and gave them a story, and the registration number and location of the Disco. The sky had cleared, and the wind had dropped, and the houses of Milford lay sprawled over the hill. Someone was burning rubbish near Tesco's, the smoke a black column in the blue air. I waited for the woman on the other end.

'We've got someone there now,' she said. 'You're lucky.'

'I am, I am,' I said, full of geniality.

She seemed to be talking to someone. Then she came back on and read me the registration plate. 'Land Rover Discovery?' she said. 'You want it relayed to Achnabuie, Scotland?'

'That's it.'

'Our representatives inform me that the vehicle is not in a towable condition.'

'It's only fifteen years old, excellent condition for year.'

'Yes,' said the lady. 'But apparently it's on fire.'

Pause for the heart to sink. 'Ah,' I said. 'Thank you. Don't bother, then.' And rang off.

A parting shot.

Or perhaps an opening one.

Wee Georgie was steering. He looked as if he was thinking his own thoughts, if you could call them that.

I was angry. I was bloody furious. What was I supposed to do without a car? I said, 'You want to check your truck, too.'

'Our Davie drove it away. It was him drove it. Rally driver, is what our Davie wants to be. Great boy, our Davie —'

I nodded and did my best to smile and said, to change the subject, 'So have we got a load of fish?' Bastards. *Bastards.*

'Feels like it,' said Georgie, giving the wheel a twitch. 'She was empty when I left her in Drummie.' The Haven was shrinking astern, a sheet of water leading into the bristle of the loading piers and oil refinery cat crackers. Ireland was over the horizon ahead. 'Oh great, we're in the money and we're going hame.'

Achnabuie, then. Without a car. Perhaps I could borrow a

bicycle. And Gavin Chance Marine could surge back into the market, as long as I did not die of a heart attack or ride into a tree.

'But I'm a wee thought peckish,' said Georgie, leaning against the wheelhouse bulkhead, vast, filthy, every inch a captain. 'Check out what's in the galley and the hold, would you?'

What was in the galley were dirty plates in the sink and baked beans in the locker. I closed the locker, threw the plates out of the scuttle and undogged the waterproof doors into the hold. A blast of fishy chill rolled out at me as I walked in. The hold was paved with green plastic boxes nested in bins packed with ice. I pulled the lid off the nearest box. An eye looked up at me, set in a metal-grey head. I stuck in a hand, got my fingers into a set of gills and pulled out a four-pound cod. Its eyes were bright, the slime still on it. I took it up to the wheelhouse.

'Fresh fish,' said Georgie. 'Give it here.' He locked on the autopilot and vanished into the galley. I stood at the wheel and watched the seas run long white tongues up Skokholm's grim rocks beyond the starboard windows, and did some thinking.

The chart plotter screen said we were 312 miles from Achnabuie, 240 from Drummie. The *Gleaner*'s holds had been empty when Georgie had tied her up in Drummie. Two hundred and forty miles was a fair two-day run for her. The hiss of fish in hot fat came from the galley. I said, 'How long would it take to catch a holdful of fish?'

'Like this?' said Georgie. 'The rest of your fecking life.'

'Not eight hours, then.'

'No way. You want beans?'

'No salad?'

'Piss off.'

'Beans is fine.' But I was not thinking about beans. The police muscles in my mind were twitching.

Cod is difficult stuff. Everyone wants it, and there is hardly any left in the sea. This is true of most fish, of course, because fishermen have been very greedy for a very long time, and they have twisted the politicians' arms with great skill, claiming to be simple hunter-gatherers engaged in their traditional calling of voting in marginal constituencies. These simple hunter-gatherers now drive around the shallow seas in dirty great fish-hoovers armed with electronics that can determine the whereabouts, species and size of a ten-inch fish at a range of fifteen miles. The fish have for their part made no technical advances for several million years. So most of them have now been caught, and fishermen are feeling their absence, and the brilliant minds in Brussels have imposed on them a quota system. I seemed to remember hearing someone in Oban telling their whisky that all the EU cod quota was gone for the year. Which would mean that either the fish in the *Gleaner's* hold had been caught in the middle of the Atlantic, where no cod exist, or off Norway, which is a long way away and busily patrolled by efficient Norwegian Fisheries Protection boats. Or that it was black fish; which if you did not know means fish caught over quota, and very illegal indeed. This, my inner policeman told me, was the most likely explanation for our holdful of damn-near-flapping cod.

For there had been no time for the *Gleaner* to be fishing. So this was not a fishing trip, but a delivery. They had not gone into Milford Haven to land fish; the first thing a boat does when it goes alongside is to unload. They had gone in to refuel.

At this moment the chart plotter told me our heading was WNW, a course that would take us clear of Skokholm and the South Bishop, where we could turn right and point the nose towards Georgie's motherland. If the fish had been caught in Scotland and was on its way to Scotland, Milford seemed a longish detour for a refuelling stop.

I reached over and punched buttons on the chart plotter.

Once, charts were printed on paper. Nowadays the simple hunter-gatherers of the sea use chart plotters, which are flat screens in the wheelhouse. Thanks to the ancient earth magics of GPS and radar and AIS, your plotter will tell you where you are, where you are going and when you will get there, and where the other boats are and where they are going, so you do not run into them in the middle of the sea. All this stuff is linked to an autopilot, which will steer you from waypoint to waypoint.

I pushed buttons below the screen. And there were the waypoints, slung round the hammerhead of the Mull of Galloway and down the Irish Sea; no hanging around fishing there. To the south of our present position were more waypoints, dotted round St Govan's Head, Caldey, Worms Head, and in to Swansea.

I thumbed the GPS log. The spidery black figures told me that the Swansea waypoints had not been used.

I knocked off the autopilot and tossed the wheel's spokes through my hands. Skokholm shifted from the corner of my eye to behind my head, and the long pitch of the deck turned into a roll as the Atlantic swell moved from the nose to the beam. I settled the bow somewhere to the west of St Govan's Head, and thumbed the AUTO button. The autopilot clicked back on. 'Hey!' said my esteemed skipper, appearing from the galley with a plastic plate in each hand. 'Whattha feck?'

'Altering course,' I said. 'We're expected in Swansea.'

'What?'

'The hold is full of nice cod,' I said. 'It is going to Swansea, and it is certainly black fish.' I took the plate out of his hands and put it on what in the days of paper charts had been the chart table, and ate. 'And when we get to Swansea we will find out who those people were who stole your boat and turn them in. You go to jail for black fish. And you pay bloody enormous fines.'

Georgie ate for some time with his mouth open. Finally, he said, 'There's money in it.'

'But you want your boat back free and clear. If you don't want to turn them in, you can use them as a lever.'

'Lever?'

'You catch them delivering and receiving black fish. You say, we'll forget about it if they'll be nice to you.'

He frowned. He did not look convinced. 'What about the money?'

'You'll have the boat.'

He scowled, sticking out his lower lip. 'Aye,' he said. 'Well. We'll see.' And he went back to eating.

Which was about as good as I was going to get, for the moment.

I did not like people who landed over-quota fish. I liked there to be living things in the sea, not dead things on slabs. Furthermore, and perhaps more important, I was fed up with people thinking I was a clown. A good black-fish collar would be very impressive to my former colleagues on the Force.

But Georgie wanted money. He would take some persuading to turn the bad guys in. What we needed was paperwork. I started poking around. There was a shelf of almanacs and regulations books. 'All these yours?' I said.

'Aye,' said Georgie, peering through his eyebrows like an ox in a thicket. 'No. No' that yin.' He jabbed his fork at a school copybook, strewing beans across the plotter's screen. 'Never seen that yin before. It's not mine. Never seen it in my life. Not —'

I tuned him out and picked the book out of the shelf. It was nearly new. The first page bore a few notes in the crabbed, laborious hand of someone who used his hands for fighting, not writing. *Sirius Gleaner*, Drummie, it said. Pickup instructions, then. From whom? Then it said '0100 Loch M.' Wherever that was. Melfort? Maddy? There were thousands of them. And after that: '0800, South Quay, Merc truck, MOX, Mr Greely.' There was a date and a mobile number. The date was tomorrow. It was all coming together nicely. 'And that's all the paperwork there is that's not yours?'

'Aye.'

'Fish has a paper trail,' I said. 'Any fish without paper is black fish. And they'll take the boat, and they'll fine you so you have to sell your house, and they'll put you in jail.'

He did not even look up. He said, 'There will be money.'

And there, of course, he was right.

I sat and ate. And after a while I found I was frowning.

My trained senses told me that tomorrow, the *Gleaner* was due to land a cargo of black fish in Swansea. But this act of detection was not what was causing me to frown. Nor was it puzzlement, or the headache consequent on having my head slammed into a metal deck. Mostly, it was a very odd idea.

Greely was a name I had heard before in connection with fish. But not black fish. Oh, no. Just precisely exactly the opposite.

It could not be true.

4

Miranda Bonneville-Clark might have had a thing for policemen, but she had underestimated the hardship of being married to one. There were the hours, and the fact that her husband's mind was usually somewhere dark and dirty and not on her. And there were other difficulties, mostly her brother Johnny.

Miranda was a good gardener, with a homesteader's instincts under her glossy exterior. She persuaded me to dig a vegetable garden and plant things in it. We did it together, because we were in love. She probably would have been happier on a thousand acres; but part of our togetherness consisted of running a cottage economy, far from criminals and their detection. I did cabbages and parsnips. She did herbaceous borders and drifts of rambler roses. It was in the waft of these that we sat one Saturday morning in June, at the height of our mutual affection. She was pouring coffee into my cup from a china pot and looking at me with her bright blue eyes, and laughing at my jokes in a way that was a constant reminder that we had shared a bed last night, and that there was no reason that we should not climb back in again after breakfast.

'Hmm,' she said, as if struck by a thought.

'Hmm what?' I said, feeling close and personal.

'I was thinking we should do something about Johnny.'

It is a measure of our closeness at the time that I did not instantly get in my car and drive off. Johnny Bonneville-Clark had been to Eton, where despite the best efforts of his teachers he had acquired the notion that he was one of the Masters of the Universe. As one of these, he had allowed himself to fail most exams and wriggle into a low-grade university. Here he had neglected to learn anything useful, like welding, making furniture or painting walls. But he had found plenty of drugs, and discovered that he could make a living selling them. A man of his talents could hardly fail to fall under the influence of his own merchandise. He had ended up in hospital, partly because of an overdose and partly because of large sums outstanding on his account with a family of Streatham junkies' sundriesmen.

On receiving the telephone call, his parents paid his debts and shipped him off to the Priory, where his devoted sister wrote him weekly letters telling him that he was a fool, but that even so there was no need to listen to those vulgar people in the therapy group. When he emerged blinking and chain-smoking into the light, Miranda was waiting at the door in her Alfa convertible. She had immediately driven him to their parents' house, which was also near Lymington, and had been built by Georgians with a sense of their own importance almost as strong as the Bonneville-Clarks'. Here he had allowed himself to be persuaded to take up residence in his old wing, and had continued his glittering career.

As a man-about-the-Solent, Johnny rapidly developed a name for brightness and rapidity. In particular, he loved to entertain the crews of visiting racing yachts to games of poker. He took on their rakish Transatlanticisms, became heavily tanned, and acquired a new personality in the seafaring mould. His sister and his parents were relieved, seeing this as evidence that he was getting plenty of fresh air and exercise. Actually, it merely masked the fact that gambling had taken over from drugs as a compulsion. But it had, and to the bookies he did go. Naturally, this led to the pawnbrokers, where one evening he pledged his daddy's de Lamerie candlesticks with a view to using the proceeds to resolve an unsuccessful speculation involving Manchester United and the UEFA cup. I found out about this because on seeing the candlesticks the pawnbroker had called me. The reasn he had called me was that I held an annual lunch party for the pawnbrokers of Solent City and their wives. This was by no means police procedure; but there was plenty to drink, and a jovial atmosphere, and it meant that when anything in the burglary line was going down, one of them rang me instead of me having to ring all of them.

Anyway, that night when I rolled in there was Johnny, greenish and blinking in the striplights. 'Gavin!' he cried, thrilled. 'Will you tell this chap it's all right?'

'No,' I said. 'Now get off home, or you're nicked.'

He got. And his bookie did not get paid. So Johnny got a slapping from some nasty hard people. And the marks of it were plain for his mummy to see, and his mummy talked to his sister, and they both sighed and bailed him out again, and decided something must be done.

And there we were on the lawn, and Miranda was pouring the coffee and stroking my knee with her beautiful and persuasive fingers.

'Darling?' she said.

'Yes, darling?' I said.

'Johnny needs help,' she said. 'He's so sort of *aimless*.'

I nodded and smiled, always a good policy when faced with a topic in which you are not interested.

'So I've been talking to Mummy and Daddy, and Johnny's really excited too.'

My nod a little shallower. My smile less sincere.

'Because we all agree that you're it.'

Electricity shot through me. 'I'm what?'

'The ideal partner.' The eyes smiled forget-me-not blue. The mouth was red and wide, made fuller by the slight pout of a sister's worry about her little brother. 'Daddy says he'll help you set up a brokerage. You can sell yachts. You can insure them, too. He'll give you some fabulous contacts.'

I had opened my mouth to say no way, over my dead body; but I shut it again. Miranda's father was a big shot in Lloyd's, the mighty insurance market. Lloyd's had provided him with plenty of millions. And to tell the truth I quite wanted some millions of my own. Not to put too fine a point on it, visions of sugar plums danced in my head. And Miranda could see them hop.

'He just needs someone firm,' she said. 'I don't know anyone firmer than you.' Lowered eyes. Blush, almost. In a moment of clarity, I reminded myself that I was a policeman, twelve years' service. And I was being invited to become the partner of a lowlife hooray in a yacht brokerage, yacht broking being an enterprise in which large sums of other people's cash notoriously lie around waiting to be scooped up by the morally toxic. I opened my mouth to tell her not on her life. My phone rang. 'Dear boy,' said a voice, smooth and rich and deep, the voice of a world-girdling sailor, or someone who wanted to sound like one.

'Johnny,' I said. 'We were just talking about you.'

'I bet,' he said. 'And I wanted to say it's a very good idea. And if you don't want to come in, just remember that you were an accessory after the fact in my getting away with nicking those candlesticks.'

'But I wasn't.'

'Oh, yes you were. The pawnbroker saw you with me.'

'But you put them back.'

'No I didn't,' said Johnny. 'I mean I took them in later. He knew I was okay. He could see we knew each other.'

'Wait,' I said. I had the pawnbroker on speed dial. I called him and said, 'The candlesticks.'

'Hello, Inspector,' said the pawnbroker. 'Lovely pair.'

'They are strongly moody.'

'But he was your brother-in-law,' said the pawnbroker.

'Still is,' I said. 'Bring 'em back.'

'But the money.'

'Do you want to bring your wife to lunch this Christmas?'

Silence.

'Unless those candlesticks come back to their owner,' I said, 'I will tell your wife about Carole.' Carole was his secretary, and he had been into more than her filing cabinet.

'Not many policemen about like you, Inspector,' said the pawnbroker.

'Lucky for you.'

'I'll put them in a taxi.'

I switched the call to Johnny. I said, 'First money you make goes to the pawnbroker. He won't charge you interest.' I rang off.

'So you'll have him?' said Miranda.

'I suppose,' I said, in the voice of a condemned man accepting the hearty breakfast. 'But no bad behaviour.'

She smiled. 'He's so stupid,' she said. 'He needs someone like you.'

But somehow the magic had gone out of the morning.

Naturally, the bad behaviour started almost immediately. Johnny set up an office in Lymington, and another in Pulteney, and had lots of long lunches with insurance men in the City. And I became a yacht broker as well as a policeman. So between flogging boats and watching Johnny and detecting crime, I spent very little time at home. Which was when Miranda met Tony Greely.

The first I knew about it was when she took me out to dinner at a restaurant called Greely's in The Docks, which is what they called the new waterfront development on the old tannery site in Pulteney. The joint was new, done in pale wood, unvarnished. The tables were rickety and the chairs had a spindly American look. The air smelled slightly of fish. In the smell sat the local MP and some footballers and their wives from the apartments overlooking the basin.

Miranda threaded sinuously through the tables to a vast silver coffin. The top of the coffin was transparent. Under it lay the corpses of fish. A cod had a little green label on its gills. 'Line-caught, south Norwegian inshore fishery,' it said. The bass was line-caught, too, and came from Poole, and they had vegan farmed salmon and hand-smoked squid and sail-dredged Fal oysters.

'Tony is deeply committed to ocean conservation,' said Miranda, as if she was reciting something she had learned by heart. She looked round, her face actually shining with excitement. An overreaction to mere fish, I thought. I have never been very good at keeping such thoughts to myself. So I said so.

Her teeth came together with a click and she gave me a pitying smile and drew breath to tell me I had erred. But before she could speak, the kitchen door opened and a man came out. He had dark ringlets and a blue canvas slop and red canvas trousers tucked into black hip-waders. He looked like a suburban great-aunt's idea of a Handsome Fisherman, and my idea of a bit of a ponce.

'Tony!' cried Miranda. 'Tony Greely, this is Gavin Chance.'

Tony brought the focus of his glittering eyes in from infinite horizons. She kissed him on the mouth, and made him sit down at our table, and told me what an amazing guy he was while she looked deep into his eyes. I began to realise I was not part of the conversation. 'He is the owner of this restaurant,' she said. 'And eight —'

'Twelve,' said Tony, showing her his good side.

'— twelve others. It's a chain. But it's not like, oh, McDonalds, you know. Explain, Tony.'

Tony smiled the smile of someone truly delighted with himself. 'Fish is a primal food,' he said. 'I had a shack on the beach in Alaska. We cooked fish we caught in water we could see, using gear we had built. That's how it's meant to be. So I thought: why not do it in Britain? Strike a blow for sustainability. Fish sourced from healthy populations. Simply but beautifully cooked. House wines chosen with consummate care, perfect for the fish.'

I found I was feeling slightly nauseous; the fish, perhaps, or the house wine, which was a low-rent Chilean sauvignon at twenty-five quid a pop. I said, 'You have terrific eyes.'

He batted his lashes. 'Thank you,' he said, with what he probably thought was simple dignity.

'I mean eyesight,' I said. 'To be able to see all the way to Norway. Like the label on the cod says.'

His smile froze. 'Well, er,' he said. '*Bon appétit.*' And he stumped back into the kitchen, waders and all.

Miranda was looking at me stonily, as in granite, not sapphires. 'That was unnecessary,' she said. She was right, but it did not help.

I drank twelve quid's worth of wine in a single gulp. 'Ponce,' I said.

'He is a visionary,' she said. 'You are a policeman.'

The wine began to work. 'And yacht broker,' I said. 'And insurance agent. And babysitter.'

Miranda's smile came back, in order to reveal the sharpness of her teeth. She said, 'You are in the presence of someone who seriously cares about the future of the oceans, and all you can do is be negative.'

'I beg your pardon,' I said, and got up. 'I think I'd better go.'

'Yes,' she said, still smiling. 'And stay gone. Because you should know that I am sleeping with Tony and he is sensitive and marvellous in a way that you just can't imagine.' And I could tell that that was it, the way you can tell a smack in the teeth is a smack in the teeth.

So I got a fiercely expensive taxi back to the cottage, and packed all my stuff into a remarkably small case, and left. I had nowhere to go, and I couldn't face a bed and breakfast. In the end I moved on board a Rival 38 that the brokerage was listing for an owner who was spending his holidays in Barbados.

Not that I spent much time on the boat, or even worrying about Miranda and her new friend. Because I was in the middle of dealing with a man from London who was supplying heroin to a man from Bournemouth. They were nasty violent people and I did not like either of them, but they were very hard to bust, because London handed over his bag to Bournemouth by leaving it on the top of a bus. As London got off by the Winter Gardens, Bournemouth got on and collected the gear. To pay, Bournemouth put a big bet on with London, which Bournemouth always lost. The problem was catching both of them at once.

So I spent a lot of time on buses, thinking. And I eventually managed to replace the bag of smack with a bag of icing sugar while it was unattended on the bus. This upset Bournemouth, because it led him to conclude London was trying to rip him off. And later that same day Bournemouth stuck a knife into London, and was caught because I was close at hand, taking an interest. Not classic police work, of course. But things went quiet after the funeral, and Bournemouth was going to be an old man by the time he got out of prison.

But you do not need to hear about this now. Because we were on our way to see a Mr Greely, who was waiting for delivery of a load of fish that had been illegally trawled off the bottom of the sea. He was probably the wrong Mr Greely. Nonetheless, I was treasuring the tiny possibility that these raped and plundered specimens were destined to wear labels that said they had been caught by disabled Inuit using sustainable whalebone jigs.

So far, my life had been a progression from frying pan into fire. Now that was going to stop, I thought, as Worms Head receded astern and we rode the flume of the Bristol Channel tide down to Oxwich Bay. From now on, I was back with the good guys. But I was not going to hand the case over to the law straight away. I was going to find out where the fish was going.

It was late when we hammered across Swansea Bay. The channel markers were winking like ruby eyes as we slid down the black channel. The city lights reached out for us, blue-white and dirty orange. Last time I had come into Swansea I had been a yachtsman, and we had turned left, into the marina. This time we turned right, into the lock that took us up into the King's Dock, a working harbour whose only visible part was a grey steel shed floodlit white. Georgie yawned, farted, and said, 'I'm turning in.'

I said, 'What if those guys from Milford are there to meet us?'

'Wake me, and I'll kill them,' said Georgie. His free hand was behind his back. He brought it round, and I saw that clasped in the leg-of-mutton fist was a four-foot adjustable spanner, the business end sharpened on both sides until it closely resembled a battle-axe. 'I did it on the engine room grindstone,' he said. 'They won't like it.'

He was probably right. I did not like it myself, and it was on the same side as me.

'Money,' said Georgie. 'You have to fight for it.'

I gave him a perhaps unconvincing smile and took myself to one of the stinking bunks abaft the wheelhouse. I put a copy of the *Daily Sport* between my head and the brownish pillow, and lay with a nipple in each ear trying to work out how to run away. Then of course I went to sleep.

It was the engine starting that woke me; that and Georgie's voice, then a strange voice, answering. Raising my head carefully, I peered out of the scuttle.

The quay was half dark. The shed loomed grey and forbidding in the rain. In front of the shed an eighteen-wheel reefer panted fumes. There was a driver and another man, both of them talking to Georgie. Neither of them was Tony Greely. I got the impression that Georgie felt outnumbered.

Policemanlike urges stirred in me. Time for evidence-gathering. There was no lettering on the truck. I wrote down its registration mark, which did indeed start with MOX, as per notebook. Then I stuffed myself into oilskins, pulled a woolly hat well down over my eyes, and walked on to the quay.

The lorry driver glanced at me, saw a fisherman and paid no attention. I said, 'Start loading.'

Georgie gave me what was almost a grateful look and said, 'Aye.'

I said, 'Got a forklift?'

The lorry driver said, 'Yes.'

'Let's see your paperwork.'

The lorry driver said, 'What paperwork?'

I said, in tones of stressed forbearance, 'The paperwork.'

The lorry driver looked tired, but not hard. He felt in his pocket, and his mate closed in, so I knew the driver was about to come out with the money.

Out came the envelope. I was planning detective work, not bribe-taking. But I noticed that I was holding out my hand, and taking the envelope, and sliding it into my breast pocket. 'Go and help the deckie,' I said to the driver's mate.

The hatch cover was off. The derrick was going. A pallet of green fishboxes came up out of the hold, swung on to the quay, settled. Each box bore the word GREENREAP on its side. I watched the forklift drive round the end of the truck and start for the pallet. The wad of money was a nice weight in the pocket —

'Good morning, sir,' said a voice.

I turned round and nearly jumped out of my boots. A policeman was standing there, high-vis jacket brilliant in the lights. I said, 'Good morning,' hoping he could not hear my heart clattering around my ribcage.

'What,' said the policeman, 'is in those boxes?'

He flicked his torch at them. They lay there, piled six high on the pallet. For a split second, I considered telling him that this was an investigation in progress. But he would laugh in my face. 'Fish,' I said.

'Let's have a look, shall we?'

The forklift had stopped. The driver was watching as we walked across. 'Whole catch going to a restaurant chain.

Greely's. We're just doing what we're paid to do. That right?' I said to the driver.

'Greely's. Yeah,' said the driver, his face silvery with rain, or it might have been terror. And despite the extreme peril I felt a surge of astonishment and triumph. It was the right Greely.

Fool.

The policeman put on a glove. He popped the lid of the box nearest him. 'Fish,' he said. 'And what kind of fish is that?'

The triumph ceased. I was part of a fair-sized crime. I felt sick. I peered into the box. And felt suddenly better.

The yellow light-disc shone on silver scales. The fish's tail was small, the wrist where it joined the body slender, the muscles undeveloped because it had never had to fend for itself off Greenland, or hammer its way up the rapids of the Shiel. 'Salmon,' I said. 'Farmed salmon.'

'Because that's what Greenreap does,' said Georgie, coming alongside. 'Farm salmon. You can see their farms everywhere north of Kintyre. They're a big outfit. In salmon farming, that is —'

'Yes,' said the policeman, staunching the flow. And he went back to his car, and got in, and rolled away.

I helped load the fish in a warm glow of relief. He had not asked for ID or paperwork. He had looked in the top layer of innocent farmed fish that masked the seriously valuable and seriously criminal fish underneath. And he had extracted from the lorry driver the sacred name of Greely. My investigation could continue.

The glow lasted for the next ten minutes as we finished loading the boxes into the lorry, and the lorry drove off into the South Walian drizzle. 'Well,' I said as it vanished. 'All's well that ends well, eh?'

'Aye,' said Georgie. He was looking out of the wheelhouse window. A police car was drawing out from behind a shed. As it pulled away, I saw the pale oval of the driver's face. It was the policeman who had inspected the fish. I said, 'He must have stuck around to watch.'

Georgie said, 'I hate a polis. I do.'

I shrugged my shoulders at him. The police are a representative cross-section of people. Some are nice. Some are nasty. And some are as evil as the dirtbags they are meant to be chasing.

But I did allow myself to wonder why this officer had felt it necessary to oversee the loading of a lorry with what he thought was farmed salmon, but not to make any further inquiries. Too good to be true, really.

If I had thought about it harder, I might have noticed that things which seem too good to be true usually are not true. But I noticed nothing except that we had shifted some fish and I had the drop on Tony Greely. And a pocketful of his money.

Not very clever, really.

5

The lock opened. The *Sirius Gleaner* slid in. The lock closed. The water went up. The lock opened. The *Gleaner* slid out into Swansea Bay and hammered southwest at eleven knots. I counted the money from the envelope on to the chart table. There was a lot of it.

My phone rang. I did not recognise the number. But that is usual for secondhand car salesmen and yacht brokers. 'Gavin Chance,' I said.

'Good morning, Mr Chance,' said a voice that was neither cheerful nor uncheerful. 'We met earlier.'

'I don't think —'

'Uniform branch,' said the voice, and it perfectly matched the policeman who had inspected the fish. 'Calling on behalf of someone who wants his boat back.'

'Boat,' I said, through lips that had gone suddenly numb. It would be better if Georgie did not overhear even one side of this conversation. I opened the wheelhouse door and went out into the blast of rain and wind, swallowing hard to summon enough saliva for speech.

'You there?' said the voice.

I noticed that one of the wheelhouse windows was sliding down, and moved away under the shelter deck. 'Yes,' I croaked. 'How can I help?'

'By returning the boat to its owner,' said the flat police voice.

'I am happy to say that the vessel has now been restored to Mr George Strother, who is indeed its owner,' I managed to say. 'After, I may say, a complex and exhaustive investigation.' I tried to sound definite, but the base of my stomach was somewhere around my steel-capped boots.

'Yes, sir,' said the voice. 'I am aware of the background. I think you should make further inquiries about this. It will then become apparent that the boat you are in was not yours to sell. Think of this as an informal approach.'

I said, 'So arrest me.'

'It may come to that,' he said.

'Hold on a minute,' I said, a chink of light dawning. 'Are you freelancing?'

There was a long, cold pause. Then the policeman said, 'There are worse things than being arrested,' and rang off.

And I sat and watched a rivet on the shelter deck and tried to work out which way was up.

He was freelancing all right. I was not sure I wanted to find out who for. But it seemed reasonable to assume that they were the people who had lit my car. I had the feeling that the solid ground on which I had been standing was turning to quicksand. It was a feeling recognisable to many who had dealings with Johnny Bonneville-Clark.

I had the little brute on speed dial. Most people he worked with did. When you were involved with Johnny Bonny there were always questions that needed answering.

But Johnny knew this, so his phone went straight to answer: *Hi*, said the mellow voice. *Terribly sorry, can't take your call. Do leave a message.* Which would naturally be a waste of breath.

I said, 'We need to talk about who sold the *Sirius Gleaner*,' and hung up. Then I went back to the wheelhouse.

The *Gleaner* was barging into a steep grey sea. Over to starboard the low hump of the Gower crawled by, hellish slow because we were pushing tide. The money was gone from the table. 'Hey!' I said. 'What about me?'

Georgie smashed a wave with the boat's bow. The water sailed down the deck and slammed into the wheelhouse windows. 'Aye,' he said, and pulled some notes from the breast pocket of his boiler suit. Five notes; red ones. He looked at them, put one of them back, handed the rest over to me.

'Two hundred quid?' I said, shocked. 'I found your boat. They torched my car.'

'Aye, well, that's it,' said Georgie. He seemed to have got over his diffidence on the quay at Swansea. This was Captain Strother, pocket full of money, master of his destiny. He squinted at me, perhaps to see how pissed off I was, and doubled a large fist on the console in front of him. I scowled, and beat a retreat. But later, in the privacy of the *Gleaner*'s filthy head, I inspected the wad of notes I had taken the precaution of scraping off the top of the pile. Five grand. Enough for some kind of wheels, and to pay the premium on Georgie's insurance.

For unless I was much mistaken, more bad things were about to happen to the *Sirius Gleaner*, and for the sake of my arms I very much wanted Georgie to have peace of mind.

And of course there was the wickedness of landing black fish, and the need to make a case against Tony Greely. Though that seemed less important than staying alive.

We plugged on westward, turned right round St Govan's

Head, and took the tide north. That afternoon we passed the gannet-iced pudding of Grassholm, sank the white blink of the Bishops and Clerks over the starboard quarter, and launched ourselves across the grey void of Cardigan Bay. Somewhere between Arklow and Holyhead my phone rang.

It was a woman. More than a woman: Miranda. She said, 'Is that you?'

I said it was, and asked what I could do for her.

'You rang Johnny,' she said. 'I was ringing in case you were trying to bully him.'

'I wasn't,' I said. 'I wanted to know where he found a boat we sold.'

'Which one?'

'You wouldn't know.'

'He told me a lot of things.'

I drew a breath. That was Miranda, always wanting to know everyone's business. I said, 'A fishing boat called the *Sirius Gleaner*.'

'Oh, *that* one,' she said. 'Didn't he tell you? Some partner you are. He won it.'

Beyond the wheelhouse window a gannet dived on a fish. It stood as much chance of coming up pink as of this being true. 'He never won anything,' I said.

'I know. But I can feel your anger. It's not helpful. The game was poker.'

'So this loser sailed the boat on to the table.'

'Don't be pathetic,' snapped Miranda. 'Of course he didn't. He gave Johnny an IOU for sixty thousand pounds. And he didn't pay. So Johnny went and took the boat.'

I said, in a weary voice, 'Took.'

'You wouldn't have, would you?'

'No,' I said. 'It's illegal.'

'For God's sake don't be such a policeman,' she said. 'He

showed some guts for once. Oh, by the way. Daddy says, where's his repayment for your startup loan?'

I said, 'When Johnny pays me my share of the commission on the boat he stole I will pass it right on. By the way, have you seen Tony Greely lately?'

'Mind your own business,' she said. The phone went dead.

I shoved it in my pocket and inhaled sea air. It was cool and clean and no help at all. Johnny's winnings were his own business, but it would be hard to prove that they included the *Gleaner*. The man he had nicked the boat off obviously shared that view. And now I needed an insurance premium for Wee Georgie, and a loan repayment for Sir Edward Bonneville-Clark. Let alone the fact that Georgie and I had pocketed a fat envelope whose rightful owner was the proprietor of the fish we had landed at Swansea, who was presumably the man from whom Johnny had nicked the boat, whose hired hands were in the habit of carrying guns.

Oh, dear.

I breathed more air, and hoped I would see Johnny soon, so he could explain all this to me before I killed him.

The wind was over the tide, and the water looked cold and grey, and the Isle of Man was crouching somewhere over the horizon off the starboard bow. 'Teatime!' shouted Georgie, in high spirits with his pocketful of money and his boat back, poor simple gorilla. What the hell was I going to do?

First things first.

I rang the underwriters at Lloyd's and arranged insurance for the *Gleaner*, said insurance to lapse if premium not paid in cash within four days. Which once again brought to mind that between us, Georgie and I had pocketed sixteen thousand quid of someone else's money.

Still, at Achnabuie you were hard to find. I cooked us some eggs and sausages, and went and crashed out for a few hours.

When I awoke, things seemed slightly clearer. I walked into the wheelhouse and said, 'I'm going into the hold.'

Georgie shrugged, and resumed his inspection of the dark sea ahead. Personally, I wished to see that nobody else had left anything lying around below, like a few tons of undersize lobsters or a couple of magnetic mines. So I walked into the hold – not so cold now, the refrigeration plant off to save fuel – and pulled the big switch.

Cold bluish light flooded the metal room, forty feet by sixteen, with a roller-table down one side and a slush of old ice in the bins along the other, frozen into a sort of rubble piled up against the sides where it had been slung after the unloading at Swansea. It was a normal, tidy sort of fishing boat hold: not ancient, not derelict. A useful boat, really, the *Gleaner*, a good service boat for a fish farm. A credit to the vendor, always assuming it was the vendor's to sell. No lobsters. No mines.

I walked down to the back end and undogged the door that gave on to the trawl deck and flashed my torch around. This was the platform where they had emptied the cod end of the net when the *Gleaner* had been trawling. But she was not trawling any more, so nobody came down here, and there was nothing except rust, and broken boxes, and old net. At the forward end, the deck rose to the railings aft of the wheelhouse. At the aft end was the churn of the wake and the black sea.

It was a nasty place, dark and cold and derelict, and it caused a deepening of my gloom. I pulled out my phone. It was not worth ringing Johnny's home number, because his sister would be hovering over the phone like a polar bear over a seal-hole. There was another number, a mobile he used for work. Since he never did any work, it was never worth ringing it. But I selected it anyway, and pressed the button.

The trawl deck was noisy with the hammer of the diesel. I

walked over to the side to get away from the noise, and leaned against the port rail. There was rubbish heaped up against it, bags, part of an old trawl, weed and dead crabs, an odd starfish pale in the flashlight's beam. A telephone was ringing somewhere. It seemed to be coming from the pile of old bags. The voicemail message kicked in. The ringing stopped.

I rang again. So did the phone. The voicemail kicked in. The ringing stopped.

I had a foot on the iron ladder up to the wheelhouse. I paused. So did my heart. I taught myself how to breathe again, and bent to look at the pale starfish.

It was not a starfish. It was a human hand. The hand was attached to an arm. An arm in a sleeve of navy-blue cloth.

I crouched by the hand and gave it a heave. It was stone cold. The bags slithered. They were not bags. They were a body. A human body, wearing what seemed to be a blazer and jeans.

I did not want to touch it. I started up the steps. Then I went back and bent and was nearly sick all over the corpse, which for some reason seemed as if it would be a very terrible thing. But I took a deep breath and grabbed it by a cold wrist and dragged it into the white glare of the hold, and turned it over so I could see the face. Though I already knew whose face it was.

It was the property of my ex-brother-in-law and partner in brokerage Johnny Bonneville-Clark.

Had been.

The body seemed hard to drag. In the light, I could see why. There was a boat anchor tied to the right leg.

The lights were roaring into my head, and the engine was trying to hammer the top off my skull. I turned, very deliberately, and walked a careful-drunk walk back to the wheelhouse.

Georgie was where I had left him, gazing out of the window at the marching pyramids of sea. Off the starboard bow was a green light over a white; someone trawling, and beyond him the white blink of the Mull of Kintyre. I opened my mouth to tell Georgie he had a corpse in his hold.

He said, 'I'm knackered. You've got her,' and stumped off to the cabin. And I closed my mouth, and looked at the little boat-shape on the plotter, and the line projecting its course inside the Mull and into Campbeltown. I felt numb and dazed, and my mind was working slowly. Into Campbeltown police station and a murder inquiry. It had to be murder.

Hold on. Hold on. Mr Bonneville-Clark was a known abuser of Class A drugs. Overdose was a possibility. A probability, even.

So he had tied the anchor to his own leg?

The grey seas marched under. I tried to pretend this was not happening. No luck. There was a way of checking. It was just that I did not fancy the hold.

Get down there.

I waited till I heard the clatter of Georgie's snore rise above the diesel. Then I locked on the autopilot and went back down.

It was Johnny, all right; a strange, collapsed version of Johnny, the sporty gear sodden rags, the flash-handsome features gone sideways, then set into a horrible caricature of themselves. The eyes were open in nasty little crescents, which for some reason upset me badly. In the police I had seen bodies, some of them heavily mangled. But none of them had been as unpleasant as this one.

I started with the anchor. It was tied to the leg with a length of polypropylene rope made fast with a wild profusion of half-hitches. Not a seagoing knot. Not a knot Johnny would have tied, no matter how stoned he had been.

The realisation settled in me like cold water. Someone had tied an anchor to Johnny and slung him over the port corner of the deck abaft the wheelhouse. Probably they had thought they were putting him in the sea. But they had put him on the trawl deck instead.

Bloody Johnny. He couldn't even get himself murdered properly.

What now? It could still be natural causes. Suicide, perhaps. While stoned. Against reason, hope bloomed.

He was lying face-up on the deck by the bins. I bent and rolled him over.

Hope died.

The hair on the back of the head was matted with something that shone black in the blue-white light. It was oddly parted, from the way the body had been lying. And in the middle of the parting was a little black hole. Just at the nape of the neck, the hole. Not natural causes, then. And not suicide.

It was murder. The chill settled into my bones. Not just murder. I had seen this kind of thing before, in Bosnia. Execution.

Big trouble.

Huge trouble.

I bent. I ran my hands over his cold, stringy head. There was an entrance wound, no exit wound. The bullet was still in there. It was important to preserve the evidence. There was only one thing I could do. I pushed the body into one of the bins, shovelled ice on to it and turned the cooling back on. Then I went back into the wheelhouse.

It was warm up there, and a pale dawn was dimming the flash of the Mull of Kintyre. I sat in the fat leather chair and made myself think like a policeman.

When we told the Campbeltown police, they would ask questions. These would turn up the following answers. Johnny had been my business partner. The business had not been thriving, and we were known to have had strong differences. The Campbeltown police would not take long to work out who I was. Once a crap policeman, always a crap policeman. I had motive. I had opportunity. I was as good as nicked.

And while I sat in a cell helping them with their inquiries, things would be happening. Whoever it was that Johnny had stolen the boat from would be keen to take it back again . . .

I thought of the man who had looked at me when we had been in Milford lock, the pistol-butt against the belly. I thought of that nasty clotted little hole in the nape of Johnny's neck. I was being stupid. I should go to the police and take my chances.

But policemen had journalists' numbers in their mobiles. Going to the police would mean publicity. And publicity would mean that whoever had killed Johnny would know where I was. Say I managed to convince the boys at Campbeltown nick that this had all been a horrid misunderstanding. I would come out of the interview room and walk into the drizzle. And *boom*.

No way.

The sun crawled out of the sea and into the cloud. The Mull rose to port. Georgie came out of the cabin, yawned and farted long and loud. I went and spooned Nescafé and four sugars into a dirty mug. 'Aaah,' he said. 'Aye, it's a lovely day. I have my boat back. There is a satisfaction in it, a great satisfaction, and soon we will have a hold full of fish, and sell it. It's a great life. I love it, because it's great —'

'No it isn't,' I said.

'Wha?' He was not used to contradiction.

So I told him. I told him how Johnny had come by the boat, and what I had found in the hold, and what I had decided to do about it.

I watched the knuckles whiten on the grab handles by the throttles. His eyes were narrow and exceptionally nasty. 'Shite,' he said, to whom and about whom he did not make clear. 'You mean all that time, in Milford and Swansea with polis everywhere, he was lying on the trawl deck?'

'They tried to throw him into the sea,' I said. 'They missed.'

There was a silence.

'So what are you going tae do about it?' he said eventually. I got the impression that this was only partly a challenge. The rest of it sounded like a cry for help.

I had been considering how to respond to this question. I had evolved something straightforward, if untrue. 'We should really go to the police,' I said.

The cry for help receded into the background noise. He said, 'If you go to the polis they will take my boat away for months and I will kill you. Because they will put everyone in the jail and we will —'

'Yes,' I said, to stop the flow.

'Anyway,' said Georgie. 'You were a polis yourself once. So what's wrong with you go and find him?'

'Find who?'

'This guy who stole my boat. And killed this man.' His resolution seemed to be hardening. 'And tell him it's mine again.'

'He may not listen.' I could not get Johnny's face out of my mind.

'Then make him,' said Georgie.

'And how am I supposed to do that?'

'You may think of something,' said Georgie. 'Me, I'm fishing.'

'My partner is in the hold,' I said. 'Dead. Killed.'

'It's all right,' said Georgie. 'I'll keep him in the ice.'

I stared at him. 'Ice?'

'To stop him going off, like.'

I said, 'You'll need a crew.'

'I'll get one. Aye. I'll keep him down in the ice. In plastic. Anyone asks, I'll tell them he's a shark.' Georgie's shoulders shuddered somewhat. Apparently he was laughing. 'And when you get me the papers of the boat I'll give you the corpse and you can do what you want with it.'

'You haven't got the papers?'

'Your partner said they'd come later. You should ask for them. Him being dead, and all. I need the —'

'Yes,' I said. 'You do.'

He went into the hold. I heard him singing. There was the crackle of polythene.

I sat slumped in the navigator's chair. It seemed like several weeks since I had slept. When he came back, I said, 'They have killed Johnny. Why wouldn't they kill you?'

'They can try,' said Georgie. He sounded sure of himself now. With violence, he was on home ground. A moored yacht went past the window. A grey town rose ahead. 'Here's Campbeltown. You can go and find me my papers, and good riddance.'

'Where are you going?' I said.

'I told you. Fishing.'

A cloud of gulls floated over a couple of trawlers alongside the pier. Georgie jammed the nose in to the concrete and wound the stern in, and I climbed the quay ladder as soon as we had the lines on. I looked down at the hatch under which my brother-in-law lay wrapped in plastic waiting for Judgement Day. I said, 'I'll call.'

'Ye will,' said Georgie. He had been using his phone on the way in. A couple of men in jeans and rigger's boots were stumping down the pier, bags on shoulders.

I turned my back on him and walked away. I had the feeling that I was waking from a nightmare. Johnny was in Hampshire, charvering someone's wife in a Jacuzzi. Soon he would ring and explain his new disaster and try to borrow money.

The phone did indeed ring. It was Miranda. She said in a cold voice, 'I don't want to talk to you, obviously. Is Johnny with you?'

'No.' Well, he wasn't.

'What's wrong with you?'

'Me? Nothing.'

'You sound as if you've swallowed a brick. He was supposed to be having breakfast with Daddy. To discuss your business.'

'He's missed a meeting? I'm amazed.'

'There is no need to be sarcastic.' She sounded halfway between irritated and worried. 'He's an idiot. But he tries a lot harder than you give him credit for. I hope he's all right.' Suddenly I wanted to tell her the truth. I opened my mouth, but she had rung off. Just as well.

I walked up the quay and across the park to the bus station, feeling bad. It was Sunday. Everyone seemed to be indoors, and a thin wind was whistling over the grass. When I looked back, the *Sirius Gleaner* was a black toy on the grey sea, heading for the horizon.

6

By the time the Sunday bus got me to Oban, everything seemed less real. I bought a nasty but economical pickup truck from Chucky Muck's 4×4, prop. Charles Maconochie, who did the best of his business on Sundays. Then I clattered away down the main road and bounced along the track to my little green home in the swamp. It was teatime. I sat down on the dampish sofa in the tug's saloon and stuffed the underwriter's money into an envelope. Then I stared at the wall and tried to think, and went to sleep instead. I was woken by a car door slamming. It was six o'clock, getting dark. I levered the sleep out of my eyes as Maureen came down the gangplank.

I had bought the tugboat at a distress price from a slow man whose wife had decided that she was not willing to wait ten years for him to convert it into the houseboat on which she would have her children. It was a shell, the conversion about one-eighth done. On my first day of occupation I had woken in the dank steel bunk to hear a knocking on the door. When I went to open it, there in the rain was a tall, broad-shouldered woman with red hair, frowning with embarrassment at the intrusion. 'Hello,' she said. 'I'm Maureen. I thought you mightn't have any milk.' She held up a bottle.

'Come in, come in,' I said. She came, and I saw her eyes take in the rumpled bunk, and the empty Bell's bottle, and the brass clock on the steel bulkhead, which said 11.45. 'Bit of a mess,' I said.

'You've only just got here,' she said, instantly demonstrating her talent for giving the world the benefit of the doubt. 'Will I make tea?'

I started to tell her that I would do it myself, but she was already under way. She pulled out cups. From the middle of a cloud of kettle-steam she gave me the lowdown on Achnabuie. I had planned to move the tug a bit closer to civilisation. But as she went on, the idea began to recede. Finally, she said, 'And what do you do for a living?'

'I'm a yacht broker.'

'So it doesn't matter where you stay?'

This was true. I poured us more tea. She looked at me with the green eyes. There was something nervous in them. She said, 'And that's what you'll be doing here?'

The rain had stopped. The sun chose this moment to make an appearance. It lit up the hills and the sea, and the bright red hull of a fishing boat upside down on the foreshore. It even manufactured a small but brilliant rainbow. I said, 'I think so.'

She nodded. She said, 'I don't suppose you'd be needing an assistant?'

I looked at her hard, to make sure she was not joking. She looked steadily back. I could have hugged her. But I made myself say, slowly, 'Can you type?'

'I did a computer course. And I do a bit of carpentry.'

'The business is in a period of consolidation,' I said.

'You mean there's no money.'

'Hardly any.'

'Ah, well,' she said. 'A woman could go mad here. I'll give it a week or two, see how it goes.'

That had been the best part of a year ago.

As I said, Maureen is a large girl, well-proportioned, with a lot of red hair kept in place with midge repellent. That morning, the one after I had got back from the *Gleaner*, she was wearing jeans and walking boots and a green fleece that matched her eyes; scarcely catwalk gear, but she made it elegant and stately. She said, 'You look awful.'

I said, 'I am awful.'

'Wait you a minute,' she said. And ten minutes later she was loading the table with eggs, bacon, toast, beans, tomatoes and (from God knows where) a large bowl of raspberries and cream. 'Well,' she said, sitting on the sofa and watching me narrowly, to see that I ate everything up. 'Tell me about it.'

This was a wonderful woman. I felt entirely at ease with her, and there were no secrets between us. But it would not have been fair to speak to her of corpses. 'We found the boat,' I said. 'We took it back.'

She gazed upon me as if she was trying to see into my head. 'Was there trouble?' she said.

'Trouble?' I said, round the last of the eggs.

'Only I see you have a new car.'

'The other one caught fire.'

She nodded, as if this was to be expected. Then she said, 'Who lit it?'

'Lit it?'

She swiped the dirty plate with an impatient hiss. 'Someone's been ringing,' she said. 'Four times. A man with a strange voice. He wants to talk to you.'

'Misunderstanding,' I said. I was sleepy again.

'He understood all right. He said you had sold his boat after it had been nicked off him and he wanted it back.'

'Nicked?'

She sighed. She said, 'You can tell me or not. But it's just as well they don't know where you stay.' She let that sink in. 'What are you going to do?'

'Talk to them.'

'They didn't sound the talking kind.'

I knew I was about to take steps which would be impossible to retrace. Already had. I said, 'What was the name and the number?'

She pushed a bit of paper across the table at me. It was an Oban number. The name was Smith. I did not believe it was real.

'Oh,' she said. 'And I brought my old computer, it's better than yours, I don't use it any more. I've put your stuff on it. It's all wi-fied up and that.'

'Thanks,' I said, like a drowning man thanking a liferaft. She shook her head, and smiled affectionately. I gave her a fat envelope to take to the bank, and she was gone.

My peace of mind went with her. I sat and tried to be calm. Gavin Chance Marine was registered on the south coast, and listed boats worldwide. As Maureen said, nobody would find me at Achnabuie unless they knew where to look.

But I could not stay at Achnabuie for ever. Because if I did not get after this Smith, Georgie would get after me. Those jellied crescents of eyeball watched me accusingly from the deck. Like Georgie said, it was time to be a policeman again.

But policemen have other policemen to help them, and are backed up by the law, which tells bad people it is very very illegal to kill them. I was not a policeman. There was no reason to assume that whoever had killed Johnny would consider it a big deal to kill me as well. I went across and switched on Maureen's computer.

There were seventy emails. I picked up the phone. There were a lot of messages. I started to go through them. A few people wanted to see a few boats; they could wait. And there was Mr Smith, once, then once again for luck. *We need to meet,* the voice said. I could see Maureen's point about the accent. The vowels were squashed, perhaps slightly Welsh. *You will be aware of the reasons. You should come prepared to fulfil your obligations.* In other words: give me my fish money and give me my boat.

This was worrying, because I did not have either.

I needed to start at a beginning. So I turned my face to the computer and Googled Tony Greely.

There was a lot of stuff about sustainability and the planet, and a picture of him, smiling, probably because he had caught sight of his own reflection in the camera lens. 'Tony wears an earring in his right ear in the immemorial manner of fishermen the world over,' said the puff. 'He says, "It is in case I fall overboard from one of my all-wood sustainably built boats, fuelled by filtered cooking fat. My mates will have somewhere to plant the boathook when they haul me aboard. I like to think that my Greely's restaurants are an earring for the world's oceans, and that my customers are the boathook that will save them."'

Pull the other earring, Tony, I thought. It has got bells on it. I Googled on.

And stopped.

I had arrived at a page showing the launch of Greely's in Poole. There were a lot of people standing on the Town Quay admiring a dirty great halibut hanging from a crane, and Fishboy Greely posing next to it with a frying pan in one hand and a lemon in the other. Everyone had a champagne glass. There were a couple of soap stars with warm smiles and cash-register eyes. Miranda was there, of course, radiant in neat jeans and a deep-cleavage top, gazing adoringly at her Fishboy.

But there was one person beside her and Greely that I certainly did recognize. He was standing to attention, his peaked cap under his arm, his face mild and blank. He was wearing a police sergeant's uniform. And the reason I recognised him was that he had been driving the car that had watched the *Gleaner* unloading at Swansea Docks.

I zoomed in. The picture went to pixels before the number could be seen. Anyway, I had not bothered to get the number when we had been on the quay at Swansea.

Same guy, though.

Never mind policemen. This is a one-man informal murder investigation. Look for means, motive, opportunity.

Means, then. A bullet in the back of the head (here I shivered, remembering the nasty little black dent in the clotted hair). A .22, probably. Speedy, efficient, very little mess. The kind of thing you got in Serbia, not Swansea. Whoever did this had killed people before.

And would again.

That bad thought back again. Move on.

Motive. Pretty straightforward. Johnny had gone around cheating most people and robbing the rest. His business style would certainly lead people to wish him dead. And the people on the lock at Milford looked like people for whom the wish and the deed were highly adjacent.

Opportunity. That was the one, really. God knew where Johnny had been during the last days of his life. I would need to check with Miranda. *Good afternoon, Miranda. You know your brother? The one I am supposed to bully while he steals? Well, he's dead, but don't tell anyone.*

There would be obstacles.

An engine sounded outside. Not the usual Achnabuie wheeze and clatter, but a deep, disciplined purr that spoke of good maintenance and a regular service schedule. I put my head above window level and found myself looking at another half-Battenberg 4×4. A constable in a high-vis jacket was panning a potato face across the harbour. His eyes locked with mine. He advanced.

For a moment, I felt my innards swoop towards my boots. Wait a minute, though. This was only a constable, alone. I was merely a concerned citizen on the end of a visit from the law. So I opened the door, assumed an expression of puzzled innocence, and said, 'Good afternoon.'

The potato face remained fixed on me, though the eyes moved to and fro. 'Good afternoon, Mr Chance,' said the mouth. They all knew; of course they did.

'Come aboard,' I said, leaning casually on the rail.

'No need,' said the constable, as if I had offered him a bite of reptile. 'I believe a Mr John Orkney Bonneville-Clark is your business associate?'

The blood left my head. I said, 'What's he done now?' to avoid a direct answer.

'We have an enquiry as to his whereabouts.'

'You can add mine to it,' I said.

'When did you last see Mr Bonneville-Clark?'

'Ten days ago? I could look in my diary.'

'Yes, please.'

I went and fetched the diary, and showed him. 'At the Southampton Boat Show. Mr Bonneville-Clark was running a stand we had.' For a couple of hours, anyway. Then he had got drunk, and fallen over in Joe Coral in St Mary Street.

'Thank you, sir,' said the constable, making a note and closing his book. He advanced, and handed me one of the nastily-printed little fliers that the police use instead of visiting cards. 'If you should chance to hear from or of Mr Bonneville-Clark, perhaps you would contact me on this number.'

I was not a murder suspect, then. I felt a dangerous elation. I said, 'He moves in a mysterious way.'

'Beg pardon, sir?'

'I mean you never know, with him.'

'Ah.'

The policeman got into the 4×4 and Battenberged off through the dreary ranks of shrouded boats. I went back into the cabin. That had been the start of the process of massing up details that when a body showed up would make a picture of the final stages of Johnny's life. It was a process as stupid as a machine, but it would be thorough. And in the end it would lead to the bullet in Johnny's head; and to me as the man most likely to have put it there.

Unless I found who had really put it there.

The coppers of Britain were as the grains of sand, and I was one man with a rusty computer. I grinned encouraging at my reflection in the screen. A rusty computer was better than none.

The phone rang. I answered it. It was a young voice, enquiring about a boat. Captain Maxwell's boat. I took this as an excellent omen. '*Lorne Lady*,' I said, glancing out of the window to check the thing was still afloat. 'No current survey, but she's like a piece of furniture.' This was true, if the furniture had been sitting in the rain for thirty years and had not been that comfortable to start with. So the young voice told me it was called Henry Heap and made a date to view the boat the day after tomorrow, and I went to tidy it up.

I rowed out to the mooring in the punt, climbed up the side and into the cockpit. The pump sucked dry after three swipes, which was pretty much what you would expect in a hull built in Early Fibreglass an inch thick. The engine started second go, and blew out cooling water that left a hint of oiliness on the sea. But if you do not get oil in a Perkins' cooling water, it is a sign that there is no oil in the engine.

I got out the bucket and brush and started on the gullshit that lay over all horizontal surfaces. And as I chipped my way down to the pale-blue non-slip, I made my own mental picture of the events leading to the demise of Johnny Bonny.

Johnny had stolen a boat from a fellow gambler and sold it to Wee Georgie. The original owner had stolen it back. When it had left Drummie it had been empty. When we had repossessed it, it had contained black fish in Greenreap boxes, for delivery to the representative of Greely's restaurants in Swansea. And also the body of Johnny Bonneville-Clark, with a bullet in its head.

I hacked at the last stubborn fragment of gullshit. A lot of this was very hard to understand: like, for instance, the coincidence that the fish from the *Gleaner* was heading for the boyfriend of my ex-wife. But (said the phantom of Sergeant Moulton, my instructor at the Police College) you got to prioritise, Gavin. You got to pick up a corner and find out what the hell. And first you got to decide which corner.

So I gave the deck a final sluice of seawater, and hauled the sails up to check for mildew and birds' nests. Then I dropped the mooring and shoved the boat in gear and motored in to the pontoon, so Henry Heap would not get a look at her from a distance and be affronted by her various dings and scrapes. I planned to sell the *Lady* straight off the pontoon. If this sounds ambitious, it was not. You would be amazed at the casualness with which your marine punter brasses up twenty-five grand; which was the sum Captain Maxwell had in mind. But Captain Maxwell had his fantasies.

Once the *Lady* was tied up and looking her best, I went back to the tug, turned on the computer, and began to scrutinise Greenreap.

The company's website was a charming affair, featuring happy salmon symmetrically arranged round a logo that combined the poshness of Harrods with the rustic charm of Balmoral. 'Sustainable fish for a new age,' said the blurb.

> 'Greenreap supplies organic salmon to the retail and restaurant world. Most farmed fish is the product of three times its own weight in sandeels and other feedstocks. Greenreap uses a minimum of fish-derived feedstocks, and a maximum of vegetable-derived feedstocks. Ours is high-quality, low-impact fish, produced by our farms in beautiful areas of Britain where the employment we provide brings real advantages to less advantaged populations. Greenreap. We all win!'

The usual fish farming operation, then, lightly greenwashed. No mention of black cod.

On another page was a map of the west coast of Scotland, with little green blobs indicating fish farms. The southernmost was in a group of rocks to the north of Islay.

Time to dig deeper. I pulled the phone to me and dialled.

'Hello?' said a voice.

'Gavin,' I said. 'Chance.'

'Ah,' said the voice, more guarded now. Edwin Bentley worked in the pisciculture department at Bristol University. Nice guy, excessively tall, very kind to children and animals, rightly suspicious of yacht brokers.

I said, 'What do you know about Greenreap?'

'Fish farmers,' he said. 'Why?'

I said, 'They say they're organic or vegan or something.'

'I doubt it. You can't feed salmon on anything but fish. If you feed them pig meal they taste of pig meal. The punters don't like it.'

'And you can't farm, say, cod?'

'Not yet. Why are you asking?'

'They want to buy a boat,' I said, improvising.

'Ah.' Losing interest now. We chatted awkwardly for a minute, and parted. I sat and thought: if I was a fish-farming company, would I improve my margins by laundering black fish? It seemed a bit drastic.

Christ, I was tired. Every time I closed my eyes I began to drift away. And every time I drifted away, I saw those jellied crescents in Johnny's collapsed face.

Whisky would fix it.

But I had given up whisky.

But this was an emergency.

There was a bottle in the cupboard. I hauled open the door and looked at it. Teacher's, half full, sticky dust mantling its shoulders. I put out my hand. I picked it up, and sloshed some into a glass, and tipped in some water, and poured it down the hatch and felt the depth-charge bloom and flare. One did not quite do the trick, so I took another back to the sofa. And this time when I closed my eyes all I could see was a deep, comforting redness. Better. There were things about this that were not good, of course. Whisky was not good, and the fact I was not thinking about bodies did not mean there weren't any. But at least there were no eyes. No eyes was good. I had some more whisky.

I went to sleep. It was a deep sleep, started by exhaustion and deepened by whisky. But the whisky turned. And some time later I found myself staring into the dark with red-hot eyeballs, listening to the pulse beating in my head.

I knew what you did now. I was right in practice. You got a

handful of aspirins and a pint mug of water, and you went to bed, and hoped you would go to sleep —

A movement. Somewhere in the dark, a movement. The tug was a houseboat nowadays. But she was afloat. And she was not one of your new giant tugs. She was small enough to stir a little to the sea, and to pull at the warps when the tide ran. By now I understood the way she moved. For instance, I could tell that the tide was at about half-ebb.

And that someone had just stepped on board.

7

My heart gave a batter in my chest. I drew one breath and held it. Nobody I knew would have stepped on to the tug without a shout. Nobody I knew and wanted to see, that is.

I rolled off the sofa and on to the carpet. I began to think very fast. My head was hammering, my mouth dry. If these were the Johnny people they would be good. They would cover the exits. Then they would send in the man with a .22 target pistol to do what he did.

The exits they knew about.

I was already moving down the companionway, bare feet, hands and knees. The adrenalin was sweeping the whisky away. I crawled down the alleyway between the cabin doors. Glass broke behind me. Someone coughed, and I managed to make the cougher into a man the size of a small family saloon car. The cough might have been the last sound Johnny had heard before the bullet slammed him into the black . . .

The door. I was up against the steel door at the aft end of the alleyway. The tug was moored facing inland, into the ebb. I lifted the big steel handle. I had oiled it last week. You had to oil things at Achnabuie, or they crumbled to red powder.

Bless Achnabuie. The door swung open: a watertight door leading into the crawl-space under the towing deck where the propeller shafts ran. Dark in here, dark as the inside of a cow, slippery with grease and oil, stinking rank of bilge. I heaved the door shut. Too hard. Clang. A shout on the other side. But I was dogging the hatch with my greasy fingers, heaving myself down the shaft, getting just enough traction on the oily metal to propel me where I needed to go.

Then I was at the place on the back end. The place where I had taken one of the winches out, not to service it but to sell it, and stuffed up the hole with some hay in a fertiliser bag to stop the rain coming in. Through the hole I went, flat on my belly on to the towing deck. I could hear hammering from below. I stuffed the fertiliser bag back into the hole and lowered myself over the stern, very quiet. The sea was cold enough to sting. I clamped my teeth and kept on lowering, trying not to gasp like a seal as the icy water hit my chest. I let myself sink nearly all the way and floated away down the tide. The whisky was mere rags in my head. Christ, it was cold. The tug was shrinking. There was the dark loom of people on the deck. I put myself right down into the water.

Ahead, I could see what I needed: the pontoon, with the shape of *Lorne Lady* dark against the overcast, bless her fat old heart. I drifted down with the tide, sank under the pontoon, held my breath for an improbably long time, saw a paling in the water, came up on the far or blind side. Speech came across the water as I gripped a mooring cleat and hauled myself on to the shitty boards, keeping my head down. Then I was untying figure-of-eights, head still down, bow first, it being downstream, then stern, and scrambling into the cockpit as the ketch drifted gently off the pontoon and out into the harbour, and the tide caught her, and away she drifted towards the dogleg where the wooded point came out to make the narrow called Caol Ban. I lay on the cockpit sole, out of line of sight, and looked up at the stars, which were of course thickly cloaked in cloud.

A reddish glow started to dance up there, and I could not think what it was. Then the masts wheeled against the overcast, and round we went into the back-eddy the tide made when it ran round the point, and I knew that the hull of the boat would be out of sight of the shore now, so I stood up and looked back, and saw that the red glow in the sky was caused by flames: a large number of flames, leaping out of a nasty oily orange glow. A glow centred on my tug.

I put my hands on my head to stop it exploding. I was homeless, jobless, and penniless except for a pocketful of change and a wet credit card and an extensively marinated mobile phone. Furthermore it seemed that someone wanted to murder me. It was not a comforting feeling. In fact it was bloody annoying.

All right, I thought. We will take this as a message from God. I will head for Loch Mor, and analyse the doings of Greenreap, and acquire full details of its association with murderers and Tony Greely. And then I will destroy the bastards.

This was not natural bravery, you understand. It was just that it was plain to me that if I did not kill them, they would kill me. And of course I had been at the whisky.

Stealthily, I pulled out a bit of foresail. A little breeze was blowing from the south. I felt it bump the genoa, felt the deck tilt under my feet and the wheel firm up under my hands as water poured over the rudder. The wake began to gurgle. Jupiter hung big and yellow in a hole in the clouds. The dark shadows of the land dropped astern. And we were sliding into the great dark smooth of the Sound of Jura, with the flash of Sker Vuile off the starboard beam.

Somewhere over the water, the Paps of Jura were propping

up the sky. Somewhere to the northwest beyond the lighthouse, the ebb was roaring in the whirlpools of the Gulf of Corryvreckan. But out here in the dark I was sailing *Lorne Lady* over a quiet black sea, and the whisky was an echo in the back of my mind, and for the moment the night was full of peace.

Like the peace that comes when you have jumped out of a seventeenth-floor window, and before you hit the pavement. Not a very peaceful peace. But better than being burned alive, or getting a .22 bullet in the back of the head.

There was stuff to do.

On with the autopilot. Below into the cabin. Take an inventory. Pockets, empty. Galley, sim card from phone rinsed in fresh water and drying over cooker. Mould, bilge, three tins of Captain Maxwell's baked beans. One can of Captain Maxwell's Theakston's. Two tins sardines, half a handful of tea bags, a locker full of blankets slightly mildewed. Fuel, enough. Water, some.

When I went up into the cockpit the lights of Craighouse were strung over the horizon ahead. The sky was lightening astern as I sailed past the harbour buoy, rolled up the genoa and lassoed one of the visitor's moorings under the distillery. And suddenly the adrenalin was all gone. Now it was five o'clock in the morning, and I had been up most of the night wearing clothes that had dried on my body, on the run from someone who wanted to put a bullet in the back of my head. I was knackered.

I had not even begun.

So I went below and rolled myself in a few blankets, and closed the eyes of Gavin Chance, fugitive, and prepared to wake up as Gavin Chance, cruising yachtsman.

The alarm went off at eight o'clock. I stumbled to the galley and made tea, no milk of course. After a mostly protein breakfast of beans and sardines it was nineish. So I took the boat alongside the big concrete quay, pulled up my hood and walked round to the Jura Stores, where I bought a couple of bags of groceries. The whisky on the shelf called out that it had certainly saved my life last night. I ignored it in a studied manner, paid with a credit card now dry but uncomfortably close to its maximum, and returned to the boat.

The morning was charmingly picturesque. Behind the straggle of houses, the hills of Jura rose golden with bracken into a sky whose pure blue was touched with a high ripple of cirrus. The glass was falling. I shook my head cruising-yachtsman style, and ostentatiously unfolded the Loch Linnhe charts, so anyone interested might think I was heading for Fort William. Then I stowed the food and rummaged through the lockers to see what we had in the way of equipment.

There was a mackerel line, a patched inflatable tender, and a pair of collapsible oars. It all looked very flimsy after the solid gear on the *Gleaner,* but it was better than nothing.

About halfway up the tide, I started the engine and went forward to let go the mooring. A small red fishing boat was puttering across the harbour. It seemed to throttle up when it saw me, and an arm came out of the wheelhouse and waved. I knew the boat, and the arm. I pulled my hood up and sat down on the coachroof and waited. The fishing boat put out fenders and positioned itself neatly alongside. Maureen's red head came out of the wheelhouse. She tossed me a bow line. 'Good morning,' she said.

'Come aboard,' I said. 'Come below.' I was in mortal fear of being recognised, and Maureen's boat was a familiar one around the Sound.

We went below. Maureen sat on one of Captain Maxwell's

taupe velvet banquettes and peered at me and said, 'Are you all right?' Then she burst into tears.

I went and sat beside her. She took my hand in both hers and put her head on my shoulder and said, 'I was so worried.'

'Me too,' I said, feeling awkward.

'I thought you were dead,' she said.

'I'm not.'

She sniffed. I gave her one of the Captain's tea towels. 'They came last night. They told me your boat was burned.'

'Who came?'

'The police.'

'Highly vigilant,' I said. 'Credit to the Service. So what did you tell them?'

Maureen blew her nose on the tea towel. 'I told them you probably left the gas on,' she said. 'I told them you were not a very tidy person. I had a look round the harbour. And I saw that the *Lady* had gone and I rang the Stores and they said she was here.' She frowned. 'You do know that there's someone coming to look at her tomorrow?'

'Indeed,' I said. 'Put them off, could you?'

'Aye.' The frown had not gone. The fine green eyes had a troubled look. 'Now will you tell me exactly what is going on?'

'No,' I said.

'Aye, well.' She sat and looked sad.

'Did you tell anyone about me leaving in the boat?'

The eyes fired up again. 'I did not,' she said. 'I told the policeman I did not even know if you were there. I did not tell him that Welsh Smith guy rang up at teatime yesterday and asked were you at Achnabuie and I said you were not —'

'Shit.'

'Aye. And I did not tell the police that the *Lady* was missing from the harbour even though she had been there the day before and Captain Maxwell isn't very well so it wouldn't have been him took it out. So either they will think you weren't there or that you were burned to bits in the fire.'

'Shit,' I said again.

'I hate that word. So I tried to ring you but you're on answer —'

'Soaking wet,' I said.

'Aye. So I thought, he'll need a phone. So I brought one. And where are you going?'

'Oh, not far,' I said.

'Gavin Chance, you will maybe realise one day that you can't go on like this,' she said. 'A trail of devastation is what you're leaving.'

I nodded. The conversation was following a familiar course. But I could not avoid the eyes, which were now at a temperature suitable for welding. She said, 'When are you going to learn that people care about you?'

I opened my mouth to answer, but I could not think of anything to say.

'So,' she said, and fished in her bag. 'Phone, and charger. And a cake.'

'A cake?'

'You'll need a cake.' The eyes filled up with tears again. We tried the sim card in the phone. It worked. She dabbed her eyes and smiled in a strained manner and said, 'Please don't get yourself hurt. What would we do without you?'

Live peaceful, happy lives free of debt and anxiety, I thought. But before I could say anything, she was out of the cabin and over the side. And by the time I was on deck she was gone. A bundle of oilskins and a couple of fleeces lay where she had thrown them on the cockpit sole. I waved to her. She did not wave back.

So I let go the mooring, feeling, in the middle of this shitstorm, oddly happy. I had dropped on Maureen out of the blue. And she had become a friend.

Out of the harbour I went, past the line of little islands, and moved the wheel between my hands until the forestay rested on the sea to the east of Islay. At first I used the engine. But I was supposed to be a cruising yachtsman, and the wind was still in the south-southwest, so I pulled up the mainsail and sheeted it in hard. The beginnings of the Sound of Islay opened up to starboard, a broad sheet of dark water narrowing to the quarter-mile ribbon separating Islay from Jura. The tide was running, shoving the boat into the funnel. I hauled on the genoa sheet. The sail came off the roller with a thump, and *Lorne Lady* dug her stout shoulder into the sea and began to truck on with a powerful, ungainly surge. The Black Rock buoy went past, towing a gurgling trough of tide. And on the tide washed us northward, the breeze funnelling up from astern, so I cracked main and jib sheets and we moved over the ground at ten knots by the antique grey screen of the GPS.

The sky had clouded over, and dirty wafts of drizzle were riding up the groove of the Sound of Islay, blotting out the Kintyre hills astern. I clambered into the oilskins Maureen had brought.

As soon as I was well inside them, the phone gave me the text bleep. I dug it out from under the layers. The screen said CHECK VOICEMAIL. MO. The voicemail was somewhere in an exchange, not affected by tugboat fires. I dialled in, punched in the pin number. I had one new message. *Just in case you're alive,* said a flat Irish voice. *Don't get used to it. It won't last.*

I put the phone in my pocket with a hand that shook. The light had gone out of the day, and I felt cold and stupid and frightened. The tide swept us past the Bunnahabhain distillery. As the shores of the Sound diverged the wind went obtuse and fluky. The squalls joined up, and soon the rain was falling steadily from a grim, dark sky.

There were fishing boats on the sea ahead, dragging their trawls through the surface of the Tarbert Bank in case there was anything left alive out there. Loch Mor and the Greenreap fish farm were round the corner to the southwest, or left. But I was a cruising yachtsman taking a late break in the holiday highlands, and nothing to do with fish farms. So I put the helm up and turned right, following the Jura shore round, and was soon heading out of the big open sea and into the dark interior of West Loch Tarbert.

Loch Tarbert is a maze of pools and channels that just about cuts Jura in half. I crept along its south shore, dodging rocks until I found a bay sheltered from the breeze. Here I dropped the anchor. When I stopped the engine the silence flooded in: a huge, deep, lonely silence that poured down from the mountains and joined the boom of the sea on the skerries in the loch mouth. There are caves here where the ancient Scots parked their dead en route for burial on the holy islands of Oronsay and Iona. And there was a hollow in my head where poor bloody dead Johnny lay. And a hollow in my stomach, because tonight I was going to go and play commandos. Once, I enjoyed that kind of thing. Not any more.

I put it off for as long as possible. But in the end I got fed up with reading last year's almanac and pulled out the charts, of which the Captain had a practically encyclopaedic collection, and studied Loch Mor and its outliers. Once I had the entrance to the loch clear in my head, I leaned back on the settee. A genuine commando would doubtless have done a few pressups, eaten some energy foods and prepared himself mentally for bloodshed. My own preparations consisted of wishing there was some whisky on the boat, and being glad in a grudging way that there was not, for I had a feeling that ice-cold sobriety was about to be de rigueur. I had had a night interrupted by attempted murder, and a day with a very bad telephone call, and that kind of thing can take it out of you. So I dozed off.

When I awoke the light was fading and the tide had turned. I made a heavy snack of bacon, eggs and beans, and had a try for the weather forecast, but there was no VHF reception. So I pulled on as many clothes as I had, and went on deck and blew up the dinghy and lashed it to the coachroof grabrails. Then I started the engine, let the windlass haul the anchor up, and headed out of the loch, counting rocks and taking what I hoped were clearing bearings off what I presumed were headlands.

It was properly dark now. Beyond the mouth of the loch the world was as black as a cellar. The bow rose, then fell with a crunch. Spray blasted port and starboard. I realised that there was a heavy sea running, and found that I was whistling a tune between my teeth, and stopped quickly, because whistling brings wind, and there was plenty of that already.

The GPS was a dim grey rectangle. I found myself wishing for a modern chart plotter. Well, I could wish all I liked. But I was still checking my position against the light on the Islay side of the northern entrance to the Sound, confirming it with GPS latitude and longitude as I ran down on the waypoint I had put off the entrance to Loch Mor.

The wind had gone south and picked up. It was bad all the way across the mouth of the Sound, for the tide was ebbing now, and the funnelling wind blew across it, squeezing the waves tall and close together so the *Lady* corkscrewed horribly, dipping her chainplates in every trough. After five miles the wind had a flutter in it, as if it was being combed by hills, and the *Lady*'s motion eased. This should have been consoling.

But I knew that what was giving the shelter were the skerries round the mouth of Loch Mor. So it was hard to feel really cheerful.

The GPS bleeped. I was a mile off the waypoint. The land was a clotted darkness to port. To seaward, the night gave a feeling of emptiness. As I watched a squall must have passed, for a ruby came into view, and a little chip of emerald: the trawlers, still trudging across the banks, with beyond them the yellow loom of the lights on Colonsay pier.

But I was not admiring the view to seaward. I was looking ahead. Pale streaks were coming and going in the dark off the port bow. That would be the swell breaking in the outliers of Loch Mor. I swallowed with a mouth turned to cotton wool, and hoped I had keyed the waypoints in right.

The tide was taking me south. I corrected, got the waypoint on the nose again, squinted at the chart with the red-shaded flashlight. There was the scatter of rocks down to port, ledges running into the sea from the loch entrance like pincers from a prawn's claw, with a channel down the middle. The first waypoint was well to seaward of all known hazards. The next was well into the entrance, and there was another in the body of the loch a cable's length off the dotted fish-cage symbols.

The sea walloped in again as I came up on the waypoint. I put the wheel over to port. The cockpit deck rolled violently as the nose came round. The breeze was on my right ear now, mixed with the slam and boom of the waves on the skerries to starboard. The deck steadied. There were lights beyond the shrouds, glittering in water that was no more than rippled. Yellow lights; fish-farm working lights, maybe. I throttled back until the engine sound was a soft clatter.

At the next waypoint I turned forty-five degrees out of the channel, showing my side to anyone who might be watching from the fish farm. The sounder showed a bottom rising from the deeps. We were halfway up a ten-foot tide. So I waited until the numbers showed three metres, came head to wind, knocked the engine out of gear, and waited for the boat to start drifting astern before I let go the anchor.

Then it was time to be a cruising yachtsman again. So I turned on the anchor light and pulled the dinghy off the cabin top, dropped it over the side and put the painter on a stanchion. After that I took out the Captain's binoculars and pointed them at the farm.

Captain Maxwell had not stinted in the glasses department. These were Monk Commanders, with a knack for soaking up all the light that was going. They showed an ordinary fish farm: a circular cage of netting surrounded by staging, anchored just off the far shore of the loch. On the shore were a couple of huts and something that might have been a cold store. There was a workboat on a mooring, and a jetty with a trawler alongside. There were lights on the trawler's deck, and men moving. I saw boxes rise on a derrick.

At this point, Oban Coastguard squawked out of the VHF. Southwesterly force seven, veering westerly gale force eight soon, they said. Rain. Visibility poor, very poor in rain.

God bless Scotland, I thought. The only place in the world where there is no need to write down the forecast. A squall howled across the loch, blotting out the trawler and the men on the jetty. Lovely night for a long row. But it would have been worse in a flat calm under a full moon.

I went below and turned on the cabin lights, and made a cup of tea without any whisky in it, and ate some of Maureen's cake, and waited.

After half an hour I heard an outboard. The motor throttled back. Something banged on the hull. 'Anyone there?' said a voice.

I pulled down the hood of my coat and went into the

cockpit. A flashlight hit my face. I shone mine back. A round-faced youth was sitting in an aluminium workboat. 'Helloo,' he said. 'Howya doin?''

'I was heading for Colonsay,' I said. 'But I thought, breeze going up, I'll come in here instead and see what happens to the weather.'

'Aye,' said the boy. The white disc of the flashlight ran over the boat. 'So you're cruising, is it?'

'That's right,' I said.

'Rather you than me,' said the boy. 'The lads said would you like a fish?' He held up a salmon: six pounds' weight, narrow farmed-fish wrist to its tail.

'That's really kind,' I said, and rummaged in my pocket.

'On the hoose,' he said, and tossed the fish into the cockpit. 'Well, have a good night. There'll be boats in and out, but you're out of the way here.' And away he roared, having convinced the cruising yachtsman that he was an honest fish farmer packed with highland hospitality. Which he probably was.

I went back below and cut a fillet off the fish. It had the authentic chemical taste of farmed salmon straight out of the cage. I ate it anyway. The bulkhead clock ticked round to midnight. The wind wailed in the rigging, each gust a semitone higher than the last. The workboat howled back down the channel. I turned off the cabin lights. Anyone watching from the shore would be thinking that the cruising yachtsman had turned in, bless his silly heart. I crept out into the cockpit and trained the Captain's glasses on the fish farm.

The trawler was gone. Nothing moved. The men had gone home. That was what you did at a normal fish farm.

But if the cargo we had landed in Swansea was anything to go by, Greenreap was not a normal fish farmer.

Now zero hour was upon me, I was properly frightened. I

started to argue with myself. It was entirely possible that the *Sirius Gleaner* had merely got hold of a bunch of Greenreap boxes. Fishboxes spread round the world like rumours, swiped off quays, shuffling from port to port until it is no big surprise to find a Vladivostok box in Newlyn —

Shut up, Chance, I told myself. You are trying to convince yourself out of this little reconnaissance. Do it.

And there I was over the side, fitting the oars into the dinghy. I untied the painter and gave a pull. The wind took me away. The *Lady* became a pale line that faded and vanished until all that remained was the anchor light at her masthead, a single golden star in a skyful of racing clouds. When I looked over my shoulder, I saw the quay coming up at me. I was pretty sure I had the place to myself.

But pretty sure was not the same as dead certain. I had crawled around rocky places in the dark with the army in Bosnia, and in Bournemouth when I had been a policeman there. But there had always been the army or the police to fall back on.

Not tonight.

The quay came up fast. I pulled along to where it ended in a rough beach of boulders. Here I tied the dinghy to a stone and climbed up the beach.

It was dark. Even now my eyes were used to it, it was hard to know where everything was. The glimmer in the shed window had gone. The rain was pouring down, slanted by the breeze. I found the quay. As far as I remembered, its outside edge made a line to one of the sheds. The rain roared on my oilskin hood as I moved forward. By the time I saw the shed, I could just about reach out and touch it.

It was more a box than a house, windowless, made of a shiplap of rough planks. It looked like the kind of place you would store tools. I moved on, heading sideways. My foot hit something, and I went flat on my face on wet stones. The thing I had tripped over was soft, but firm. It might have been a corpse. I wriggled away from it, panicking. Then I told myself to shut up, and gave it a blink of the red torch. HYDROGEN PEROXIDE 50% APPLY BY BATH FOR SEA LICE INFESTATION, said the lettering on the big plastic bag. So far, so legitimate. When I finally found the door there was no padlock on the bolt. The torch showed nets, chemicals, spare bits of angle iron. I closed the door and moved on, more confident now, using blinks of the torch to locate myself.

I steered well clear of the hut with the windows in case they had left a watchman, who would be sceptical of my prepared excuse, viz. that I had rowed over to thank one and all for the salmon. Anyway, I was more interested in the cold store, a squat metal building from whose nether regions came the purr of a generator and the hum of a reefer unit. Even in the wind and rain it smelled of fish: fresh fish, new caught. I torch-blinked my way round to the door, pulled down the latch and let myself in.

The store was full of the familiar green boxes. There was a pile of them in the middle, and another stacked up against the right-hand wall. I peered inside. A five-pound salmon gazed back, and so did a group of its friends, identical, nose-to-tail, legitimate fish-farm stock. I moved the red disc of the flashlight to the central pile of boxes. It was bigger than the other pile; much bigger. I stood on a box to look in at the top.

This time, it was not a salmon that looked back. It was a fish like a square tennis racket, with two little eyes in the middle of the flat bit. A skate. Skate is commercially extinct in most British waters, and only idiot criminals without consciences fish for them.

I went through the boxes. There were cod, haddock, whiting, all presumably out of quota. I sat and thought about it, in the chill and the smell of new fish. There was only one explanation. Boats were landing their by-catch here, which is to say the fish they caught by accident when they were after something legal, like for instance prawns. And someone would stop by and collect them up, and ship them off somewhere for sale to Tony Greely or equivalent.

At this point, my heart gave an uncomfortable lurch. Fish is a highly perishable commodity. Someone would want to get this load to market as soon as possible. Which would mean lifting them from here tonight.

I found I had already backed away from the boxes. I was out of the door, closing it carefully and quietly while the rain clattered on my hood, moving as best as I could towards where I had left the dinghy. Which was not very good, as it turned out. For my foot hit a rock, and over I went again, dealing myself a wallop on the cheekbone that blew stars into my head and set me whimpering and telling myself to shut up.

I rolled on to my side and started to get up.

The world went white. Someone had turned the quay lights on.

I lay there, letting my eyes adjust. Out in the harbour, beyond the lights, I saw the port light and steaming white of a big boat coming in. The red light grew a green on its left. The btoat was heading on to the quay. Coming alongside. A man came out of one of the huts, zipping his coat. I heard him swear as the rain hit him. Then the boat came into the glow of the working lights and water boiled under its transom, and the man from the hut took a stern line.

But I was not watching the man from the accommodation. I was trying to burrow into the ground, and when that failed on account of it being granite, I was moving at a low sideways belly-crawl into the inky shadow behind a big boulder, unable to take my eyes off the boat.

For the boat was the *Sirius Gleaner*.

8

I lay with my face against the rock and did a lot of worrying. My dinghy was tied up to the boulders under the boat's starboard bow. But the working lights threw a hard black shadow over the shore, and nobody was going to see the dinghy, unless they looked, and there were better things to do than gaze at the scenery on a night like this. So perhaps that was all right. But what I was really worried about was the *Gleaner.* If the boat was taking on cargoes of black fish, that might mean that the Milford crew were back in control. In which case, what had they done to Georgie and his lads?

The derricks started up. A forklift ground out of one of the sheds, moved into the cold store and started ferrying fish boxes down to the quay. The derrick lifted into the glittering rain and lowered them into the hold. Figures moved stiffly to and fro, yellow oilskins gleaming in the lights. There seemed to be three of them. One was enormous, the other two merely huge. Was Johnny still in the hold? Had they sunk him in a deep dark hole in the North Channel with the time-expired gas shells and drums of nuclear waste? He would fit in nicely.

I sat behind my rock and began to shiver as the wind howled

and the rain battered my hood. I have no idea how long it went on for; hours, it felt like, but it was probably twenty minutes. At last the forklift stopped rolling and vanished into its shed, and there were shouts from the quay, and the lights went out, and the *Gleaner* backed away into the night.

I ran down to the dinghy and pulled it out into the teeth of the wind. After ten minutes of hard rowing and green water over the nose I was back aboard the *Lady*. I had the engine running, me on the foredeck by the clattering windlass, not caring who was watching. The anchor came up. The *Lady* heeled thirty degrees as a gust caught her bare poles. I pushed the throttle forward, lit the GPS and ground towards the waypoint at the mouth of the loch, rain drumming on the side of my head.

Even in the loch the waves were sharp and awkward. I did not want to think what they would be like in the open sea.

I soon found out. To my left, a roar and a boom, and white spray jumped twenty feet in the air and blew heavy over the cockpit and ran away down the drains. The next blast came past my stern. The one after that arrived unbroken by rocks and skerries. The *Lady* rolled her starboard rail under, then back the other way. I wound the helm hard down, and the nose came round and plunged into a trough, and the back end reared high, high above my head, and I thought, hell and damnation, this thing is going to dive to the bottom of the deep black sea.

But the wave rolled under, and the nose came up and the stern went down. For a moment the wind dropped, baffled by the next wave. Then the stern began to rise again, and I felt it slide sideways, and I was hauling the wheel the other way. At a time like this the big danger is broaching, which in case you have never done it means getting sideways-on to the wave so it can roll you and knock the masts out of you and perform other undesirable actions. I let a few feet of line off the foresail reefing drum, and gave the sheet a tweak, and a lump of sail unfurled with a bang like a dropped guitar. The boat steadied. Next time she came up on a wave I saw a white stern-light ahead, and a gleam of green transom. I was following the *Sirius Gleaner*. Which was after all what I had set out to do. So I swallowed dry-throated, and kept my eyes off the wind-speed indicator, which was reading thirty-eight knots across the deck. This is a full gale – all right for a fishing boat like the *Gleaner*; but your cruising ketch, even a hefty lump of Early Fibreglass like the *Lorne Lady*, generally finds itself a nice sheltered anchorage in a breeze of this nature.

But it seemed important to find where the *Gleaner* was heading. And the way to do that was to follow her.

So I followed, cold and wet and at some points knee-deep in the water that sloshed into the cockpit from the breaking crests. The waves rolled under, big as hills. And always the *Gleaner*'s stern light floated like a white star far ahead.

There was plenty to do, of course. We were running before a gale up the western shore of Jura. At the northern end of Jura is the horrible Gulf of Corryvreckan, which on the flood makes a race that the Admiralty Pilot says is a danger to small vessels, which in the Admiralty's view are destroyers. Happily the tide had turned now, so we did not have the Corryvreckan to worry about. That left me free to worry about a scatter of rocks and islands up there. They are mostly lit, but on a night as thick as this they could have the Blackpool Tower on them and you would be none the wiser. And after that was Loch Linnhe, heading up to Fort William. Fort William is what passes for civilisation round here, and would be an unwise place to land black fish. So we would be heading somewhere lonelier than that, I thought, as the *Gleaner*'s light swam in the blackness beyond the pale rag of jib. Somewhere nice and quiet, with perhaps a quay for landing the fish and a bit of a road for a refrigerated van.

I squinted at the GPS and the chart, and for the fiftieth time that night cursed Captain Maxwell for being too mean to fit a chart plotter.

And on we went, on and on, for hours. I was not thinking about black fish or bodies in ice. I was thinking about keeping the *Lorne Lady*'s tail to the sea, and the nasty rocky Garvellachs bearing northeast, and my eyes on the kind grey glow of the GPS screen where the magic numbers were flicking —

The GPS went out.

I hit it with the heel of my hand. Nothing: blackness. I hit the autopilot button. Nothing happened. I pulled the flashlight out of its clips and swept it over the dials. The battery meter said seven volts. No good, no good. There would be another battery for engine starting, though.

Then I remembered that there was not. And that the reason was that Gavin Chance, God's gift to broking yachts, had taken the starting battery off the *Lorne Lady* and put it in the Land Rover when the Land Rover battery lost a cell. Which meant it was now a pool of acidulated plastic among the ruins in a Welsh scrapyard. Not here, where it was needed.

No power. No GPS. No way of starting the engine. No bloody nothing. I gazed into the dark and cursed myself.

Up ahead, I caught a bright twink of white light.

Darkness, during which I counted one-chimpanzee, two-chimpanzee, up to six. Then the twink again, high ahead. Shit. *Shit.* That would be the light at the southern end of the Garvellachs. Nasty, long, rocky, sharp, precipitous islands, the Garvellachs. Still, it was a position check. I began to feel happier. To the west of the Garvellachs was open water, without hazards all the way up Loch Linnhe. The *Gleaner* would head up there. I watched the stern-light, unrolled a little more jib to make sure I did not lose it. A squall blew in, a strange, curly squall, with rain. It blotted out the Garvellachs and laid the *Lady* far over to starboard. I put her back on course, following the stern light, waiting for it to curve to port, left, into safe water.

The light moved to the starboard side of the forestay.

I checked my course. It was steady. The *Lady* sank in a trough. Next time she came up, the *Gleaner*'s stern light was further to the right.

No, I thought, with a deep sinking of the heart. Stop it. Not possible. He was heading down the eastern side of the islands.

The east side of the Garvellachs is not clear water. It is a funnel between two sets of unlit rocks. No problem in daylight. No problem on a clear night, even, GPS or no GPS. But in a howling gale with sheets of rain and no instruments, on a boat where to take your hands off the wheel to keep up a dead reckoning plot would be to ask for a broach, a big, big problem.

Only one thing to do. Whoever was steering the *Gleaner* was sitting in her nice warm wheelhouse, watching himself on his plotter as he moved gently down the firth. He knew where he was going and how to get there without hitting anything. All I had to do was follow him. Which was the plan anyway. I grinned a cold grin at the rain. Fine.

The stern light faded in a squall. The *Lady* dug her side in, and I heaved at the wheel.

I let off a few more feet of reefing line, got the jib sheet on the winch and hauled. I felt it pull the boat forward. Stay on his tail, I thought. If there is enough shelter where he is going for him to land a lot of boxes of black fish, there is enough shelter for you to anchor.

There was the merest wedge of north in the wind, now; enough to keep us on the port tack. I concentrated on keeping that light just visible to the left of the forestay. And on we went: the nose plunging downwards, the light gone behind a black hill of water, the lull as the following wave masked the breeze; then the nose up, the light again, the roar and boom as the sail caught it, ratatat of rain on the back of my hood, and down again.

An hour it went on; an hour and a half. I was seriously cold now. Then, suddenly, the light was gone.

I was so slow with cold that it took some time to work out that it had gone behind the sail. I heaved the helm down, and there it was again, closer now, too close, so I could see it reflected in the green paint of the stern. Then there was a flaw in the wind, and I saw high and to my right something dark and solid, with white water bursting at its base. My heart slammed at my ribs. The next wave came under. Just ahead of the bow it turned white and crunchy. I knew that this meant something very bad, but I was too cold and weary to work out what. Then the sail flapped and boomed and lost its air, and there was a roar of water that turned white all around, and under my feet the boat went down what seemed like for ever, and at the bottom of the drop, still falling, we hit something with an enormous crash. Then there was a clang like bells and something whipped my ear, and against the sky I saw the masts came down, and a great glossy flood of water gush out of where the companionway had been. And I thought, in my freezing half-coma: I have put the boat on a rock, and I am going to bloody well drown.

Then the world turned over, and I was in icy salt, and there was nothing to breathe.

When you drown, your past life is meant to flash before your eyes. As usual, I seemed not to be doing a proper job.

Nothing flashed before my eyes except darkness that stung. Visions were replaced by extreme terror. Of course I was not wearing a lifejacket. Of course I was wearing a suit of industrial oilskins and rigger's boots designed for agriculture, not yachting, with steel toecaps that told me in persuasive terms that they wished to take me to the bottom of the sea. I opened my mouth to shout for help. Extra water rushed in. I drew breath to do some good coughing, but I breathed water, not air. So I choked, and panicked, and struggled, and heard the blood in my ears and saw it behind my eyes, red, lightening to the brilliant white of death —

Not death. A flashlight beam. My wrist was caught on something. I got my other hand to it. It was a thick thing, swathed in plastic. A human arm, whose hand was gripping my wrist.

I felt myself heaved. I felt myself dragged over something round and rubbery, and land face first on boards. Something hit me in the stomach, hard, and I retched water and took a breath of broken glass. I lay with my face in what I now understood was the bottom of a boat, and coughed and heaved until I was strong enough to realise that I was shuddering with cold and soaking wet. And I said, 'Where's my boat?'

'Sunk,' said a voice. 'Lucky you're no' with it.'

There was something familiar about the voice. I managed to roll over. The sky was dark, dark grey, and spinning. Between me and it was a head and mighty pair of shoulders, pulling at a pair of oars. A familiar head. I began to feel iller. I said, 'Georgie?'

The hood moved. The voice said, 'Do I know you?' It was definitely the voice of Wee Georgie Strother. My ears were full of water, and some of it seemed to have got into my brain, because nothing was making sense.

He stopped rowing. He peered into my face. The dinghy went beam-on to a wave. He said, 'Gavin?'

'Yes,' I said. 'I'm bloody cold.'

'Gavin,' he said. 'Gavin Chance. What the hell are you doing here, Gavin Chance? Was that you on that boat? That hit the rock and went down? Was it —'

'That was me,' I said, to quell the torrent. 'Here I am. Now row.'

The arms began rowing again. I could hear the slosh of the water, the boom of the waves. And another sound: a sort of sniffing. Then he said, 'Christ, Gavin, thank God you've come,' in a small, choked voice. And I realised that the sniffing noise was the sound of Wee Georgie, hardest of the hard, weeping.

I said, 'What's wrong?'

And he said, 'What isn't?'

At which point I stopped receiving, because everything began to spin, and I vomited, and went into a sort of demi-coma. I was dimly conscious that someone hustled me up the side of a boat, and that I ought to be very, very worried about something, but I could not place what. Then the air got warmer and smelled worse, and whoever the someone was pulled my clothes off and I fell on a bunk and passed out.

When I opened my eyes I did not know where I was. Then I recognised the buttocks of the woman on the wall. This was the cabin of the *Sirius Gleaner*. And things began to trickle back into my mind.

I put my feet on the deck and waited for my head to stop whirling. Outside the scuttle I could see grey daylight, a bay corrugated with waves, a rocky beach with a bungalow and some sheds. And something on the beach: something that might have been a dead whale, if the whale had been dark blue, and had once been ketch rigged. Something that was definitely the wreck of Captain Maxwell's charming cruising yacht *Lorne Lady.* I am not much of an insurance person, but it was hard to see her as anything but a total loss. Just at the moment, though, *Lorne Lady* was a long way down the worry list.

I got up cautiously, hobbled across the cabin and managed to get the door open by using both hands.

Georgie was slumped in the skipper's chair in the wheelhouse. When he heard the door open, he looked round. There were big black bags under his eyes, and he looked twenty years older than when I had last seen him. I said, 'Thank you for pulling me out of the sea.'

He said, 'I saw you come into the bay. I saw you round up.' He pointed to a rocky ledge chucking spray into the sky in the anchorage's mouth. 'I knew you had to hit. What in hell were you doing?'

'I was following a load of black fish and I had no electrics. And what exactly were you at?'

He scowled. Reflex made him open his mouth to tell me to mind my own business or he would break my arms. It was hard to imagine how that would make them hurt any more than they hurt already. Then he sighed and looked miserable and dropped his hands on his knees and said, 'I needed the money.'

'You did.'

'I mean,' he said, 'there was all that money in Swansea. And then we were off the Mull, trawling, and nothing was comin' up. And a wee boat pops out frae God knows where and a man comes aboard with another man, big man. And he said did I ken whose boat this was, and I said mine, and he said wrong, his, and he shows me the papers with his name on them. And he said we should have a charter agreement. I'm to pick it up today.'

I was getting nervous. I said, 'I can explain.'

'No need,' said Georgie, dully. 'He said did I want real trouble? And I said no. And he said that was up to some lads who had to go back to Ireland to decide, but if I did what I was told it might not come to that.'

'Ireland?' The narrative style was difficult, as usual. But this time it seemed to contain actual information.

'Ireland, he said. So he said now I would be working for him. And I said all right, then. And all the time I was thinking of that body in the hold, and how I didn't want to end up like that.'

'And it's still in the hold?'

'Aye,' said Georgie, with a slight return of his old fire. 'Like you said, it's got someone's bullet in it. Yours, maybe.'

'Not mine.'

'So you say. Anyway,' said Georgie, 'I was a free man two days ago. Now I'm workin' for some bastard and he put the fear on the boys who came to work for me and they've gone hame. And I've got some kind of clown on board and I'm doin' the fetch and carry and it's not feckin' safe.'

'Why not?' I was pulling Maureen's telephone to bits. It was wet inside. I rinsed the sim card in the galley sink and put it to dry.

'Because they don't care who they kill. And they're all mobbed up with the polis. Christ,' said Georgie, 'how the hell did I get into this?'

'By being greedy and selling that fish at Swansea,' I said, with only partial accuracy. 'You've only yourself to blame.'

'Black fish is only by-catch,' said Georgie, sniffing. 'If we didn't land it, we'd be throwing it dead into the sea. It's the politicians handin' out the bollocks, not the fishermen.' There was a pause while he considered the iniquities of the situation. Finally he said, 'What are we goin' for to do?'

'Find out what's happening,' I said. 'And get you your boat back.'

'Aye,' said Georgie, thumping the chair arm with his oil-drum-sized fist. 'Aye we bloody will.' Then he began to look worried again. 'But they're hard, hard.'

'Not as hard as me,' I said, which we both knew was pathetic. 'So you need a deckie, right?'

'No.'

'Yes you do. It'll be me. All right?'

He looked at me. His mouth opened, then closed. 'All right, then,' he said.

'Right,' I said. 'So what are your precise orders?'

'Collect fish from point specified,' said Georgie. 'Deliver where instructed. Which will vary.'

'And what about . . . that?' I pointed in the direction of the hold and the remains of Johnny.

He shrugged. 'Like I said, still there. Nobody knows.'

I nodded, thinking: I should damn well hope not.

'There is a thing,' said Georgie. 'The boss seemed a bit curious about you, like. He'd like for to meet you, really.'

'Who is he?'

'Name of Smith.'

'Welsh accent?'

'Talks a bit funny, aye.'

'I've been wanting to meet him.' Which was not strictly true.

'Aye.' His anxious air had returned. This Smith had had an impact, all right. 'You'll need your clothes. I put them in the engine room.' He scuttled off and came back with the bundle. The clothes were stiff with salt and smelled strongly of diesel.

As I forced my way in they emitted a fine white dust. The socks had shrunk, so I pulled the seaboots on without.

'Right,' said Georgie.

The *Gleaner* was tied up alongside a concrete quay. The rain had stopped, but the wind roared in my ears as I heaved myself on to the coping. Georgie stumped ahead, leading the way to a white bungalow that lay on a patch of tarmac in the lee of an outcrop of rock.

It was a charming spot for a holiday cottage; though there was something less than charming about the bungalow. The garden was tarmac, the windows plastic, the yard round the back concrete, tidy the way a funeral parlour is tidy, with a big shed humming the way a mortuary hums. Georgie led me to the back door and knocked, tentatively for him. The door opened immediately. A woman of fifty held it on a chain. She had narrow eyes and hard vertical lines in her jowls. She looked as grim and tidy as the bungalow. 'It's Georgie, Mrs Smith,' said Georgie, and if he had had a cap he would have been twisting it in his hands. 'With Gavin.'

The woman looked at me. I looked back. I felt I was being counted and found deficient. She said, 'Take your boots off.'

I left my boots by Georgie's alongside the scraper. The woman observed that I was not wearing socks, counted me again, and found I added up to even less than before. She said, 'Do you know who you're going to meet?'

'I don't even know his real name.'

Her jawline hardened. She said, 'Strother, go in.' She turned to me. 'I suppose you can read?'

'Just about.'

She handed me a scrapbook. 'Go on,' she said. I opened the brown plastic cover. There were newspaper cuttings inside, yellowing behind sheets of plastic. One of them was the front cover of the *Observer* magazine. It bore the portrait of a man with his hands folded on a table. He would have been about forty-five. The eyes were pale blue. The hair was cropped short, and the face spread away for a great distance on all sides of the nose, which was long and narrow. The mouth was small and pink. The hands were enormous, with a wedding ring on the usual finger. I looked up at the bulldog woman. The ring matched the gold band on her hand.

As I leafed through the scrapbook, a memory stirred and grew. The man in the photograph had been famous. He was Major Horace Davies, the Man with No Nerves. He had been a soldier in the Royal Logistics Corps, with odd links to law enforcement in Northern Ireland. He had got his real name from his parents, who were extremely Welsh. The redtops had given him his name after he had walked up to a couple of armed Irish terrorists in the last days before Stormont, and the Irish had been so shocked by his size and general demeanour that they had failed to open fire. The arrest had briefly made him very famous. I and my fellow policemen had been astonished that he had not dived for the nearest cover. What on earth was this national hero doing in an outfit dedicated to the laundering of black fish?

'That's who you're going to meet,' said the woman. 'So make sure you show him a little respect.' She spoke as if he was ill, or in some way diminished since the days of his heroism. 'Now. Get in.'

I went.

9

I walked into a big living room with a picture window overlooking the bay. There were brown swirls on the beige carpet and china Bambis on a rough stone mantelpiece under which burned a coal-effect fire. Georgie was standing in the middle of the carpet, looking agonized. I went to stand beside him. In the far armchair of the three-piece suite a big man in a brown suit was frowning at a copy of the *Daily Telegraph*. I said, 'Good afternoon.'

Major Davies looked up at me with his pale eyes and did not answer. If he had been the one who had burned my tug, he should have been surprised I was still alive. But he did not show any emotion. He had a presence that spread from him like chill spreads from ice. He waited long enough for me not to get the idea that he was continuing a conversation I had started. Then he said, 'Explain yourself.'

I said, 'What do you mean?' Next to me, Georgie went rigid. I knew he thought this was a man whose questions you answered without asking any of your own.

Davies said, 'You come round the point in a gale and wreck

your boat on my beach. And now Mr Strother says he wants to employ you. What's your name?'

I allowed my eyes to rest on his. It was no problem to make them look somewhat nervous. I said, 'Gavin.'

'Gavin,' he said, gazing. The huge white fingers tapped the magazine. 'Gavin Chance, late Inspector. Now ship and yacht broker.'

I nodded, to cover up the sinking of my stomach. How the hell did he know this?

He said. 'Apparently you were once a useful police officer.'

'That is very lovely to hear,' I said.

He gave me the icy glare. It froze Georgie, but not me. He said, 'There is nothing worse than a failed policeman.' Except possibly a national hero running black fish, I thought. 'Do you want the work? It involves making collections from fish farms. Not hard.'

'No,' I said. 'I mean yes. I'll take it.'

The little mouth became a rectangle full of teeth. It was not precisely a smile. He said, 'Can I trust you?'

I said, 'Yes.'

'Quite,' he said. He gazed out of the window, where the wreckage of Captain Maxwell's boat was grinding on the ledge in the bay. 'You've messed up my beach.'

'The insurance will deal with it.'

'They may,' he said. 'If I find I can trust you. If not, I shall be forced to give them my opinion that your mishap was the result of gross negligence.'

Again the silence. Again a sort of shudder from Georgie. This was a frightening person, no error. But he was making me angry with his great blank arrogance. I tried to keep the anger down, but it got round the side. I said, 'One thing.'

'What?' He did not look at me.

'Why did you burn my boat?'

'Burn?' he said. 'Boat?' He was frowning, as if puzzled. It was the first expression I had seen on that large acreage of face, and it was strangely convincing.

'Your people set fire to my boat,' I said.

He said, 'Not my people. But I can understand how someone might come to feel it was necessary.' The cold eyes held mine. I realised he was as angry with me as I was with him. And though it was not sensible, I was pleased.

He took a deep breath. The anger went, and his face was blank again. 'Tell you what,' he said. 'Why don't you have a look round?'

'Round?'

'You'll want to see what you're getting in to. Check out the fish store, perhaps.'

I said, 'Yes. Maybe.' How the hell had Johnny thought he could play poker with this reptile?

'Go on, then.' He went back to the *Telegraph*. The audience was over. Georgie went out first, like a rabbit out of a dog's home. The woman averted her eyes as I passed through the kitchen. I heard her bolt the door behind me.

Georgie and I stood in the yard by our boots, looking at each other. 'He likes you,' said Georgie, shaking his head.

'What do you mean?'

'He didn't kill you.' He walked off back to the boat.

And there I was, standing in the yard, deeply puzzled. What was puzzling me was this. Major Davies might easily call himself Smith for business purposes. He might easily run a fishmonger's business on the side, and have a tame policeman who supervised his landings for him. But I could not see him protecting his investments with .22 bullets in the back of the head, or indeed burning boats. And the voice issuing threats on the voicemail I had picked up in the Sound of Islay had not been his. Perhaps, I thought, Major Davies was being hoodwinked by an acquaintance or acquaintances I had not yet met.

Perhaps I should have asked him.

But that would have been a stupid idea. If Johnny's body was there because of him, I would need shutting up, perhaps by the same means as Johnny.

Meanwhile, I was in a splendid position to continue my inquiries into Greenreap's business model.

The concrete of the yard looked as if it had been scrubbed, possibly with a toothbrush. *Pictures at an Exhibition* trickled out of the window where Mrs. Davies was washing something and listening to Classic FM. I strolled off round the buildings, breathing deeply to clear my mind of the interview. Tidy garage for the forklift. Tidy pile of Greenreap fish boxes. Tidy whitewashed breezeblock building, windowless, humming, connected to the quay by a tidy concrete road. Big insulated door in the middle of the wall. A cold store. The fish store.

I pulled the door open and looked inside, as per the Major's instructions. There was not much to see, except that it was less tidy than the rest of the place. The Greenreap boxes were in there, one pile small, salmon, another large, black fish, and a big untidy pile of boxes and tarpaulins in the corner, piled in to reduce the amount of empty air that needed cooling. Perhaps the Major was worried about his carbon footprint. There was something on the ground, on a pallet of its own. My heart gave a bump. I thought it was Johnny. But it wasn't. It was an enormous fish: a tuna. I had no notion there was tuna in Scotland. I walked over to the boxes, found some haddock. Salmon this side, black fish that. Waiting for the lorry. It was cold in here, full of the hum of the refrigeration equipment. There was a sound behind me. I turned back towards the door, a bright square in the dim grey wall. A figure stood silhouetted in the brightness. Its arms moved. I said, 'Hey!' The square grew narrower, became a slot, went out.

I stood there with my heart thumping and my mouth open. I had been sleep-deprived, burned out, shipwrecked, half-drowned and pissed off. Now I had walked into a cold store and someone had shut the door. I heard the clunk of a hefty catch. I was a total bloody fool. It was hard to imagine things getting any worse.

Until the lights went off.

I felt my way round the boxes to the door. It was black as the inside of a cow, properly dark. I found the door, felt round it. The latch was on the outside. So was the light switch.

It was cold in here.

Not freezing, of course. Freezing a fish is not good for it, whatever the late Clarence Birdseye may have said. To keep a fish in prime condition it needs storing just above zero. But you can kill a human being by storing him just above zero, though it can take a day or two.

My fingers were already getting cold.

I found my way back through the inky dark to where the tuna had been. I sat on it and tried to think things through. My maths teacher once told us that the human brain works best at a temperature of 37° Fahrenheit. Mine was certainly moving fast. Partly, it was thinking that the Major had probably murdered Johnny after all, and that he was about to do the same for me. Partly, I was thinking that it was bloody silly to survive a full-gale shipwreck, then die of exposure in a little dark room. But mostly I was concentrating on being frightened.

Conserve body heat, I thought. Generate more. But there were no piles of blankets flung idly in a corner. There were only some boxes and pallets and plastic bags, and ninety-odd boxes of black fish, and the tuna on its pallet.

I was beginning to understood the extreme respect Georgie seemed to feel for Major Davies.

Christ, it was cold.

I got up. I walked backwards and forwards. I ran on the spot. I tried to have thoughts that would keep me warm. But they were all about freezing.

I tried to find positives in the situation. The Major seemed to be a person who knew the value of a pound. So perhaps he would not want to turn down the temperature, because turning down the temperature would freeze his fish, halving its value. He would keep it cool. And while mere coolness would kill me eventually, it would take a long time, during which the fish would undergo as much deterioration as me; more, possibly, since I am not averse to sashimi, even if I have to gnaw it off the bone. So I went to the door, and shouted, 'Soy sauce!'

Silence.

'Wasabi!' I yelled. 'I have a knife! I'm cutting up your fish!'

More silence. I went back to the tuna. I had read somewhere that tuna are warm-blooded. I wondered if I should climb inside, like an Inuit with a caribou. I pulled out my Swiss Army knife and cut a small hole in the tuna and stuffed my hand into its guts. They were cold. So I got up, and wondered if I was really hungry enough to eat a raw salmon, and decided I wasn't, yet. Then I decided that Inuit practice did indeed present an opportunity. So I jogged over to the door and shouted, 'I'm getting inside the tuna!'

There was a silence. Then someone coughed. 'Stay outae the tuna,' said a voice, faint through the door.

'If I stay in here, I'm going in the tuna,' I said.

There was a pause, possibly for discussion. Then the door opened a crack, admitting a dazzling stream of daylight. The light flicked on. A man came in; not the Major, but a stubble-faced man in a woolly hat. 'I'm out of here,' I said.

'Aye,' he said, as if locking people into chill houses was all in a day's work. 'Boss says next time he gets any verbal out of you he'll put you in for a week.' But I felt a sort of manic glee. I had bluffed him, and he had let me out. Some poker player.

It wore off. The odds were that he would have let me out anyway. A rap on the knuckles was all it had been. By the time I walked out of the yard, I was pissed off again. Who did this Major think he was, dishing out knuckle-raps?

I found I was on the quay. The *Gleaner* was burbling gently alongside. Georgie stuck his head out of the bridge window. 'Where you been?' he said.

'In the cold store, thanks for asking.'

'Oh, aye,' said Georgie, not a sufferer from prurient curiosity. 'You comin' to sea?'

'As soon as possible.'

'You want to talk to the big man again?'

'No. I want to find out exactly what he is doing and fuck it up, and him too. All right?'

'Sounds fine,' said Georgie. 'Stern lines.'

And I hobbled down the quay and took off the stern lines.

When I got aboard I put my sim card into Georgie's phone. It still worked, though with some suprising crackles. I left a long message on the voicemail of Captain Maxwell's insurers, telling them about the unpleasantness with the Captain's boat. Then I consulted the notes the Major had given Georgie.

There was a collection to be made from the Loch Mor fish farm. Then there was a delivery, to Holyhead this time, for eight thousand pounds, cash. I went back to the wheelhouse. The *Gleaner* was thrashing down the channel. To starboard the Garvellachs reared like a stegosaur's backbone from a brilliant blue sea. Jura stretched away on the port bow. The sky was a pure, deep blue. It was even possible to be happy you were alive, if you dismissed from your mind all thoughts of ex-wives, bodies in the ice and cold stores. I said, 'Can we drop into Achnabuie?'

'No way,' said Georgie. 'He'll see it on the plotter. He checks the plotter, he told me. So he can see where we've been. He said he didn't want any mixing up of business with diversion. He —'

'Yes,' I said, to stem the flow. 'How many times have you been up and down the Sound of Jura?'

'Thousand?' said Georgie. 'Fifteen hundred? Let me see —'

'No,' I said. I leaned forward and switched the plotter off. 'He's a soldier. He doesn't believe you can do anything without machinery. It is a nice clear evening. You can get through the Sound of Luing and on down without radar and satnav?'

'With my eyes closed,' said Georgie. 'Like anyone else.'

'So we'll go to Achnabuie and on up, and he'll never know. I mean, do you want to be loading in daylight?'

'No way,' said Georgie. 'Pickup's at four in the morning.'

'Well then.'

'Aye.' He gave me a sort of a look. And I saw again that as far as Georgie was concerned, I was the man who knew what he was doing when the world got complicated. He said, 'Would you look at this?' He passed me an envelope, flap open.

I pulled out the papers it contained. It was a charter agreement between the Major and Georgie, duly signed by both parties, dated a week previously. I said, 'It's like he said. You're chartering the boat.'

'Aye,' said Georgie. 'A formality, he said. Pending dispute resolution. I don't quite get it.'

'The dispute resolution bit is bullshit. The rest of it is like this. If a Fisheries boat finds you with a load of black fish, they'll fine you half a million quid and take your house. And he wants to be sure it will happen to you, not him.'

'Aye,' said Georgie. 'Thought so.' He sounded almost relieved. I explained things, and he had a boat. In his mind this amounted to a partnership.

I had a shower, nice and hot thanks to the waste heat from the reefer units that were cooling Johnny's ice. Then I rang Maureen. She sounded very pleased to hear my voice. I was pleased to hear hers, too.

We crawled into Achnabuie as the sun was sinking. And there she was on the quay, ready to take the lines. She handed me a bag of groceries and said, 'The whisky's in there,' with that look people give people who are suspected of being too fond of whisky.

I said, 'It's for Georgie.'

Her face cleared, and she gave me her beautiful smile. Then I walked down the quay with her and had a look at the tug.

I had fitted that tug out myself, personally nicking the chairs from the village hall and the pipe lagging from the abandoned classrooms at Achnabuie School. It had not been much, but it had been home.

Maureen was beside me, the back of her hand touching mine. She said, 'I didn't want to tell you. But the man from the insurance came, and said it was petrol, and they were no' going to pay.' She had taken on the air of a redhaired bear defending its young. 'So I gave him a piece of my mind but I don't think it helped. You might have got killed!' She seemed about to cry. Then she went bright red and said, 'That's me, then,' and walked back to her car.

I watched her go. I called, 'I'll ring.'

She said, 'Suit yourself.' Over her shoulder she gave me a smile that just about knocked me down.

'Christ,' said Georgie, behind me. 'You could get lucky there.'

I walked away from his nasty presumption and inspected the wreck.

Police tape flapped in the drizzle. The roof of the wheelhouse sagged like a pancake, and the computer was a skeleton of sooty metal. I stepped on, feeling the heat-buckled plates oilcan under my feet. The heat had burned off the paint, and the fire brigade had half-filled the hull with water, so I could see it shifting dark and evil where once my bulkheads had divided my cabins.

I stopped.

There was something white on the top of the Samson post. I walked quickly forward, my feet scuffing flakes of burned paint. The white object was a rosette, of the kind awarded to ponies at the New Forest show to which Miranda had frogmarched me during our married life. It was snow white.

How did it manage to be white in the middle of all this soot and ash?

I bent and picked it up. I had to peel it off the post. It had been stuck with gum: spearmint, by the smell of it. I stuffed it in my pocket and jumped on to the quay. I rang Maureen's mobile. She sounded happy to hear me. I said, 'Did anyone come down to the boat today?'

'Not above fifty people,' she said. 'Fire brigade, police, reporters, you name it. Why?'

'Nothing,' I said. 'Thanks, Maureen.'

'Don't mention it,' she said, and rang off, too soon, as if she had been disappointed by the content of the call.

Who was sticking rosettes on the ashes of my boat? Odd thing to do. I felt faintly threatened. But then you do, when someone has just burned your home to the waterline. I walked back to the *Gleaner* and jumped on and said, 'Let's go.'

We went.

10

We went across to Craighouse and rowed ashore in the dinghy and on to the distillery tap. I had plans not to drink. But I saw Georgie tucking in, and thought about my pressing anxieties, and convinced myself that I was looking at the cure; so I bought us a round. The eighty-shilling was all right, and so was the whisky. After the third pint, Georgie scowled at me and said, 'You know what?'

I squinted at him. 'Wha?'

'You're all right,' he said.

'I know,' I said, because the whisky made me believe it was true, and besides, he liked being agreed with by the other members of his team. So we had a steak and chips each, and rowed back to the *Gleaner*. Presumably I climbed aboard and set the alarm. I have no idea. All I know is that next thing I knew I was in a bunk with all my clothes on, and a tin alarm clock was clattering in my ear and telling me it was half past two. Then I was out of the bunk and stumping up to drop the mooring.

And away we went up the Sound of Islay on the tide, buoys blinking red on the port bow, and round to Loch Mor, hatch covers off, white light streaming from the Bonneville-Clark vault and a fine collection of black fish descending from the derrick.

This time I got a proper look at the man who came out of the hut to help with the loading. He had a square face with a broken nose, and the faint atmosphere of anxiety common to all who worked for the Major. We finished up and cast off and pointed the nose out to sea.

'Aye,' said Georgie as we turned west after the outer channel marker. 'Donnie. Hard man. Well, that's me.' And he went to his bunk.

I propped myself in the helmsman's chair and tried to keep my eyelids up as Islay crawled past to port. The tide was against us, and the bow slammed nastily in the race off the Oa, but not as nastily as Georgie snored. I sang 'God Save the Queen' to keep myself awake until we opened up the Mull. Then I set the autopilot, and the alarm clock, said a brief prayer and plunged into a deep, horribly unseamanlike sleep.

It was the alarm clock woke me again. Daylight had come, and the Mull of Kintyre was five miles on the port bow. I lurched into the galley, tipped instant coffee into mugs, filled up with hot water from the tap, and took one to Georgie.

He grunted, extended a paw, and took a swig. 'Ach,' he said, perfectly reasonably.

'Course one seventy,' I said. 'Still two hours of ebb. I'm going to turn in.' All very Jack Hawkins, really, and I got the impression Georgie was on the edge of saluting. But he restrained himself, and I went to my bunk and put my head down.

It was good to lie in a bunk, however stinking, and luxuriate in blankets, however crusty. Probably Rathlin Island streamed past to starboard. A bouncing in the pillow might have been the race off the Mull of Galloway, and a distant whiff of money the Isle of Man. But I knew very little about all this. I was deep in sleep, where I was joined by Miranda, whose teeth were unnaturally sharp when she laughed at the jokes of Tony Greely, who had a sharp gutting knife, except that the fish he was gutting turned out to be Johnny Bonny —

The phone woke me. It took me a moment to work out where I was, but as always the bulkhead girls put me straight. I pressed the green button without looking at the caller ID. A sharp voice said, 'Gavin?'

'Miranda,' I said. 'I was just dreaming about you.'

'Lovely for you.' She did not sound interested. 'Listen. Johnny's vanished.'

'So you said.' I left a silence.

'We haven't seen him. Nobody's seen him. For a week.'

'Me too,' I said.

'Are you sure?' she said.

My stomach did its lurching thing. 'For God's sake,' I said. 'Why would I say I hadn't if I had?' An open question, avoiding the issue.

'I've asked around. He was in Cowes last weekend. He said he was coming up to visit you in Scotland. And he set off. In his car. And nobody's seen him since.'

I said, 'He was my partner in a business that was packing up.' Past tense. Careful. 'I'm not responsible for him.'

'Oh. Yes. He's an idiot. But we worry.' Her voice had gone small and sad. This was Miranda at her most dangerous. 'You are responsible, though,' she said, recovering. 'At least I think you are. Daddy agrees. That's why we set you up in business. So you could look after him.'

'Wait a minute —'

'Anyway,' she said. 'If you see Johnny, tell him he's a bastard not to get in touch.'

'All right.'

'You sound tired.' Steelier now.

'I am.' I rang off before she could get under my skin, and climbed out of the bunk and made more vile coffee.

Georgie was nodding over the wheel. It was duskish. The lights of Holyhead were a line of dirty orange jewels on the port bow, and the Dublin ferry was ploughing across our nose. Georgie said, 'Where we going?'

The correct answer was 'Holyhead'. But I had had enough of being tangled up in other people's machinery. So I said, 'Aberystwyth.'

'Horrible place,' said Georgie.

'Into each life a little rain must fall,' I said, and rang directory enquiries, and found the number of Tony Greely.

When Miranda had started screwing Tony Greely I packed my bags and left the house and moved into a flat in Bournemouth. The flat was tastefully decorated in magnolia, which did not accord with my mood, so I began to spend too much time in the pub. While in the pub one evening I made a redecoration decision, and on the way to work next day nipped into B&Q and bought three gallons of eggshell as close to the colour of blood as I could reasonably achieve. I stored these in the boot of the Peugeot van I was driving at the time, and went to work.

This should have meant detecting crimes. Actually it meant clattering away at a computer, answering meaningless questions for the benefit of departments whose job it was to draw their pay and look busy. After a couple of hours of this, I knew I was going to go crazy. So I logged off and went out into Bournemouth.

It was a hot summer day, and the streets were full of people. I was not in the mood for people, so I turned out of the town centre and into the streets that run behind the seafront hotels.

There is a school down there, a nice place where the children of the people who work in the hotels go to get educated. It is full of good teachers and pupils of thirty different nationalities. I needed to remind myself that there were people in the world who did not merely draw their pay and wait to die.

So down the street I walked. But instead of children's voices, I heard male British swearing. And as I went round a corner I saw a nasty sight.

There were five big white lads and two small brown men. The white lads had the brown men penned into a corner. The brown men looked nervous, as well they might, because one of the white lads had a baseball bat and one of the others had a wrecking bar. 'Fuck off home,' said one of the white lads.

'This is our home,' said one of the brown men. 'We have simply come to collect our children from school.'

'I said fuck off home,' said a white lad, who was perhaps none too bright. 'Or we'll send you there in a fucking box.'

I was beginning to feel very depressed. Partly this was because it is not nice to see white yobs behaving in such a stereotypical manner. But mostly it was because this was a Racist Incident, which meant that if anyone survived there would be months of paperwork. I said, 'Oi.'

One of the white lads looked round. 'Piss off,' he said, and turned back to the brown men, who were now grey.

I am not a show-off, but there are times when I do not like being ignored. This was one of them. There was a skip on my left, full of building debris. From it I extracted a length of four-by-two. Then I said, 'I am a police officer.'

The were not listening. One of them took a whack at one of the brown men.

My duty was plain. I should assess the situation, conclude after a head count that I was outnumbered, withdraw to a safe distance and call for backup, recording events in my notebook until such time as reinforcements arrived. But I had been sitting in an office all day, filling in meaningless online forms. So even as the police thoughts went through my head, I found I had smacked the lad with the baseball bat round the ear, jabbed another in the kidney hard enough to hurt my wrist, and raked another with a nail that seemed to be sticking out of the four-by-two. The other two turned round to look at me. I said, 'You are under arrest,' and fumbled for my warrant card, but they were already running away. In the opposite direction, fortunately, from the brown men.

The yobs on the ground stirred, groaning. There were sirens now. I threw the four-by-two back into the skip. 'Anyone asks, you were fighting,' I said. 'What were you doing?'

'Fighting.'

A panda came round the corner. Two uniforms got out, groping for batons. They stopped when they recognised me.

'Fighting,' I said. 'Eh, lads?'

'Funny,' said the sergeant. 'When you're around they all start hitting each other.'

'It's a gift,' I said.

'Certainly is,' said the sergeant.

Then I went to the pub, and drank the first pint two-handed, I was shaking so badly. For I am not a violent person. It is just that I find it hard to take the long way round when the short way will do.

The first pint led to another. And then it was eight o'clock, and I was stepping out of the pub. I navigated through the outdoor drinkers without incident, unlocked the van door at the third attempt and started to drive. But the drink put me in a sort of reverie, and force of habit directed me not to the magnolia flat but towards Lymington. I was halfway across the New Forest before I realised where I was going. A rapid blast from a bottle in the glove compartment convinced me that I might as well take this opportunity to inspect the scene of my greatest happiness. So up to the cottage I drove; and there parked discreetly outside the gate was a black Porsche Boxster that I recognised as belonging to Tony Greely, Man of Fish. I applied once more to the bottle, in the hope that it would calm me down. It did not. Quite the reverse, actually.

I have virtually no idea what happened next, except that when I came round I was standing next to a Boxster that somebody had painted red, and that judging by the six-inch brush dripping in my hand and the paint on my jeans, the someone was me.

I put the brushes in the back of the van. As I slammed the door, I heard a window open. And there on the first floor framed by roses was the nut-brown frame of Tony Greely, stark naked, with his mouth open. I gave him the finger and drove off.

I had not finished with Greely.

So now off the coast of Anglesey I pressed the call button on my phone.

For a moment I worried that he might not take the call. But a voice said, 'Hopley Manor Hotel?'

I said, in a voice as deep and blank as I could make it, 'Mr Greely?'

'What is it regarding?'

'Fish.'

They put me through.

'Yes?' The voice was well-modulated and boyish. 'Who is this?'

I said. 'I met some of your people in Swansea last week.'

'I beg your pardon?'

'I can give you the number of the refrigerated lorry,' I said.

'Mr Smith?' said Greely.

'Who did you think it was?'

'Oh.' He laughed; nervous, the laugh. His voice became more anxious to oblige. 'What can we do for you?'

'I have another load. Flapping fresh. Excellent price.'

'Oh?' Cautious now.

'Ten K,' I said. 'FOB Aberystwyth Town Quay, four a.m.'

'That's very soon.'

'If you're not interested —'

'I am, I am,' he said. 'The truck's no problem. It's the . . . er . . .'

'Finance.'

'Yes.'

I felt I was smiling a large, radiant smile, though the reflection in the wheelhouse window looked more like a skull. I said, 'I'll come and fetch it.'

'Well,' he said, doubtful now.

'Oh, well, leave it, then,' I said.

'No,' said Greely. 'That will be, ah, no problem.'

'Fine,' I said. 'See you.' And rang off.

It was raining when we went alongside at Aberystwyth. The buildings of the town shone black and spiky under the lights. A truck was waiting on the quay. We pulled off the hatch cover, and got the derrick going, and the pallets of boxes started coming up from the hold, and the truck driver loaded them with a miniature forklift. I looked around. There was no police car that I could see. But it was not particularly pleasant to be landing fish in the deadest hour of the night, knowing that those wet Gothic windows could be full of eyes drawing nasty Welsh conclusions, and that the corpse of Johnny Bonny was chilling in the hold.

As we were loading the last boxes, a police car did draw up. A constable climbed out and walked over. He was Aberystwyth constabulary. I had never seen him before; a wild policeman, not a tame one. I thought, oh, hell, here we go. The constable said, 'What you got in these boxes?'

I said, 'Fish.'

He stooped over a box, flashed his torch, saw farmed salmon. He said, 'Let's look in one of the others.'

From the corner of my eye I saw Georgie adjust his grip on a length of four-by-two. I could practically see the flames over the edge of the frying pan. 'That one.' He tapped a box well down the stack.

I pulled off the boxes on top. The policeman looked in. The flashlight shone in the eye of a nice fresh over-quota deeply illegal cod. Georgie commenced his wind-up. The policeman said, 'More fish, then.'

I frowned at Georgie, not that he would see. I said, keeping the shake out of my voice, 'What did you think it would be?'

'Cannabis. Cocaine.' The policeman shook his head, and my blood warmed with the realisation that his library did not include the *Collins Field Guide to the Sea Fishes of Britain and North-Western Europe*. 'I hate fish.' It was four in the morning, and he was bored, and he wanted to talk. I did not. So we froze him out, and he drove sulkily away. And Georgie carefully propped his four-by-two against the wall on which I was leaning thanks to the weakness of my knees.

'That it?' said the driver, pitching his roll-up into the harbour.

'That's it,' I said. 'I'm coming with you.'

He was a small man, elderly, with the defeated look of one who was not driving refrigerated trucks as a matter of personal choice. 'All right,' he said. 'Hop in.'

I hopped. As the truck pulled away, I saw in the rear view mirror the *Sirius Gleaner* moving off the quay, bound for

Caernarfon, where she would suffer a diplomatic engine problem until I was good and ready.

The A44 unreeled in the headlights. It was warm in the cab, and smelled faintly of polish. I went back to sleep.

'Morning,' said the driver, when I woke up. It was light. We were passing through rolling green hills with big stands of trees. I said, 'Where are you delivering this stuff?'

He pulled a clipboard down from the sun visor. 'Hopley Manor Hotel,' he said.

'Ever been there before?'

He said, 'I'm just the driver, innit?'

'Short notice job?'

'They all are.'

'Ever heard of someone called Tony Greely?'

'No.' He frowned. 'The chef off the telly?'

'Probably.'

'Oh.' He turned up Radio 2. Talking to hitchhikers was not part of the job. And I meditated on the continuing rise of Tony Greely. TV reception is not good at Achnabuie, and I had never heard of Hopley Manor. I was looking forward to finding out more.

After another hour, an increasing grimness of the countryside indicated that we were entering the Midlands. It began to rain. We drove along a red-brick wall, inside which was a large building bristling with turrets. A discreetly-lettered sign said HOPLEY MANOR COUNTRY HOUSE HOTEL. There was a signature reproduced at the bottom of the sign. It appeared to read Tony Greely. This looked very like stardom. Nice work, Tony.

The driver was reading his clipboard, steering with his knees. 'The Stables,' he said.

So round to the stables we went.

The stables had once been home to a couple of dozen horses.

But the horses were gone, and the doors were rain-flecked plate glass, behind which were offices with tidy-looking women battering computer keyboards. What might have been the hay barn was now a cold store, and on the gravel in front of the store stood half-a-dozen refrigerated vans. There was big money here, and a high level of organisation.

A man in a sentry box directed the truck to the cold store. Doors opened. A forklift truck began buzzing about. I left them to it and put my head round the office door. 'Where's Tony?' I said to the dark woman with the perfect hair behind the reception desk.

'You mean Mr Greely?' she said, rolling the great man's name round her mouth like wine. 'Mr Greely is filming in the Golden Ball Bar.'

'On Scilly?'

'In the hotel,' said the woman. 'But —'

I did not hear the rest of what she had to say because the door had closed behind me. I walked past the lorry, through a gate in a wall and onto a big green lawn. At the far side of the lawn were tables with umbrellas. The tables were empty. And so was the reception, except for the glossy girl behind the counter.

I saw her eyes sweep from the top of my baseball cap to my filthy rigger's boots, and conjectured that I was not her usual type of customer. 'Golden Ball Bar?' I said.

Her eyes flicked to a corridor, and she said, 'Dress is smart casual,' but I was already walking away down the seagrass runner. The hotel was about as bustling as your average tomb, but there were voices from the Golden Ball Bar. I went in.

There were tables, a scrubbed wooden floor, the trademark Greely fish cabinets, and a blackboard menu with prices to make your eyes water. Tony Greely was standing at a range, frying something for the benefit of a TV camera. His ringlets jostled under the band of a chef's hat tilted rakishly back, and his eyes sparkled, and his teeth shone, and his gold earring gleamed like pirate treasure as it reflected the magic of his personality. 'And *cut*,' said the director. 'Lovely, darling.' She embarked on an explanation of what she wanted next, while Tony looked around for a shiny surface to admire himself in. I saw him catch my reflection in a mirror advertising Jameson's. I saw his eyes travel on, then return. I saw his mouth fall open.

'Good morning,' I said, in the voice of Mr Smith.

'Tony,' said the director, calling him to order. She turned round and hissed, 'We're busy.'

'Just watching,' I said.

'Oh.' She looked at Greely, but Greely was doing goggle eyes, open mouth and grey skin, very much like a dead cod.

'When you are ready,' I said, 'I think we ought to have a chat. Finish dinner, though, go on.'

The director looked at Greely. Then she looked at me. Then she said, 'Derek.' A large person with no hair got up from a cane-seated chair at a scrubbed-wood table, opened and closed a large pair of hands and started towards me. For a moment I wished I had brought Georgie along for backup. But I had bigger backup than Georgie. I said, 'Have you done any filming in the stables yet?'

The director ignored me. Derek came on like a shaved grizzly. I said, 'There's some very interesting stuff there.'

'Ah,' said Tony, with a sickly grin. 'It's Gavin, isn't it?' Derek stopped.

'That's me. And we've just made a delivery of —'

'Right,' said Tony, cutting me off. 'Lovely. Splendid.' Derek went back to his chair.

'And still flappin',' I said. The film crew were beginning

to relax. This was not some chancer who had slept in a ditch and was planning a death-or-glory assault on the optics. This was a noble seagoing fisherman, and his wild appearance bore testament to the perils of the deep.

I said, 'We should have a meeting.'

'But —'

'Now,' I said. I went round into the lights and took Tony by the elbow, and said, 'You look fabulous, darling. Where?'

'Thank you,' he said. 'My office. Ten minutes, everybody.'

'No more,' hissed the director, whose lips had disappeared. As we left, assistants were taking over the demonstration, providing mouthwatering close-ups of a fillet of pair-trawled bass, laundered to full sustainability and sizzling in lemon juice and fennel.

We went into an office. The door closed. Tony got a desk between us and said, 'How *dare* you!'

I stood and watched him and thought how surprising it was that such a handsome chap could turn first into a cod and now into a rat with ringlets. I said, 'How dare I what?'

He had not considered this. 'Burst in,' he said.

'Oh, that,' I said. 'There were some things I wanted to clear up. And I think your fans would be interested, too. Such as why you have been buying consignments of black fish and claiming they have been hand-speared by Native Americans. And why you have been buying them for cash. The Revenue might find some very interesting questions to ask. And you would find them embarrassing, be fair.'

'You're guessing.'

'No I'm not. I've got names, number plates, photographs.'

'Nonsense.'

'Listen,' I said, for I did not want to have to show him that I did not have any photographs, and that even if I did have number plates I was not in a position to trace them, no longer being a policeman. 'I have observed that your hotel is not very busy. And I suspect that you expanded your restaurants rather quickly, am I right?'

His lower lip came out. I was right.

'So there are creditors here and there, I expect. And I look at you and I think, here is a man in need of money. And one way of getting money is when a person rings up and says, hello, I'm a friend of your girlfriend's brother, want fish for cash? Well?'

He shrugged. He was sulking now. He would be trying to think of a way out. There wasn't one.

'The girlfriend, by the way. She all right?'

'Miranda is very well. Never better. And I don't have to explain anything to you. You're a loser, Gavin. They slung you out of the police. You led Johnny up the garden path —'

I was somewhat astonished by this. It had never occurred to me that Johnny's version of events would include me as one of the agents of his difficulties. Suppressing the urge to turn the desk on to his legs and stamp on his head, I pulled out my notebook. 'Never mind that,' I said. 'Who put you in touch with Major Davies?'

'Who?'

'You may call him Mr Smith.'

He was drawing confidence from being behind the desk. He said, 'Who on earth do you think you are?'

I made the smile as nasty as I could. His eyes shifted away. I said, 'It's not going all that well, is it, Tony?'

'What on earth do you mean?' He shoved a paper across the desk. It was open at the TV listings. There was a red circle round *The Art of Sizzle – Fish Cooking with Tony Greely.*

'Most impressive,' I said. 'Though one a.m. is scarcely prime time. And the hotel's a bit empty, isn't it? And how many people eat in your restaurants? Fifty per cent of tables full? Sixty? Big pressure. And fish is expensive, so you decide to cut corners. Or maybe you are just greedy. Correct?'

'Don't be stupid,' he said, but there was no conviction in it.

'So,' I said. 'Greed or brokeness, I don't really care. But you're buying black fish for cash, and I can prove it, and at that point bang goes your career as Mr Natural.'

'Is it money you want?' he said, reaching for a desk drawer.

'Keep your money,' I said, with something of an effort. 'Just tell me exactly who put you in touch with your Mr Smith. Or I will make you famous in a new way.'

The Son of the Sea was gone, and so was the codfish. All that remained was the Rat with Ringlets. He said, 'You can't make me.'

'That's what you think.' I leaned back in my chair and watched him. He avoided my eye, waiting for me to say something. The silence grew longer. It was fine by me. I had used silences just like it in police interview rooms. But Greely was a talker, and he was impatient to be getting back to his film. The silence would be screaming at him. He would have to break it.

He did. He said, 'All right. You ever run a restaurant?'

'Expensive business, I expect.'

'It was fine at first. Then I expanded, and it wasn't. But by then I had met Miranda and she had fallen in love with me, of course.'

I looked at him to check if he was joking. He wasn't. I said, 'Women are like that.'

He simpered. 'Well, Miranda introduced me to some really great people. Her brother, fabulous guy.' These insights into human nature could only be the result of a lifetime spent gazing at fish. 'And she knows that depletion of fish stocks is the number one problem in food resource management right now.'

'Tony,' I said. 'You are selling black fish in your restaurants because you get it cheap.'

'Not only that,' he said. 'The quota system is totally flawed. Over-quota fish gets dumped back into the sea, dead. How does that help anyone?'

'It doesn't,' I said. 'But that's not why you were buying it.' I stood up. 'So you don't want to tell me how you met Davies. I'll send along some journalists and we'll see if they can find out. We'll start with your producer.'

'No!' he squeaked. 'All right. Smith, Davies, whatever his name is, he's a card player. He'd lost money to Johnny, Johnny said. He wanted cash. And Miranda said why didn't I go into business with this guy, because then he could pay Johnny what he owed him? And she sort of talked me into it. Keeping it in the family, you know.'

'Nice warm feeling,' I said.

'One of the things Miranda doesn't like about you is the sarcasm,' he said. 'She said you had let being a policeman get to you.'

'And you haven't let being a conservationist get to you.' He scowled. 'Look,' I said. 'If you want to buy black fish that's your decision. But I am in this, and I want to find out how I got here.'

He said, 'You aren't in this.'

I said, 'You are technically correct. This is between Johnny, who . . . is . . . a moron, and Miranda, who loves policemen, and Mr Smith, real name Major Davies, who can't stop playing poker, and you, who are the handsomest and brokest telly fish cook in Britain. So why does someone working for Davies come and burn my tug to the waterline?'

He frowned. 'Your tug?'

'A houseboat. That I live on.'

Here he smiled, a smile crawling with superiority. 'I expect you got pissed and had a fag in bed,' he said.

And suddenly I was not sitting in a chair smiling across a desk like a nice ex-policeman in deckie's raiment. Suddenly I was his side of the desk with a knee on his neck and a letter opener pressing into the skin under his right eyeball, and I was interviewing a person who had nicked my girlfriend and stitched me up. I said, 'It was firebombed. By people who work for Major Davies. So I presume they were working on his orders. Who are they?'

He started to weep. He said, 'How should I know? You can't do this to me in my own hotel.'

'I am doing it. Who?'

'I don't *know*,' he said. 'I just buy *fish* from him.'

'How many times?'

'Half a dozen. Davies was in the army. He doesn't set things on fire.'

'And you trust him.'

'Yes.'

'Still?'

He made a sound expressive of ambiguity. I stood up. He put his hand to his face to check if he was bleeding. 'Make-up will fix it,' I said. 'So where did you meet the Major?'

'At a party. With Miranda. They were all playing poker upstairs.'

'Who were?'

'Davies. And Johnny. And a couple of big guys, Irish, Scottish, I don't know.'

'Names?'

'Mcsomething. I wasn't that interested.' He blew his nose on a red handkerchief. 'Why don't you ask Miranda?'

I looked at him. His pancake make-up was grooved with

sweat, and his eyes had a sick-puppy desperation. I almost felt sorry for him. I said, 'That is a really brilliant idea.'

There was a tap at the door. The director's voice said, 'Is everything all right in there?' It might have been the acoustic, or perhaps my imagination, but I got the idea that there were quite a lot of people gathered round that door. So, by the look of him, did Tony. He swelled visibly, and scowled like the Ancient Mariner, and wondered how fierce he actually dared be.

I beat him to it. 'Pretty soon I will send you copies of all my holiday snaps and recordings. And any time you are thinking of messing me about, do remember. Now, then.'

'Now then what?'

'The money you owe me for the fish.'

'Oh.' He opened a drawer. Fleetingly, I wondered if he had a gun in there. But all I could see was a packet of Tic Tacs and wads of fifties wrapped in bank plastic. He counted out ten of these bundles and handed them over. I thanked him kindly and stuffed them in my pockets. Then I climbed out of the window, marched across the flowerbed and headed for the stables.

The truck was just leaving. I got a lift to the nearest town, which was Leamington Spa, and spent the rest of the day on trains. And as we crawled through the early-autumn countryside, I reflected. The lack of guns in his money drawer was not amazing, because this was England. The bullet in the head of Johnny Bonny was amazing, for the same reason.

And it came back to the same thing again. While Major Davies was a most unpleasant person and a soldier, and therefore theoretically capable of killing, I had never heard of a major in the Royal Logistics Corps using execution to settle his gambling scores.

It was time to meet some sportsmen.

11

I climbed off the train at Lymington, found a taxi and told it to head for Sawley Pond. The ruins of heathland passed outside the window, sandy fields and million-pound bungalows, and I concentrated on trying to work out how to conduct my conversation with Miranda. Though of course it would be Miranda who would be conducting the conversation, because you might as well try to conduct a runaway elephant as a conversation with Miranda.

The taxi drove away. I started down the path to Bridle Cottage, feeling that familiar dryness of mouth and hollowness of stomach. This was almost definitely a mistake. But it would not be the first I had made around Miranda.

I could hear the clink of a spade from the kitchen garden. So I took a deep breath and walked round the side of the house. And there she was, with her back to me, dressed in an old blue jersey and a pair of jeans and leopardskin gumboots, with her hair pulled back as she forked over a bed that I had dug and in which I had grown parsnips.

I said, 'Miranda?' It came out as a croak. She did not turn. I said it louder. Still she kept digging. I noticed that the thing keeping her hair back was not an Alice band, but earphones. I walked down the path beside her, and waved.

She straightened up suddenly and pulled the earphones off her head. Her face was flushed with digging. 'What do you mean by creeping up on me like that?' she said. 'Go away before I call the police.'

I said, 'I was the police.'

She opened her mouth to tell me not to be so pathetic. But the cross square suddenly turned into a grin, and she started laughing, which was disarming. She said, 'I suppose you want some whisky.'

I did. But I said, 'Tea would be fine.'

'Stay there,' she said. 'I don't want you inside the house in those clothes. What *do* you think you look like?'

She went into the house, kicking off her boots on the doorstep. I took a few swipes at the parsnip bed with the fork. I had laid the paths in this garden when Miranda and I had been in love —

Best not think about that.

She came out with a couple of mugs. I smelled Earl Grey. 'One sugar still?' she said.

'Fine.'

She sat down on an iron chair at a French iron table. I sat opposite her. 'Aren't you going to ask how I am?' she said.

'You look great.'

She nodded. She knew. 'So what do you want? If it's money —'

'Not money.'

Her face became suddenly still. 'Is it Johnny?' she said.

'No. Not directly.'

'Have you seen him?'

'Not lately.' This was true. After all, he was wrapped in polythene nowadays.

She sipped her tea and looked relieved that I had not brought bad news, which did not make me feel any better. She said, 'He's just vanished.'

'He's done it before.'

She pulled her lip. 'I don't like it.' She sighed. 'He is a thoughtless bastard. Oh, well, he'll be back.' I saw her eyes fill up with tears.

Frankly, I nearly told her then and there. In fact I opened my mouth to do it. But perhaps the tears reminded her of other occasions when she had cried in my company, because she frowned, and said, 'This is the first day it hasn't rained, and I want to do some digging. Why are you here?'

I took another of my special deep breaths. I said, 'Odd things have been happening to me lately. I met someone called Horace Davies.'

'The Major,' said Miranda, not looking at me.

'Who is he?'

'Just someone around. He seems to know a lot of policemen.'

'Johnny played cards with him. Yes?'

'Apparently.'

'And won a lot of money.'

'For a wonder.' She shook her head fondly.

'You introduced them.'

'Yes.'

'And you introduced the Major to Tony Greely.'

'Possibly.'

'How else would they have met?'

She shrugged. 'What is this about?'

'Johnny took the Major's boat to settle a gambling debt.'

'So?'

'It's stealing,' I said, with great patience. 'Only a total fuckwit steals from someone as close to the police as the Major.

And once Johnny had stolen the boat he sold it to Georgie Strother.'

'Who?'

'Doesn't matter. But the Major took the boat back, and now the brokerage, in which Johnny is a partner, owes Georgie the value of the boat, which it can't pay.'

'So tell the Major to go away. The man's a prick. A gambling prick.'

'No,' I said. 'Because you introduced the Major to Tony Greely. And the Major has been supplying Tony with illegal fish, using Georgie and me as a front. And if it gets into the papers, the Major is destroyed, but so is Tony. Which I don't care about, but I think you might.'

She retracted the lower lip in order to chew on it. She said, 'You're a bastard, you know that?'

'Me?' I was shocked.

'You leave me. And now you've manoeuvred poor Tony into this . . . *position*.'

I decided to leave aside the question of who had left whom. I said, 'It wasn't me who put him in touch with the Major. Are you and he still doing it?'

'Doing what?' The eyes blazing merrily, the face tight over the beautiful bones.

'It.'

'Mind your own business!'

'Weekends only, I should think,' I said. 'Otherwise he's at all those restaurants of his.'

'How dare you,' she said. 'How *dare* you!' She threw her tea in my face.

I squeegeed Earl Grey from my brow and said, watching her cup-throwing hand carefully, 'I don't really see why I shouldn't go to the papers my own personal self.'

'Blackmail,' said Miranda, mouth like a letterbox. 'I should have guessed. You want money to get your disgusting friend off the hook. You're as bad as Calum Johnson and all those other people Johnny used to hang about with. Go away before I call the police.'

I got up. I had been given some information, and she had kept her pride. I said, 'Lovely to see you.'

'Get *out*.'

I bowed, which was just as well, because it meant the tea mug hit me on the top of the head instead of in the right eye. As I walked round the house that had once been half mine, she screamed, 'If anything gets in the papers Tony will sue you to bits. Now get back to your smelly police tart and stay out of my life!'

I walked out on to the road, and wrote the name Calum Johnson in my notebook. Then I looked brightly down the tarmac ribbon between the trees. It was only five miles back to Lymington. Who knew, I might get a lift?

She had been wrong about the police tart. She had not been smelly. Certainly she had a personal fragrance, but there was no rule in the Hampshire Constabulary against a waft of Chanel, or if there had been, Karen Ansty disobeyed it.

I was an inspector in the CID. Karen was a sergeant in the uniform branch. My office was a sort of cupboard open to the corridor down which Karen used to walk to her desk. It was a pleasant walk; she was a pleasant woman, who had joined the police to serve the public, realised that this was not the idea, and stayed on in the hope of persuading her fellow officers that it was. Normally I find pleasant a bit watery. But when you have just moved out on someone like Miranda, pleasantness is just exactly what you want. Also, I was quite keen on the public service idea. And that year I asked her to my pawnbrokers' Christmas lunch, which I think she found something of an eye-opener. And afterwards we landed up in the pub, having a pleasant conversation while she toyed with some white wines and I washed large whiskies down with pints of Theakston's. After about six pints, I found that the way she walked to the bar to buy her round was causing me to think of her as something other than a resting place for the eyes. There was the tilt of the hips as her weight shifted . . .

Back came the drinks. Down went the drinks. Back came some more. I do not know what we talked about, but I noticed our heads got very close together, and I was catching the Chanel of which I was speaking earlier, and thinking what an exceptionally kind and understanding person she was. And she must have been thinking along the same lines. Because we were holding hands, and I was stroking parts of her, and she was stroking parts of me. Then there was a transition, shrouded in darkness, after which I was in a bed I recognised, it being my own, and Karen was in there with me, gasping in my ear. I had a vague feeling that everything was perhaps not as it should have been, but I ascribed this to guilt, and anyway no thought could last long, given what we were up to in the old bed.

The old bed . . .

In the end it all went dark red and we were lying wrapped round each other, and Karen was giving me the lascivious smile that had taken over from her usual expression of muted pleasantness.

When I realised what it was about the bed.

The bed had been mine, but no longer was. Now it was the property of Miranda, my estranged wife, and was situated in the bedroom of Bridle Cottage, once our marital home. By an oversight, I and Sergeant Ansty were conducting our relationship in a house from which I was barred by injunction.

Whoops.

Sergeant Ansty commenced taking small bites out of my lower lip. 'I love your house,' she said. 'I love your face. I love your —'

At this moment a door burst open, and a voice said, 'What the *hell*?' It was a voice I recognised. The voice of Miranda.

I leaped out of bed. I said, 'There has been a mistake.'

Miranda was standing there in her signature long dress and cowboy boots. Behind her was a man in a dinner jacket. Not, as far as I could see, Tony Greely; it was a week-night, after all. I rose, and said to Miranda in a dignified manner, 'There has alas been a mistake.' Then I tripped over my feet and fell through the bedside table, grasping the sheet on the way down. So the sheet came off Karen, and did not cover me. And Miranda and her new friend were privileged to witness two post-coital police officers, the sergeant with eyes the size of saucers attempting to cover herself with an alarm clock, the inspector lying stylishly but not warmly clad in the ruins of a Regency bedside cabinet.

We got out somehow. Karen was sobbing, and Miranda was screeching about trespass.

'Motes and beams,' I said.

'She's so *unpleasant*,' said Karen.

And into the night we sped, dressed in towels, and avoided being stopped by the police until I drove into a lamp post in Boscombe. 'Hot pursuit,' I said.

'I guessed,' said the traffic officer, without removing his eyes from Karen, whose towel had come off.

If anyone had talked, it would have been a resigning matter. But nobody did. This did not stop Karen seeing it as an emigrating matter. She sent me a postcard from Toronto a month later. *It wasn't worth it*, said the postcard.

I was back in the nick, and nowadays there was a bottle in my filing cabinet. I knew just how she felt.

I walked into Lymington. I got a bed in a B & B, rinsed the Earl Grey out of my hair, ate a kebab and started making telephone calls about Calum Johnson.

Johnson, it seemed, was a popular figure and an enthusiastic gambler, in the sense that he arranged games of chance for those who wished to play them. He was also an enthusiastic yacht owner, being the proprietor of *Velma*, a hundred-foot schooner built in the glory days by Alfred Mylne. My last call was to Terence Lyke, a childhood friend who nowadays had a company that ministered to the needs of superyachts and their owners.

'*Velma*?' said Terence, after the pleasantries were complete. 'Yeah. Put a new baize on the saloon table last month.'

'Baize?'

'They play cards on her. Horrible big stakes. She's done up like a Moroccan brothel down below.'

'I want to talk to Calum.'

'What you have to ask yourself,' said Terence, 'is whether Calum will want to talk to you. Why?'

'My business partner used to play in his games. Now he's vanished. Can you get me on board?'

There was a silence. 'As an old friend, you mean,' said Terence.

'If you want.'

'We're not really old friends,' said Terence. 'We went to the same school, is all, and you were always in trouble. And I make my living by being discreet. That's what big boats are about. Specially Calum's.'

I said, 'Oh,' and left the Police Pause, into which the guileless victim generally plunges, and flounders his way out by telling you anything he thinks you want to hear.

Terence was good at this, but not as good as me. He said,

‘You can talk to the skipper, though. Dave Scott, that they call Scotto.’

I thanked him, and disconnected. I knew Scotto. He was a large Kiwi, married to a nice black woman called Georgia. Their children were nice too, but the wrong colour as far as the skinheads of Gosport were concerned. I had watched a brown boy running down Gosport High Street at midnight one June, pursued by a bunch of lads with empty bottles in their hands and the bottles’ contents in what passed for their brains. I had picked the brown boy up in the car and taken him home, to his relief and the joy of his parents, who were Georgia and Scotto.

So I rang Scotto and told him what I wanted. And he said, ‘We’re a man short tomorrow night. Come along and welcome. You won’t like it, though.’

‘Beautiful boat.’

‘Owned by a jerk.’

So at three the following afternoon I turned up at Ocean Village and walked down the pontoon among the plastic. And there on the hammerhead was *Velma*, 110 feet of dove-grey teak and white enamel and dazzling brightwork. Scotto was in the cockpit, a big man with fair hair greying at the temples. He lent me a razor, and a blue jersey with VELMA on the chest, and white trousers with belt and sheath knife. I transformed myself into a deckhand in the crew quarters, and went into the bow, and started to Dura-glit the brass ventilators in the deck over the forecabin.

Velma was indeed an astonishing boat. The deck swept aft in a true, joyous curve, and the two mighty masts soared into the blue sky of teatime. For a moment I was possessed by the glory of a machine like this, and felt a deep scorn for the mouldering plastic wrecks I sold at Achnabuie. Then the owner and his guests started coming aboard. And I was reminded that while the great boats of yesteryear were among the most beautiful things ever seen by land or sea, their owners were not.

Calum Johnson was the first to arrive. He was a stout man with a red face and pimples, dressed in a blazer and white chinos. He went below, and I heard him shouting at Denis the steward about a dirty glass. A couple of girls turned up, small and well-shaped, and made a fuss when Scotto asked them politely to take off their four-inch heels. Three-quarters of an hour later four men walked down the pontoon. They looked prosperous and fortyish. Two of them were big, wearing jeans and fleeces, and did not seem at all curious about the beautiful boats that surrounded them. The third was smaller. He had curly brown hair and a hard little face. He wore old deck shoes and walked with the cracked-knee gait of someone used to decks, looking up at *Velma's* mighty spars and shaking his head and grinning. The fourth was Major Davies.

This was not exactly a surprise. Still, my heart beat hard as I bent over the ventilator, buffing it powerfully, but not so powerfully as to attract attention. I did not want Major Davies to think I was following him around. Out of the side of my eye I could see a couple of other men waiting further back on the pontoon, chewing gum. They were wearing leather jackets and a businesslike air. One of them was enormous, the other merely huge. The smaller man had shoulder-length hair. He kept his hands in the pockets of his jacket. The other man had a shaved head and a weak chin. He looked left and right and behind, then walked forward and handed the little man in deck shoes a briefcase. It looked like the kind of case that might be full of money. But I was not really thinking about cases of money. I had seen the slaphead with the case before, and his friend as well. They had watched me from the side of the dock at Milford, and had later lit my car.

And were very likely to have shot Johnny Bonneville-Clark in the back of the head and made a mess of throwing him overboard.

12

I turned my head away and polished for dear life. I felt the tremor as the engine started. From the corner of my eye I saw the Major's head below. Scotto's voice came out of a little squawk box in the deck. 'Cast off forward,' it said.

I hauled the bow line aboard, coiled it into a gasket coil and walked aft with it. The slaphead's glance crossed me as he turned. It did not snag; no recognition there. Last time I had been unshaven, in oilskins, and this time I was all brisk and bright, clean shaved and in uniform. How would he?

The nose came off the dock. The masts wheeled against the sky. *Velma* slid swiftly out of Ocean Village and into Southampton Water. The squawk boxes in the deck began to murmur. I and several people younger and beefier than me tailed on to halyards and hauled up huge expanses of close-seamed main and foresails, while another half-dozen people up on the foredeck hoisted flying jib, jib, and staysail. *Velma* leaned her elegant white side into the dirty water and began to slide south. The Major did not reappear.

The boat had two cockpits, one for the owner and his friends, and aft of it another, with the wheel and the instruments, for the crew. Scotto gave the mate his instructions and drifted on to the counter, where I was watching the wake slide by and keeping my back to the cash customers. He said, 'What do you want to do?'

'I'd like to watch them play.'

'Fair enough. We're going into Newtown Creek. They have drinks and a bit of dinner, and then they break out the cards.' Scotto's large mahogany face was a picture of New Zealand enthusiasm, but I sensed that he did not approve. 'We're sailing so they can say they've sailed, and so Mr McGown can have a go. Then we'll motor, so the drinks don't slide off the table. Do you want to take her?'

I took her. The wheel was a big thing, brass-bound. The mainsail soared into the sky above my head, and the foremast carried a great swelling tower of foresail, staysail, jib, flying jib. Sailing schooners is not something you get much practice at in British waters. I settled the forestay on a hill behind Cowes and looked at the wind instruments. 'Mainsheet in a foot,' I said. Someone hauled the mainsheet. The heel steepened, and I felt the nose go up, seeking the wind.

'Foresail in a foot,' I said.

In came the foresail. The deck steepened to twenty-five degrees, but the weather helm came off, and the rustle of the wake was a steady roar. 11.9, said the log, 12.0, 12.1. The jib topsail was lifting. I thumbed the squawk-box switch, and in it came, so the jib topsail was firing a stream of air across the convex curve of the foretopsail. The numbers went up. 12.3, said the log. 12.4.

Scotto nodded approvingly. I had just about forgotten he was there. I bore away a fraction to go round the back end of a Channel ferry, let the momentum carry the boat through its wind-shadow, and put her back in the groove.

I heard Scotto clear his throat. A voice said, 'Not bad.' An

Irish voice. The voice of the man called McGown. He was standing to windward of me and a little behind, gazing at the numbers. 12.5, they said. 12.6.

Scotto cleared his throat again, recalling me to my duty. 'Why don't you take her?' I said.

I gave him the course. He looked at me with his hard little eyes, and then at the sails. Then he began to bark orders into the squawk boxes.

Sheets went out. Luffs blew back, tautened again as sheets came in. He went over the whole rig, undoing my trim, substituting his own. The roar of the wake dropped a quarter-tone. 11.9, said the numbers on the log. 12.0.

More trimming. 11.7, said the numbers. 11.8.

'Losing the wind,' said Scotto. This was him being tactful with the cash customers, because the wind speed indicator showed a steady sixteen knots.

More orders. Sheets ran in sheaves. *Velma*'s heel steepened, and her bow wave sent back drifts of spray that would be wrecking my nice shiny ventilators up in the nose.

But the numbers went 12.0, 12.1. He turned and looked at me. He did not like sailing slower than me, that was plain. I could see that he was far from pleased. This was not good. I was supposed to be watching from a discreet distance, not pissing off one of the objects of my surveillance.

He liked being the man in control, this McGown. Perhaps that was why he was a gambler: to put himself in a place where things went random. Perhaps you got bored with being in control.

Personally I had no idea.

I snuck aft to the counter, and stayed there with a tough girl called Bridget and several hundred feet of beautiful white mainsheet, and tried not to attract attention.

We slid out into the Solent, rounded the Bramble buoy,

and cracked sheets for the reach to Newtown. McGown's phone rang, and he went below. At eight we were nosing into Newtown Creek, sheltered from what breeze there was. An edge of cloud was crawling in from the west, thick and dark, putting the stars out as it came. 'Dinner is served,' said Denis the steward.

And down they all went, while we flaked the sails and put the covers on and picked up the big buoy in the middle of the fairway. It was a calm night, the first of autumn. I shivered.

Perhaps it was a presentiment.

We flemished the lines and washed the decks. Then it was time for crew supper, pizzas from the wood-fired oven in the galley. I sat next to Scotto. We talked about his family. He was doing well, and so was Georgia with her painting, and his son was a boatbuilder now. He seemed to hold me responsible for this. It was surprising to be one of the good guys for a change. I found I liked it. 'So,' he said. 'What's this about?'

'Merely curious,' I said, avoiding his eye.

Scotto nodded. Your superyacht skipper is a model of discretion.

'One thing. Did you ever see a guy called John Bonneville-Clark on the boat?'

'John,' said Scotto, whose brain worked slowly except in matters marine. His face cleared. 'Johnny Bonny, you mean. Course we did. Last time he was on board he came down here and showed us a bit of paper that said it was an IOU for sixty grand. Made us all drink whisky out of his bottle to celebrate. Wouldn't take no.' He frowned. 'Hasn't been back lately, though.'

'Probably retired,' said Bridget, who was sitting on my other side. 'I would.'

It was time to change the subject. I said, 'And who is this McGown?'

Scotto shrugged his barn-sized shoulders. 'Some sort of businessman from Ireland, north, south, who knows? Likes his sailing. Likes winning, or losing, hard to tell which.' He frowned slightly. 'Might as well flush it. He's got plenty, though. Did you see that briefcase?'

'No,' I said vaguely.

'Full of cash. You go on down when they start playing, and take a peep through the scuttle from the steward's pantry. Crazy stakes. Pay off my mortgage, any road,' said Scotto. Then, in a louder voice, 'Right. Anyone for cards?'

There was a general groan. The crew cleared away the dishes, and someone put on a DVD: Cliffhanger with Sylvester Stallone. I sat in a corner and tried to work this out.

It looked as if Johnny had been telling the truth when he said he had won a lot of money off the Major. Wonders would never cease.

'Hey,' said one of the foredeck men over the DVD. 'Scott. I hate this movie. Can we go to the pub?'

'Crap, intit? Can't see why not,' said Scotto. 'If we leave you can make your own way home, and no pay.'

'Fair enough.' Three men went up the companion. There was the thud of feet on deck, and the jingle of blocks as they hoisted the dinghy over the side, and their cheery voices fading into the distance. I wished I was with them.

But that was not why I was here.

We watched the rest of the DVD; or rather the others did, jeering merrily as Stallone struck attitudes on cardboard cliff faces. I had more pressing things on my mind.

It was interesting that the Major was part of this card game. And it was also interesting that Mr McGown seemed to be the employer of the men who had stolen the *Sirius Gleaner* from Georgie. It seemed to me possible that the Major and

McGown might be partners. I had come aboard *Velma* thinking that I might find out who had seen Johnny during the events that had ended up with him getting a bullet in his head. Now it struck me that I was on the point of getting too much information, particularly if the Major saw me.

The movie ended. Denis the steward came aft and sat at the top of the crew quarters companionway smoking a roll-up. Scotto asked him how it was going.

'Big money,' said Denis from his perch. 'Silly buggers. Two nice-looking girls, drink everywhere, and it's all raise you, see you. That big bloke's down about fifty grand to the Irishman and he looks bloody miserable.'

'Denis will never be rich,' said Scotto to the crew at large. 'But he is happy in his work.' Then to me, in a lower voice, 'If you want a look, try in there.' He pointed at a door.

I went through, and found myself in the galley, empty now. Beyond it there was a sort of butler's pantry, with racks of wine and an espresso machine hissing quietly to itself. The pantry was divided from the world of the gentry by a green baize door, for God's sake. There was a little porthole at eye level. I put my eye to it.

I was looking into *Velma*'s saloon. There were oil-painted nudes on the bulkheads, a big table with buttoned-leather banquettes and a couple of upright armchairs. The cabin was dark except for the green-shaded lamp casting a yellow pool of light over the green baize table. The diners were sitting round the table. One of the girls was dealing cards. The poker rigmarole established itself. The men pushed out chips. The Major shoved out more, and the other men matched him. More cards, more money. Calum Johnson did not play. He merely sat and watched with his boiled-looking, hooded eyes, somewhere between a host and a pimp. And I noticed a curious thing. The Major was the biggest man in the room, and

I could feel the chill of his presence even through the soundproof glass of the porthole. But the man who dominated the proceedings was not the Major. The one in control was McGown. And I could see that the Major did not like it; and also that he would do nothing about it. He watched McGown out of the side of his eye, and his grey tongue ran round his grey lips, and he smiled a little smile that wanted to be liked, but was not. The Major was scared.

McGown sat and played with neat, economical movements, small motions of the head for cards, what looked like curt instructions to raise, call, jack. The Major watched him like a rabbit watches a snake.

McGown said, 'See you.' The Major shook his head. The small man raked in the money. The Major gave him the weak little smile. Strange.

And as I watched the small man, it got stranger. He gave the slightest of frowns. His head rose from his cards, and suddenly he was looking straight at the porthole in the door and into my eyes. He could not have known I was there, for there was no light in the pantry, and from where he sat there would have been nothing but reflections on the porthole glass. But the eyes seemed to look straight through the glass and into my head. I felt he knew everything I knew. And just as I felt it, he winked. Not a friendly wink, either. A wink that said I know, and you know, and what are you going to do about it?

I found myself back in the crew cabin, badly shaken. 'See what you wanted to see?' said Scotto.

I nodded. My mouth was too dry to speak. I told myself: nobody can see through glass like that. You are making this up. He's a hypnotist, is all. And gradually I convinced myself.

We lay around and dozed and chatted. The wind got up, moaning in the rigging. The pub contingent came back. The hands on the bulkhead clock crawled round to 2 a.m. Denis went through. I heard the roar of the coffee machine. Then he came back. 'They're finished. McGown cleaned them all out,' he said. 'Calum says, time for home.'

We went on deck.

There were no stars any more. The sky was black and close, and cold air was pouring out of the northeast. The engine thrummed lightly in the deck. The anchor came up. *Velma* stuck her nose out of the creek and began to power towards the mass of lights that was Southampton. The wind was kicking a nasty little chop out of the flood, sharp and cold, bursting over the nose and sailing down the deck. We scrubbed the last of the mud off the anchor, sluiced water over the foredeck, and scuttled aft to get in the lee of the deckhouse. Not in the cockpit, though. There were too many people there, and I did not want to talk. I wanted to think about the little Irishman who made the Major look flabby. To whom the Major must have lost, what, fifty or sixty thousand pounds that evening? A lot of money for a retired soldier. No wonder he was shipping black fish.

But was he compromised to the point of ordering murder? It was a big step. The Major was a bully, but he did not remind me of any other murderers. McGown, though; he was another thing altogether.

A door opened in the deckhouse. A figure came on deck. A bright Irish voice said, 'Good evening.' And I thought, stupidly, *think of the devil*. 'What's your name?' said McGown.

'Gavin,' I said.

'Thought so,' he said. Then he hit me in the solar plexus.

All the air went out of me. As my face went down some part of him, perhaps his knee, came up, and something hit me in the face and the night was filled with a meteor storm of stars. Then something shoved me violently in the chest and

I was tottering backwards across the deck and the guard rail caught me at the top of my legs and I pitched backwards into the sea.

The water closed over my head. Salt flowed into my mouth. I came up, got some sort of breath, went down again. The thoughts were piling through my head. I was a mile from land in a strong tide. The wind would have driven everyone below except the helmsman and the lookout. There was enough water flying about for nobody to have noticed the splash. As I came up I saw the pale cliff of the boat's side slide past my face. I shouted, but the smack in the stomach still had my wind and the sound that came out would have embarrassed a kitten. I saw the hull slide by, then the overhang of the counter, felt the water churned up by the propeller. Then the stern light slid past, and I was left looking skywards in an attitude of prayer.

Something crossed the sky, black on black. A line. A rope.

I flung my hands up full stretch and hooked it with my fingers. It was a wet rope, stretched taut. Towing something. There was a clatter in my ears: the sound of a small boat moving through water. The sound of the dinghy the pub party had not taken the trouble to haul back on deck. Sloppy bastards.

Sloppy lifesaving bastards.

I tightened my grip on the rope. The water was cold enough to numb my fingers. I was being dragged through it at the best part of ten knots. The numbness made me slacken my grip. I slid sideways down the towline. There was heat in my fingers, and something seemed to tear, and I was vaguely worried it was skin. But there were other things to worry about, like what would happen if I spared the skin on my hands and let go, out here in the middle of the Solent.

I had an idea. It was not a clever idea, but I was half-drowned and very cold and being dragged through the sea, and this is not an ideal set of circumstances for developing clever ideas. So I counted to three. Then I slackened my grip enough to let myself slide sideways down the painter.

You will probably be asking why I was not screaming blue murder for help. The answer is that breathing was taking all my time. Furthermore, I was making a plan not to be on the same boat as Mr McGown and the Major. Mr McGown was responsible for the dangerous state in which I currently found myself. And if the Major found out that I had joined the crew, he would become suspicious, and consider that I was taking too close an interest in him, and Scotto might lose his job in circumstances that would not guarantee him a good reference.

All this went through my mind as quickly as I could inhale a wave and cough it out again. Then my hand touched something that was not rope. That was, in fact, wood. The bow of the dinghy, surfing on the front of the second wave of *Velma*'s wake. My weight on the bow made the dinghy sheer about violently. Any minute now the helmsman would notice, and haul in, and there would be trouble. So I hooked my left arm over the bow, and groped for the sheath knife at my belt, and pulled it out, and sawed at the painter.

If the knife had been mine, it would have been too blunt to cut butter. But Scotto was a genuine seaman with an eye for detail, down to the sharpness of knives in spare uniforms. The blade went through the painter as if it had been pack thread. Suddenly the strain was off. *Velma* powered away, a great dark shape, stern light bright, the glow of the binnacle dim in the companionway brightwork. Or so I presume; but at that moment I was holding on to a slippery varnished dinghy in a Solent chop, and I was not admiring ocean greyhounds, however elegant they might be.

So I hung there, recovering my strength, such as it was.

And when I was ready I went hand-over-hand down the side of the dinghy, round to the transom, put two arms over the side and grabbed a thwart. Then I found a ring on the keelson, to which some blessed angel had spliced a painter, or possibly a lifting strop. I did not waste time wondering which. I grasped the rope and tied a one-handed bowline. Then I pulled it through the sculling notch, put my toe in the loop and levered myself up and in.

This sounds easy. It wasn't. And if I had not had a lot of early training with capsized boats in Poole Harbour, I would not have been able to do it. But training is potent stuff, particularly when allied to the fear of death. And eventually I was lying over the rowing thwart like a dead sheep, vomiting up the gallons of water that had come aboard inside me.

After a while, a little strength returned. I used it to get organised. There was a bailer in the boat, so I bailed, and oars, so I rowed. Half an hour later I was under the red flash of the light known as Jack in the Basket. And ten minutes after that I was knocking on the hull of *Pandora*, on which lived my old acquaintance Harriet Whistler, and Harriet was looking down at me with a torch, asking me what the hell I thought I was doing, and I was wondering how much explanation I could face giving her.

Not much, as it turned out. Harriet lent me a towel to put round myself, and I used a corner of it to dry off my long-suffering sim card, and stuffed it into Harriet's phone. Then I rang Scotto, and through an electrical storm of crackles explained that I had thought it best to leave with his dinghy.

Silence. Then he said, 'You had your reasons.'

'I did.'

'You can tell me how you did it one day.'

'One day.'

'We've been looking for you. I'll get the dinghy picked up.'

'Did anyone notice anything?'

'Eventually. You would have enjoyed what I said to the guy on the helm when he told me we'd lost you and the ding. I'll tell them to stand the lifeboat down.'

'Sorry.'

'So you should be.'

There was something in his voice that told me that as far as Scotto was concerned, our mutual benefactions were now even. So I thanked him, and tried to make conversation with Harriet, who was an intelligent jolly-hockey-sticks widow of a certain age. We had things to talk about, because when I had been a policeman I had caught some idiots nicking her tender, and neither I nor they had wanted to go to court, so they had all got very wet, and she had been most grateful. She noticed that I was tired when I fell asleep in the middle of a sentence. And next thing I knew it was morning, and I was under a duvet on a berth in a not particularly tidy saloon with geraniums on the chart table.

'I expect you'll be off now,' said Harriet, after breakfast. 'How's Miranda?'

'Managing without me,' I said.

'I thought she might,' said Harriet, sighing. 'Another egg?'

'Yes, please,' I said. It was as if last night had never happened.

But it had. It certainly had.

I got a lift ashore. I went to a junk shop and purchased a new vehicle for my sim card and phoned Georgie. As far as I could tell through the static, he sounded hung over. 'Well?' I said.

'Well what? I'm alongside in Caernarfon. Waiting.'

'So get up to Holyhead and I'll catch a train. One thing. Have you ever come across a man called McGown?'

'Sounds Irish.'

'Is. A little man. Hard. The men who stole your boat work for him.'

'I thought they worked for the Major.'

'So did I.'

'You get a lot of Irish,' said Georgie. 'On account of Ireland being twenty miles over the water. They've got their fingers in everything, being so close, you see. It's the proximity, you know? Forbye —'

'But you've never met this McGown,' I said, to make him cease.

'Not as far as I know. But —'

'See you in Holyhead,' I said. 'And we'll go and get a look at some more Greenreap.'

'Gavin,' said Georgie. 'What are you going to do with the money you got for the fish?'

'Give it to the Major. Less commission.'

'Aye.' He sounded disappointed.

'Goodbye.'

'Goodbye.' He rang off. I went to the station and took the long railroad north. As England turned into Wales the cloud turned into drizzle, and day into night. I clambered out of the train and walked across to the fish dock. The *Sirius Gleaner* was beginning to look like home. There was a light in her wheelhouse, and it illuminated Georgie's mighty features, lips moving as he spelled his way through the Daily Sport. As I made my way towards the boat, I saw a car draw up on the quay: a silver Mercedes, windows black. There are plenty of flash cars round fishing ports, so I paid it no heed. I went to the *Gleaner* and banged on the gangway and shouted, 'Hi, honey, I'm home!'

The window came down. Georgie's head came out. He said, 'Wha? Oh. It's you.'

And a voice behind me said, 'Is this the *Serious Gleaner*?'

I turned round. A square man was standing silhouetted against the quay lights. I said, 'Not exactly. Why?'

'I got a pickup to make.'

This must be the person who had been expecting the fish we had landed in Aberystwyth. I found myself mildly apprehensive; he looked more violent than most fishmongers. 'Wrong boat,' I said.

'Oh,' said the square man. I caught the glint of light on a fat gold necklace. 'You sure?'

'He told you,' growled Georgie. 'You want to look in the hold?'

The man shook his head and backed away from the quay edge, hand diving into his pocket. I had survived one murder attempt in the last twenty-four hours. It was hard to get rid of the idea that the hand was going to come out with a gun. I found myself backing round the wheelhouse. But what came out was not a gun but a phone. I saw the screen light a pasty shaved head, then twink in a diamond earring as he put it to his ear. I said, 'Let's go.'

The *Gleaner*'s engine was already running. I cast off fore and aft. As we churned off the quay I saw the Merc turn on its lights and move onto the road. I coiled down the warps and went into the wheelhouse.

'Who was that?' said Georgie.

'Don't know.'

It was curious, though. I had met several fishmongers in my life. None of them had shaved his head or wore jewellery or drove a Merc with blacked-out windows. Perhaps it was something to do with the price of fish nowadays.

The *Gleaner* jinked round the Dublin ferry, left the bloody red light on the harbour entrance to starboard, and began to thrash north, for Scotland.

13

'So what's been happening to you?' said Georgie.

This was an excellent question. I had noted that Major Davies had an associate of whom he seemed to be in awe, and that his enthusiasm for gambling was strong, and his knack for winning weak. And I had sold his fish to Tony Greely for a better price than he would have got in Holyhead. I told Georgie this, and handed over a grand as commission, which seemed to please him.

'The thing is,' said Georgie, 'what are we going to do about that?' He pointed at the hold. 'I have been thinking. Why worry about finding out who did it? I think we should tie something to it and put it overboard. I mean nobody knows it's there, do they? So why not put it in the sea? He'd be out of the way —'

'There is a bullet in him that comes from someone's gun. And I want a chain of evidence that will get them arrested before they kill us. I told you. Sooner or later the police are going to start looking for him, and they may not be very bright but they are very thorough. And at that point I am going to be in big trouble. The police absolutely bloody hate me,' I said.

'And I hate them,' said Georgie, scowling at the distant wink of the Calf of Man.

'So it's like I said. We find the man with the gun before the police do.'

'And then what?'

I emitted what I hoped was a confident laugh. 'I'm building a case. When I'm ready, I'll turn it over to the authorities, cut and dried.'

'Aye,' said Georgie. He did not sound convinced, and of course he was right.

'So now,' I said brightly, 'we are off to Drummie.'

The Clyde is held by many to be a romantic and charming artery of Britain's industrial heritage. But as we nosed the *Gleaner* through the cold drizzle next morning, I had the definite thought that I would rather have been in Antigua. But preferences count for very little when you are trying to catch killers before they kill you. So I laid the *Gleaner* alongside the cut stone quay, told Georgie not to let anyone on board, and set off up the locks.

Mr Nairn the lock-keeper was probably in the pub already, and I had no wish to remind him unnecessarily of the tragic loss of his mobile phone. I walked on up to the second lock, and knocked on the door of the woman with the lipstick. I said, 'Good morning, Mrs. Craigie. You probably don't remember, but we met before.'

'Oh I do, I do,' said Mrs. Craigie, her eyes sparkling unnervingly. 'Will you have a cup of coffee?'

'That would be very kind,' I said. She led me through to the sun lounge overlooking the canal. The prawn trawler was still there. The leaves on the ash tree growing out of its wheelhouse were turning brown. 'One lump or two?' She tittered. I tittered back. Then we talked about the weather, and she complained about the boats and the lockkeeper Nairn. I said, 'The reason I have come today was to thank you for your assistance on the occasion of our last meeting. I am not at liberty to divulge precise details, of course. But I can tell you that your help was instrumental in securing the recovery of the vessel in question.' She went slightly pink. She seemed to love being talked to in Police.

'Oh yes,' I said. 'Without you, we would have found ourselves in a troublesome situation indeed.'

I noticed a sudden hard glint in her eye. She said, 'Is there a reward?'

'Not as such,' I said. 'Except the satisfaction of doing your duty as a citizen. Now there are just one or two links in the chain of evidence that must be forged before we can use it to bind the guilty men to their crime.' I seemed to be changing from Chance of the Yard into the Prophet Elijah. Get to the point. 'How many men were on the boat when it left?'

She sat forward in her chair and scowled, to indicate thought. 'I don't know,' she said. 'Three, maybe? Four? More than two, anyway. There were two cars. Shortbread?'

I picked up a stick and crunched it. It turned to Polyfilla in my mouth. She watched me, smiling her lipstick smile. Then I realised what she had said. 'Cars?' I said.

She flinched at the view of chewed biscuit. She said, 'One of them's still here. I mean you couldn't drive it. The hoodies got it. Awful battering they gave it. More coffee?' She brandished the pot.

'No. Thank you,' I said, getting the shortbread down. 'Where is it?'

She pointed out of the conservatory window. Beyond the prawn boat there stood a red BMW. A red BMW that now I actually came to look at it I would have recognised anywhere.

The red BMW of Johnny Bonneville-Clark. But with an odd sag to its windscreen, and a silvery sheen to its side windows.

'Aye, they've made a terrible mess of of – hey!' cried Mrs Craigie. But I heard no more, for I was out of the conservatory door and down the garden, through the stench from the trawler, across the lock and up alongside the BMW.

It certainly was not a pretty sight. The windscreen was crazed, and someone had stove in the passenger-side window to pop the door lock. I brushed glass crumbs off the seat with a plastic takeaway carton from the gutter, and climbed in.

I sat and looked at the silvery web of the window, and thought: this is where Johnny sat before he went on the boat.

I looked at the litter in the passenger footwell. There was the usual long-trip mulch of sandwich wrappers and empty beer cans. And because it was Johnny there was an empty Absolut bottle and a CD cover much scarred by razor blades. These were splendid clues, but only to the fact that he had been getting his courage up in his traditional manner. I went through the well methodically, seeking further illumination. There was none.

As I climbed out of the car, I saw something white on the dashboard above the steering wheel. I found I was frowning. It was a rosette, of the kind you won at a horse show if you were a successful horse.

Or that people left on the Samson post of your tugboat after it had just burned to the waterline.

These people were so sure of themselves that they advertised themselves instead of covering their tracks.

I lifted the rosette off the dashboard and stuffed it in my pocket. Then I went and smarmed at Mrs Craigie, who had the hurt look of one whose shortbread had missed its target. After that I took a deep breath, walked down the locks, picked up Georgie and went to the pub.

I could just about see Nairn in the underwater light of the bar. His friends were not around; he was by himself, on a stool, leaning against the wall. 'Buy him one,' I said.

Georgie walked over and said, 'Drink, pal?'

Nairn's eyewhites showed dingy in the yellow glimmer of the glass bricks. 'Aye,' he said.

'Double,' said Georgie. 'You're Nairn?'

'Aye.'

'How do,' said Georgie. 'I'm the skipper of the *Sirius Gleaner*. Hoi!' Nairn had tried to get off the stool, but Georgie had pushed him back against the wall. 'And I want a word.'

The barman brought Nairn a half and a half, and the same for Georgie. I remained abstemious in the shadows.

'Thing is,' said Georgie, 'my boat went on a wee holiday, and I want to know who took it.'

Nairn shook his head. I heard the clatter of his glass against his teeth as he took a swig of whisky and chased it down with beer. 'No idea,' he said.

I decided it was time for an entrance. I walked into the light and said, 'Let's go and sit down, eh?'

The eyes rolled at me. Georgie and I took an elbow each and sat him in one of the sticky armchairs under the window. The barman decided that this was an excellent moment to be polishing glasses in the other bar.

'So you can tell us,' I said. 'Or you can tell some much nastier people than us. Who took the *Sirius Gleaner* out of the canal?'

Nairn swigged again, to give himself time to think. He said, 'I'll have the law on you.'

'Never mind the police,' I said. 'Just tell us who took the *Gleaner* away, and Georgie won't hurt you.' Georgie united his enormous fingers and cracked his knuckles.

Nairn writhed in his chair and said, 'No way.'

'We've got plenty of time. We'll wait.'

Nairn put his nose in the air and ostentatiously closed his mouth. Georgie leaned forward and whispered something in his ear. A pause. Nairn said, 'Just between ourselves?'

'Aye.'

'Two bad men,' said Nairn. 'Dinny Brady and Kevin McGahey.'

'I know them,' I said. 'Kevin's the big one, right?'

'Big fella,' said Nairn. 'But Brady's the really big one.' He crossed his legs and looked agonized. 'They came in with this English fella. They were drinking. The English fella was nervous, like he was on something, you know? And Dinny and Kevin finished up their drinks right quick, because you could see he was embarrassing them. And out they went on to the boat. Can I go now?'

'Aye,' said Georgie. Nairn scuttled out of the bar.

I watched him go. Johnny had known where the boat was, because Georgie had told him. And he had taken Dinny and Kevin to it. Maybe they had threatened him. Maybe they had offered to pay him. Money, probably. Either way, he had made a nuisance of himself. And these people had taken him to sea and killed him.

Bang.

I took a deep breath, and opened my mouth to order whisky. But I caught myself at the last moment. And I said to Georgie, 'Why did he decide to tell you?'

'He wanted a piss,' said Georgie. 'My old man had the prostate thing. I know the signs. I told him, no toilet till he talked.'

We left, and pointed the *Gleaner* at the sea.

We sat in the big padded seats with our feet on the console and did not speak as Ailsa Craig grew out of the horizon to the south. Finally, Georgie said, 'What are we into?' He said it in a low, solemn voice that made me think this was a question he wanted answered, for a change. 'I mean. Folks don't murder folks for the sake of fish.' His eyes were resting on me. 'I'm no' very clever. So will you please explain to me what is going on?'

'If you don't interrupt.'

'Aye. It strikes me —'

'Shut up. Johnny nicked the *Gleaner* off the Major because the Major owed him money,' I said. 'He sold her to you and spent the money. The Major sent the hard men to pick up the boat, and Johnny showed them where the boat was, and the hard men killed Johnny.' I had been thinking, though. 'Maybe on the Major's orders, maybe not.'

'Wha?' said Georgie.

'The hard men work for someone else,' I said. 'One of the Major's card pals. A chap called McGown. Ever heard of him?'

'McGown?' said Georgie. 'No.' He shook his head. The bar-room strongman was gone. He was nearly weeping with self-pity. 'Why did this have to happen to me?'

'Because you bought a boat off Johnny.'

'I bought a boat off you,' said Georgie.

'We were both conned,' I said. He was looking angry now. 'So do you want to make noise or do you want me to tell you how we are going to get out of this alive?'

He opened his mouth. I was happy to see that the fear was taking over from the anger. 'Go on,' he said. The boat bucketed in the race south of Arran.

'I am wondering if the Major and McGown are singing from the same hymn sheet,' I said. 'I think the Major owes McGown big money, and McGown is running part of the Major's operation for him in ways that the Major might not like. Which opens up possibilities.'

'What possibilities?' said Georgie, jaw swinging.

'We could call the police,' I said.

'No polis,' croaked Georgie.

'The alternative,' I said, 'is to find out exactly how Greenreap works and grass them up to the Fisheries Protection. And then we will hand Johnny over to the police, bullet and all.'

'It's still polis,' said Georgie.

'All right,' I said. 'You have a better idea, then.'

Georgie glowered down the shelter deck into the murk. He said, 'How do you know who the polis is working for?'

And there he had a point.

It was dark by the time we hit the Sound of Islay. The lights from the tide generators winked on the shore as the flood swept us up the gut. Then there was the migraine twinkle of the distillery, and the funnel of darkness shooting us up at Colonsay. Hard-a-port, and the seaward mark of the Loch Mor channel swam into the wheelhouse window. The wink of the buoy turned the *Gleaner*'s wake to blood as we surged by. Then the road of red blinks opened before us, running down to the yellow lights of the Greenreap sheds.

'All right,' I said. Georgie pulled down the VHF mike from the deckhead. He said, 'Donnie, Georgie.'

'Georgie, Donnie,' said a voice. 'What is it now?'

'We're coming in.'

'We have nothing for you.'

'Oh, aye,' said Georgie. 'See you on the quay, then.' He pulled back the throttle. The *Gleaner* rolled up to the quay on her own stern wave. I put a little recorder in my pocket, trotted up to the shelter deck and threw a warp to Donnie. Georgie wound the back end in. We both jumped down to the quay.

Donnie was standing under a white light. His face looked

crumpled, as if he had been asleep, and the hair on the right-hand side of his head was flat. He said, 'You're not meant to be here.'

'But we are,' said Georgie. I noticed he was carrying the big spanner with the ground-down edges. So did Donnie. 'And my friend has some questions for you.'

'So shall we go into the office?' I said.

As we walked out of the quay lights a curlew yodelled long and free. I did not feel free any more. I felt as if we were walking through a maze with walls made of knives.

The office was a portacabin with a NO SMOKING sign and a smell of old rolling tobacco. There was a map of the Western Highlands on the wall, Greenreap sites marked with green stickers in lochs and on islands, maybe thirty of them. I thumbed the recorder in my pocket and went and sat in the chair behind the desk. Georgie stood by the door. Donnie hung around in the middle of the room, trying to reassemble his intellects. I said, 'Who's the boss, Donnie?'

'Boss?'

'Who do you report to? Sit down, sit down.'

He pulled a card from under the blotter. It said Worsley McGuinness. There was a Belfast number under the name.

'You're an Irish company?'

'Owned by Norwegians. Norgreen.'

'And whose idea is it to be putting black fish under farm fish?'

'Not mine,' said Donnie.

'How long's it been going on?'

'What are you, polis?'

By the door, Georgie brought his spanner into the ready position. Donnie's eyes shifted nervously, and it was hard to blame them.

I said, 'Just answer.'

'A year, maybe.'

'And how about Major Davies?'

'Who?'

'Big chap. Might call himself Smith.'

'Oh,' said Donnie. 'Him. He's the area manager for Norgreen. Both sides of the Irish Sea. Looks after the deliveries, mostly. The Norwegians don't know anything about the, er, the landed fish. They pick up salmon in their ship about every ten days, they have contracts with the supermarkets, all that. Mr Smith has local deliveries, you know, and a little bit on the side with the landed fish for himself and some Irish people.'

'And they pay you not to look too hard.'

He shrugged. 'You try crofting, see how fast it makes your million. What are you going to do about it?'

'Nothing to you.' I was sitting with my hand in my coat pockets, among the odds and ends of string and receipts and other debris. Something made of cloth came into my fingers. I pulled it out and looked at it. It was the white rosette I had found on the dash of Johnny's BMW. I heard a sort of hiss and looked up. Donnie was staring at the thing with eyes on stalks like a crab's. I said, 'What is it?'

He nodded. His mouth opened and shut. His face was grey. He said, 'Aye,' and gave me a smile that would have looked artificial in a funeral parlour. 'I didn't know,' he said. 'I didn't realise.'

'Realise what?'

He gestured at the rosette in my hand, not keeping his eyes away from it. 'That ye had . . . well. Let's just say we'll keep this between oorselves, like. I never saw you, okay? I'll do what I can tae help.' He reached for a piece of paper and a pen. 'My mobile,' he said. 'Any time.' His fingers were shaking so hard he could barely write.

I held out the rosette. 'What do you understand by this?'

He shook his head. He was a dirty white colour. 'Nothing.'

I took a step closer. 'Tell me. Now.'

He croaked, 'The cockade.'

'More.'

He looked so bad I thought he might die. He said, 'Whiteboys.'

'What about them?'

He shook his head and sat down.

I said, 'All right, then. No more of your nonsense.'

He said, 'No,' in a sort of squeak.

'Aye,' I said, keeping up as well as I could. 'Fine. Anything you want to ask him, Georgie?'

'No,' said Georgie, hard as hell.

'Let's go.'

We walked down the quay. 'Whiteboys?' I said.

'Never heard of them,' said Georgie.

As we left the channel, my phone began telling me I had missed calls. I pressed the button and put it to my ear. 'Yes?'

'Good evening,' said the flat, cold voice of the Major. 'And where the fuck are you?'

'Awaiting orders,' I said.

'I ordered you to take a cargo to Holyhead.'

I said, 'We found another buyer.'

The voice had been cold. Now it sank to absolute zero. 'What?'

I did not like the way this was beginning to feel. I said, 'We got you a better price.'

The Major said, 'You are the driver, not the negotiator. You sold that cargo?'

'Yes.'

'You had no right.'

I had a sudden memory of the gold-chain fishmonger in the Merc with the blacked out windows on the dock at Holyhead. And the chill in the Major's voice crawled out of the back of my head and down my spine. But I had seen him cringe in front of McGown, and it had broken the spell.

I said, 'So do you want me to go and fetch that fish and take it to Holyhead? Because it's going to be on the turn by now.'

'Fish,' said the Major, and now I could hear something besides ice in his voice; a cracked, ugly thing, as if something inside his head wanted to laugh at something that was not even vaguely funny. 'No. Where is it?'

My telephone started beeping again. I said, 'Hang on a moment.' This time it was Tony Greely. 'Tony,' I said. 'This is a real pleasure. But not a perfect moment, because —'

'I will tell you why this is not a perfect moment,' said Tony Greely, in a low, thin, furious voice, quite unlike the oceanic roar of a hardy British fisherman. 'This is not a perfect sodding moment because when I went down to go over that fish you brought with my staff, I found there was not only fish in there.'

'What are you talking about?' I said, somewhat rattled by his vehemence.

'I am talking about what I found in a box of sodding salmon,' he said. 'Wrapped up in plastic. In evidence bags.'

'What?'

'I wanted fish,' said Tony Greely. 'And you brought me fish. But you also brought me three kilograms of sodding cocaine.'

14

I sat there and let it all fall into place, the way an avalanche falls into place on a Swiss village. I said, 'Lucky you. Hang on,' and went back to the Major.

'I've found it. I'll get it back,' I said.

'You're right,' he said.

I turned off the telephone and tried to think.

It was not easy. What I really wanted was whisky, and an air ticket to a place where I would be out of all this, such as perhaps Mars.

'Where now?' said Georgie from the wheel.

'We'll get into Loch Tarbert and have a sleep and a think,' I said.

And into Loch Tarbert we went, and dropped an anchor round a headland out of the breeze. Georgie fried a lot of eggs and some beans. I ate them. Then I took my phone ashore in the tender, and walked uphill until I found a signal. The first person I rang was Hamish McDonald, a famous knowall I had met when we were chasing a people-smuggling outfit on the south coast. Hamish was a freelance journalist, and would talk you into mush given the chance. He picked up instantly.

'I'm at the ACPO Convention,' he said; he always thought you would be interested.

I said, 'I'm researching an army officer, slightly retired. Major Horace Davies, Royal Logistics Corps.'

'The Man with No Nerves,' he said. 'Why?'

'Back a bit,' I said. 'What else?'

'Dunno,' he said, and the interest in his voice knifed across the somnolent murmur of chief constables. 'Rumours, though.'

'Such as?'

'Very close to Special Branch, he was. And the Liverpool drug squad. They reckoned he was a sort of army-police liaison person. Totally deniable, all that. And they reckon he was sort of in bed with some paramilitaries in the North of Ireland as well. So when he walked up to those guys and took their guns away he was pretty sure of himself. Ask about him in Liverpool. You were a copper, right? You'll know someone.'

'Thanks,' I said.

'And you'll tell me?'

'Don't see why not.'

'Where are you?'

I eased my back against the rock I was using as a prop. Below me, a raised beach of white boulders glowed faintly in the starlight, as it had for ten thousand years. 'Hounslow,' I said, and rang off.

Being a policeman had just about ruined my life. But it had also left me with a few handy contacts. I called one number. It led to others. 'Harris,' said a Northern voice at last, antique and gravelly.

'Fred?'

'Who's this?' I gave him my name. For a moment I could hear the slow clatter of his breathing. Then he said, 'What do you want at this time of night?'

'Advice.'

A wheezing laugh. 'Why would I give advice to a man who will certainly not take it?'

'Maybe things have changed. Can I come and see you?'

'I can't stop you.'

'You could.'

'I am in fucking hospital,' said Frederick Harris, sometime Liverpool drug squad. 'I have got no lungs left. I blame the shite spliff out of the evidence cupboard.' A pause, with horrible coughing. Deep, hissing breaths: oxygen, perhaps. 'All right,' he said at last. 'Come and see me then. Light relief, could be good.' He gave me an address in Kirkby Lonsdale. 'And you'd better hurry up.'

'You leaving?'

The breathing again, thick and crunchy. 'You could say that.'

I rowed back to the boat. When I woke the sun was greying the sky over the Paps of Jura, and big waves were slapping the skerries to seaward. I started the main engine, pulled up the anchor with the windlass and went aft to the wheelhouse, wishing Johnny good morning as I walked over his vault. In the wheelhouse I shoved the throttle on to the stops. Beyond the skerries the waves were coming in like black walls. Finally we were out of the loch, turning to port, the Sound opening up ahead. And a couple of hours later we were alongside the burned-out wreckage at Achnabuie, and I was stepping ashore.

'Back when?' said Georgie.

'Day or two. I'll call.'

My pickup stood in the corner of the yard, untouched by fire or crowbars. I sluiced a small pool of rain off the driver's seat and got it to start at the third attempt. Gulls were scrambling into a big wind from the northwest. The Major had been on the radio. Georgie was off on a tour of legitimate collections from Greenreap farms between Loch Mor and Tiree. He was welcome to it.

I tried to find a comfortable place among the broken springs, and ended up padding the seat with the road map, which meant that after I turned off the M6 I got lost in the moors and hollows round Kirkby Lonsdale. So it was four by the time I found the hospital. I made my way through a car park busy with the population of the north British uplands bearing suet puddings for their ailing kin. At the reception desk, I said to the woman, 'I am here to visit Frederick Harris.'

In a sheet of plate glass I saw a figure in rigger's boots, filthy jeans and check shirt to match, donkey jacket, uncut hair and seven-day beard from above which glared two blood-red eyes. Apparently it was my reflection.

The receptionist seemed used to such sights. She said, 'He's in the side ward.'

The Fred I had known had looked as if he ate pies four times a day, washing them down with beer. The Fred in the bed was white, with black hollows among the prominent bones of his face and the tube of an oxygen rig under his nose. I said, 'I didn't bring any fruit.'

'I can't lift it anyway,' said Fred. I saw a morphine pump by his side. 'What was it, then?'

'You were on the Liverpool drugs squad when a Major Davies was hanging around.'

The eyes closed. 'Captain then,' he said.

I said, 'How did a soldier come to be mixed up with the drugs squad?'

'Why do you want to know?'

'I am writing a Regimental History.'

He opened the eyes again, drew breath to tell me not to be

so stupid, decided he did not have enough lung power for it. 'Prick,' he said.

'Thank you.'

'Not you. Davies. I mean, clever bloke. But always thinking about Davies. Remember the Weinstein seizure?'

'No.'

'Four hundred kilos of Colombian. Suspected Irish paramilitary involvement, because by then they were forgetting about politics and concentrating on steady work like drugs. Holby, guy running the investigation. Superintendent. Some of the evidence went missing. Screwup in the evidence cupboard, someone miscounted the bags, I don't know. But Holby was running the case, so Holby got blamed, and that was the end of him. And Davies, well, Davies was deniable, so he got denied. And what's deniable can't be accountable. Very good organiser, Davies. Fast. Quickness of the hand deceives the eye.' The eyes closed. The breathing was tiny.

I said, 'Water?'

'I'd drown.' A whisper. 'But you know what? He knew all these Irish villains, one very bad man in particular. He used to play cards a lot. Bridge with the officers, poker with the bad guys, that was Davies. And the card boys said playing with Davies was like playing with the Bank of England. Unlimited funds.'

I nodded, holding his eye. A captain earns about forty thousand a year.

'And there was word,' said Fred, 'that some of the gear from the Weinstein bust was getting back on to the street. And I always wondered, did the card boys mean the Bank of England or did they mean Boots the Chemist?' The last word was lost in a horrible bubbling wash of coughing. The white parts of his face turned grey. He waved at the nurse bell.

I pressed it for him. He stared at me with wide, drowning eyes. I pressed again. He was on the way out. And here was I, asking him silly questions.

I said, 'What was the bad man's name?'

The eyes open. The mouth open. The chin tremulous. No breath.

I said, 'Was it McGown? In an outfit called the Whiteboys?'

The eyes open. They looked surprised. They closed, opened again. A signal. *Yes.*

I said, 'Thank you, Fred.' And I took his hand, the cold, bony hand, and held it until the nurse came in and pressed another button and hustled me out and pushed the door shut in my face.

I stood there looking at that door. We had been driving around the sea with Johnny's corpse on ice, and somehow I had got used to that. The Fred thing was harder.

I turned round and went out to the yard and climbed into the pickup. I was going to head for Scotland again, in the aimless way that you head for bed when you are tired. Then I felt phantom breathing on the back of my neck, and a phantom pain where the bullet went in, plus there were thirty-three paid-for minutes on my hospital car-park ticket. So I rang the Police Benevolent Fund, and gave them my old rank and number, and asked them to put me in touch with a Chief Superintendent Holby.

'Holby?' they said, and there was a clatter of keys. 'Retired. Long, long retired.'

'Do you have a current address for him?'

'Honey Cottage, Chagford, Devon.'

'Shit.'

'I *beg* your pardon?'

'Slight cold,' I said. And I slid out of the car park heedless of the parking minutes remaining, and found the M6, and headed south.

But not for Devon.

It was ten o'clock when the pickup clattered past the sign in front of the Hopley Manor Hotel. The famous signature gleamed briefly gold in the single working headlight. I waded through the gravel and up the steps to the desk where the receptionist averted her eyes and told me Mr Greely was in the Golden Ball Bar.

There were people around now, though not many. There was a mere handful in the Golden Ball Bar, night-out couples talking in low voices. Tony was sitting at one of the tables, drinking a glass of someone else's wine and batting his eyelashes at the female half of the couple, who looked impressed. The male half was looking surly, understandably, since he was paying seventy-five quid a head to get his girlfriend chatted up by a ponce off the telly. I said, 'Evening, all.'

The diners gaped. Tony turned, and his face sagged. He opened his mouth to say something unpleasant, remembered the diners and stuck on a smile. 'A word?' I said. Then, to the diners, 'I'm the boyfriend.'

The bloke looked surprised. The girl looked interested. 'Just his little joke,' said Tony. He hustled me out of the dining room and into his office. 'How *dare* you,' he hissed. 'How dare you fill the place up with drugs and insult me in front of my customers.'

'Be grateful. He was going to hit you,' I said. 'As for the drugs, you could have given them to the police if you'd really wanted to.'

He looked sulky. There was no way he would have called the police, because the police would have leaked to the press, and the press would have been curious about how the fish had arrived, never mind the drugs. There would have been large numbers of questions to which he had no satisfactory answers.

I said, 'So. Do you want to hang on to the coke?'

He screwed up his face, as if incredulous. 'Do I *what*?'

'You got it by accident. I expect you'd like it off the place.'

'Wait a minute,' he said. 'That's an easy hundred grand's worth of, er, stuff. You delivered it to me in good faith.'

'Keep it, then,' I said. 'And work out how to sell it. Or maybe you'll use it yourself? And I'll call the police, and you can tell them what a great big mistake it all was.' I smiled at him soothingly, though he did not look very soothed. 'Or if you don't want that to happen, I'll take it off your hands and give it to the person it was meant to go to.' The rodent look was back on his face. I said, 'And if you have a plan to shop me to the police, your black-fish purchasing is all nicely documented, and will arrive with the food editors of all newspapers and VGTV the morning after my arrest. It's all there.'

'Nonsense,' he said.

Which of course described it nicely. But he could not be sure.

So I said, 'I am knackered. I want a room in your hotel. And tomorrow I will leave like a bad dream and your life will once again be a golden thing.'

He appeared to swallow a lump of something unpleasant. He said, 'Wait here,' and left the room. I tried a couple of the drawers. They were locked. A maid came in. I followed her upstairs to a room done out in turquoise and more seagrass. The view from the window was kitchen dustbins, and the bed was single. I did not care. It had been a hard day. I crawled in and passed out.

Next thing I knew the window was pale grey, and it was raining, and the phone said it was 0730. I showered and shaved, crawled into my filthy clothes and went downstairs.

The coffee was pretty good, and there were sustainable kippers. I ate three, signed a bill, and waded back through the gravel to the pickup. There was a plastic bag in the passenger footwell. I peered inside. It contained more plastic bags, fat, with white powder in them. I gave a cheery double toot and drove off.

It was an odd feeling, driving the motorways of England with six pounds of cocaine in a clapped-out pickup truck. So I turned off the M5 at Dursley, bought gloves, plastic, paper and a label, wrapped up the bags, took them into the post office and posted the parcel to Scotland. And then I drove to Devon.

Honey Cottage sat on the side of a steepish valley, contemplating a range of farm buildings converted into houses and a slurry lagoon transmogrified into a swimming pool. The door knocker was a brass hand holding a globe, lightly polished. The garden was tidy, but not oppressively so. The man who opened the door was the same. He was wearing blue jeans and a cardigan over a check shirt, and reading glasses shoved back on a head covered in close-cropped grey hair. The eyes were grey too, sharp and hard. He raised his eyebrows and waited, blocking the door. I introduced myself. 'Late Southampton CID,' I said. 'I want to talk about Major Horace Davies, Royal Logistics Corps.'

The eyes narrowed a fraction, or perhaps it was my imagination. He said, 'You'd better come in.'

Inside, the tidiness was less pronounced. There were brownish landscapes on the walls and a half-empty bottle of wine with the cork stuffed in standing on a pile of books. 'Sorry about the mess,' he said. 'Tea?'

I accepted, and he went into something that was probably the kitchen. I looked at the photographs; you do, if you are a policeman. They were of Holby, and a couple of young girls who must have been his daughters, and a clever-looking dark woman in a print dress. A kettle boiled. The tea came in cups with the teabags still in. There was nothing feminine in the place. I wondered what had happened to the woman in the print dress.

He said, 'My wife died. Cancer.'

'I'm sorry,' I said, somewhat freaked by this act of mind-reading.

'And I am writing a history of West Country policing. What can I tell you about Davies?'

'I heard a story about him,' I said. 'About you and him, actually. After the Weinstein case.'

The eyes hardened. 'You did,' he said. 'What are you nowadays? A reporter? Or just a clown?'

The clown bit showed that he had done his research. 'Not a reporter,' I said. 'An interested party.'

'How?'

'I'll tell you later,' I said. 'What I would like you to do is tell me about your relations with Davies before you resigned.'

No movement in the long, narrow face. Then he said, 'Are you recording this?'

No point lying. 'Yes.'

'Then stop. Let's see it.'

I took out the recorder, switched it off, put it on the coffee table. He pulled it towards him, assured himself it was not running, and said, 'What do you want to know?'

'What happened?'

'After Weinstein? It was cocaine coming ashore in containers of pineapples, canned. We ran a joint operation with Customs and the army, surveilled and followed until we were at the distribution point. Davies was liaison and coordination when we went in. Very successful we were too. Twenty-one arrests, nineteen convictions. Half a ton of cocaine seized. Davies organised the delivery of the drugs to our evidence cupboard. The prosecution used it, of course. Then it was shipped down to the Customs incinerator for destruction. And it turned out that what arrived at Customs was a couple of hundred kilos light of what had been seized. We investigated, Christ did we investigate, and I did what I could to keep it private. I have to say that I was somewhat worried by Captain Davies's role in the whole business. You know what it is with drugs; people can go native. So I started after him. But as soon as I did there were politicians screaming and yelling, and a lot of stuff blowing up in the Irish community in Liverpool, and I was a racist and a fascist and God knows what else, and I got a word in my ear to shut up because there were security implications, operations half completed, I should wait until I got the word before I resumed the investigation. But the word never came.'

He fell silent, head bowed, looking at his feet. Finally, he said, 'It is perhaps true what was said later, which was that I did not pursue the investigation with sufficient energy. But you try summoning up sufficient energy when you've got the Prime Minister's representative on earth screaming in one ear about Irish sensibilities and the hospital in the other ear telling you your wife has got three days to live and a visit might be nice.' Another pause. 'So I was slow. But Davies's friends weren't. They put their tame hacks on to me, and next thing I knew there were politicians everywhere and I was writing a letter of resignation.' There were angry red spots in his cheeks as he pushed a vinyl album across at me.

It is strange, the way the forces of law and order like to show you their scrapbooks. The stuff in the Major's had been adulatory, but nonsense. The stuff in Holby's was also nonsense, but it was not adulatory, not at all. If they had been my cuttings, I would have used them to start a fire, and then gone looking for the people who had written the stories, and cooked them on it. There were remarks about pissups in breweries. There was a detailed picture of an incompetent senior officer surrounded by shadowy druggies. There were local politicians calling him a racist. There was an inquiry, to which he did not show up.

His eyes followed me greedily as I turned the pages. Evidently he knew the book backwards. I closed it with a chill in my heart quite different from my usual sense of looming disaster. I said, 'This is bullshit.'

He said, 'I told you. My wife died.' He shook his head, gazing at something far beyond her picture on the mantelpiece. 'I joined the police because I wanted to help people. In the end I couldn't even help her. I can't say I was . . . in control of things. It wasn't very good.'

'The police should have helped.'

'They gave me counselling.' A smile like a piano keyboard. 'Obviously that was very useful.'

'So you just left.'

'And waited,' said Holby. 'And now you are here. And I will tell you what you want to know. But don't tell me about anything for which you wouldn't want to be held accountable in a court of law.' His eyes blazed briefly. 'Or I will perform a citizen's arrest on you. Understood?'

'Yes,' I said. And I knew that I had at last met an honest copper. I said, 'You say there was Irish involvement. Political?'

'They would have said it was. But in the Troubles they said they were thieving and dealing to raise money for the war effort, and maybe it was true. Not afterwards, though. Just a bunch of scumbags, dirty little fingers in all pies. But nobody in Ireland would touch them, and they had help in England.'

'Any names?'

'I'm not giving names to you.'

'McGown?'

He blinked. He said, 'Very good.'

'And two men called Brady and McGahey. And an outfit called the Whiteboys.'

He opened his mouth to say something surprised. But another emotion caught him, and he looked away. The light caught a tear sliding down his face. I felt terrible. This was the only surviving decent human I had met in a week, and I had made him cry. I said, 'Sorry,' then realised how bloody stupid it sounded.

'They found Mary's oncologist,' he said. 'They made him lie on the lawn of his house in front of his children. They kicked his face in and dropped a white rosette on him. It didn't make any difference, she would have died anyway. But they wanted it to hurt.' He pulled a handkerchief out of his sleeve and blew his nose. 'So I am going to be very pleased if you can do anything about these people. And not very surprised if they kill you. Because you have come all the way down here I will assume your intentions are good. But all that stuff when you left the Service, well, I think you're a bit of a clown.'

I said, 'It wasn't the way it sounds.'

'No,' he said. 'Probably not. Do you want a drink?'

I opened my mouth to say yes, and said no instead, and got up. He gave me a card and a mobile number, and as far as his face was capable of expression, looked as if he was sorry I was leaving. He said, 'If there's anything I can do to help get those men,' and shook my hand. And I went out of the door and started up the truck, and when I looked round he was in the doorway, waving, and I thought that perhaps I had made what passed in my life for a friend.

Under false pretences, though. I had told him that one of my final acts in the police force, for which I was famous, had not been the way it sounded. But if I was honest with myself, it had.

See what you think.

15

It is not easy to be a serving police officer and a yacht broker at the same time. This is particularly true if you are drinking two bottles of whisky a day, and those of your friends who will still talk to you keep telling you you are having a nervous breakdown. That was roughly the state I was in after I had been a year in the flat in Boscombe. I had never got round to painting it red, so it was a drab box where I spent as little time as possible. But my computer was working fine, and in its silicon imagination Gavin Chance Marine sold beautiful yachts from an office under whispering palms. One morning the mobile rang. 'Bruce Laing,' said a voice. 'I've got to go to Hong Kong, and I've bought a boat, so I want to sell the old one. How about it?'

Naturally it was fine. Laing was an acquaintance from the days before I had lost interest in competitive sailing. His boat before this one had been stolen. He had come to me as a friend in the police. I had advised him that if the police got mixed up with the recovery, he would be unlikely to get it back that season, if ever. And I had offered to do what I could, informally.

Naturally he had been pleased. So I looked at the weather and the tides, and started telephoning. And found it on the twenty-third call, in St Peter Port. So I took a day's holiday, flew to Jersey, and found the boat in the hands of a remarkably stoned French hippie. I told him not to be so silly, gave him his fare home, and brought the boat back to Poole on the next tide. Laing had been impressed. And here he was, putting his money where his mouth had been.

So after I came off duty that day I pulled my cleanest blazer out of the pile on the wardrobe floor, ironed a pair of jeans and pulled on my go-to-meeting deck shoes. Then I had a swig of Bell's, crunched half a dozen Extra Strong mints and hopped into the bent Sierra.

The boat was a Da Gama 60, a Charlie Agutter design, a great big sloop more luxurious than most houses. Bruce was a tanned person who seemed not so much brisk as in a big hurry. We had a short meeting in the boat's cockpit.

I said, 'How much do you want for her?'

'She's got a lovely survey,' he said. 'What do you think?'

I looked at the perfect teak under my deck shoes. I raised my eyes to the majestic rig. I thought of the mirrored stateroom with en suite head, and the Philippe Starck galley, and the washing machine, and thought: whatever I suggest, he will want more. So I said, 'Nine hundred thousand.'

'Pounds?' he said. 'You're joking. A million three.'

I smiled ruefully. 'I'll do my best,' I said.

'I'm sure. No hurry.' He handed over the keys and went ashore.

Well, my flat was horrible, and Johnny's creditors kept shouting bad words through the letterbox because he had given my address as his. So (and I confess that this had been in the back of my mind when I suggested the nine hundred thousand pounds to Bruce, because the boat would not sell at that, let alone a million three) I had a floating home, rent free, with a few days' supply of Bell's in the lockers. And that would have been a nice breathing space, had it not been for Morgan's Ice Cream.

The Morgan's Ice Cream van with Henry its scoopmeister stood in the corner of Wardell's Boat Yard. Wardell's was the last old-school yard in Poole Harbour, and was an economical place to park a tender and an N-reg Ford Sierra. One evening in June I arrived in the yard fresh from the saloon bar of the Saracen's Head, and noticed a short queue in front of the Morgan's van. This was odd, because Henry's notion of hygiene consisted of picking his nose clean before he plied the scoop. I was in the state of drunkenness that likes to stamp its personality on anything faintly unusual. So I went over to have a look.

The queue had gone by the time I arrived, but Cyril Dobson the yard gofer was there, shaking his antifouling-spattered head. A figure moved behind the glass of the ice cream van. It was too slim for Henry, and too tall. I walked up to the window and opened my mouth to order a small vanilla cornet. But my voice seized up, and my mouth remained open.

Henry was not in the van. In his place was a girl. She looked twentyish. She had flawless skin the colour of Cornish ice cream, amber eyes set at a slight tilt over high cheekbones, and blonde hair done up in a chignon harpooned with a paintbrush, artist's, not decorator's.

'Yes?' she said, her perfect mouth curving into a smile of infinite understanding.

The drink kicked in. My voice came back. 'Happy in your work?' I said.

'Is all right.'

'Where are you from?'

'Belarus.' She handed me the cornet. 'One pound twenty, please.'

I ransacked my brain for ways of keeping the conversation going. The range was limited. In the end, I said, 'What's your name?'

She smiled kindly, no doubt observing what was on my mind. 'Irina,' she said.

'Why don't we have a drink after work?' I saw the smile start to turn dismissive. 'On my yacht,' I said.

'You have yacht?'

'Watch out for him, hur, hur,' said Cyril. 'He's a copper.'

'What is copper?' said Irina, a small frown marring the perfect brow.

'Plod. Fuzz. Police,' said Cyril.

'Oh,' said Irina, looking as if she had been slapped.

'But I am off duty,' I said. 'And I insist that you accompany me for a drink on board.'

Her face was blank now. She shrugged and nodded. Perhaps the cops in Belarus did not do irony. I said, 'But only if you're thirsty.'

She smiled. I rocked back. 'I am often thirsty,' she said. 'For instance now. Is knocking-off time.'

'Hur, hur,' said Cyril, a keen watcher of Carry On films. She locked up her van. I led her down to the tender, and we motored out to the Da Gama, a warm breeze spreading blonde tendrils across her elegant throat. I helped her up the stern, tied up the dinghy and unlocked. 'Yours?' she said, amazed.

I shrugged modestly. I made some charming canapés of Mother's Pride and cheese. We washed them down with whisky. She said, 'What is your age?'

'Thirty-six,' I said. This had been true a few years previously.

'Is good,' she said. 'I have twenty-five years. In Belarus we have saying. For good relationship, mistress should be half age of man plus seven years, minimum.'

I nodded, hypnotised by her astonishing beauty. This was not my boat, and I was drunk, and the rest of it. But she had used the word 'mistress'.

Deep in my brain, a couple of cells not yet knocked out by alcohol offered the opinion that this was all a bit rapid. I told them to shut up, but they made me bring the conversation back to something a bit more general. I said, 'When did you come to England?'

'Two weeks.'

'And do you like it here?'

The beautiful mouth grew fuller. The amber eyes brimmed with unshed tears. She said, 'So very much. But I am illegal.'

'Illegal?'

She put out her hand, a beautiful hand, long, the nails perfect ovals pink as cowrie shells. 'I have no passport, no visa. A man called Dave brought me on fishing boat.' Now she was on her knees. 'But I must stay, for I have agreed to sell ice cream for Mr Morgan and I am loyal person.'

The brain cells told me that there were probably other reasons she wanted to stay. But their voices were faint in the roaring flood of lust chemicals. I took her hand and patted it and said, 'There, there,' or words to that effect. She came and sat beside me and filled my glass and hers. I said, 'When did you last eat?'

'I had one vanilla cone, in mid day,' she said. 'Mr Morgan will be angry.'

'Never mind him,' I said. 'Now we are going to have some food from the freezer and I will take you ashore and I will see you tomorrow evening after work.'

'Work. As police. You will report me.'

'I will not,' I said. 'I promise.'

She gave me a radiant smile. She said, 'I am lucky, I have found good man.' Then she leaned over and kissed my cheek with her lovely soft lips, and darted below and cooked us dinner.

Actually she was a terrible cook. But when you are drinking on my scale you do not eat much. She seemed hungry, hunching over her plate and looking up from time to time to smile at me. After dinner I took her ashore so she could drive the ice-cream van back to Morgan's. That night I hardly slept. Next day I crawled into work and ate some speed out of the evidence cupboard to keep myself awake, and interviewed a confession out of a lad who had come into the pub to spend the money he had nicked from a paper shop down the road. At last the lad was in custody pending remand, and I was off and away.

It was sixish when I got back to the yard. My heart sank. There was no ice cream van. Then I saw a slender figure get up from the bench in front of Cyril's shed, dust off the bottom of her tight white jeans and come towards me, wearing a dazzling but nervous smile. Most of the men working on their boats stopped what they were doing to watch. Frankly, I was extremely proud. And I got prouder when she kissed me on the cheek and said, 'Let's go to ship.' As she stepped into the tender, I observed through the whisky and the rag-end of the speed that she was carrying a biggish bag.

An overnight bag.

I cleared my throat and started the engine. I said, 'No ice-cream-selling today?'

She turned pink and lowered the lashes. 'No.' A tear.

'What happened?'

'Mister Morgan,' she said. 'He want me to go into bed with him.'

'Nasty man. Did he sack you?'

'Yes. He was angry by what I told him.' The amber eyes came up at me under the lashes.

'What did you tell him?' I said.

'That I was taken.' She took my hand.

And that was just about that. With Irina, resistance was futile.

Not that I minded. That night we slept in the stateroom. I looked up at the mirror on the deckhead and saw her slender person sprawled over my unslender frame. A sort of crazy glee bubbled up in me. Onward! I thought. Irina stirred in my arms. 'I hate ice cream,' she said. 'I love you.' And the crazy glee got stronger.

Next morning I woke up to find she was padding about the boat in nothing but an oversized Musto, and she looked vulnerable and beautiful and good enough to eat. I said, 'Do you want to go sailing?'

'Sailing?' she said. Her smile had become a little fixed.

'I have this lovely boat,' I said, suppressing the thought that it was not mine in any way, shape or form. 'We can go to the West Indies. Panama, the Pacific. Not dreary old England.'

'I am liking England,' she said.

'I'm not.' I climbed out of bed and invigorated my coffee with a sharp blast of Bell's. Once I had necked the restorative, I picked up the mobile and rang the station. 'Touch of flu,' I said. 'Won't be in.' And rang off, and turned off the phone. 'What have we got in the way of food?' I said.

Irina was eyeing the lockers. 'Some bacon, eggs, bread. Five whisky.'

'Plenty,' I said. There was half a tank of water, a quarter-tank of fuel. And sails, of course. The world lay at our feet.

'Can I go to shore?' she said.

'No need,' I said. And I hauled up the tender, hoisted the enormous mainsail with the charming electric winch, and dropped the mooring. 'We're off!' I cried. And Irina smiled back, in her tight white jeans, leaning on the uphill coaming of the cockpit. The jeans were faintly grubby now. Never mind, there was a washing machine.

I unrolled the jib. The wind was westerly, force three. I felt the kick of the wheel as the sails filled, watched that great white tower ease over against the true blue of the sky, heard the water roar from the transom. A pure happiness filled me. I celebrated with more whisky.

Irina said, 'Do we go far?' There was a sallow look to her face, and dark shadows under her eyes. Tired. After last night it was hardly surprising. I put my arm around her delicate shoulders and pointed out the long sweep of beach heading up to Studland, the chalk pillar of Old Harry mourning his fallen wife. 'Sad,' I said.

'Maybe,' she said. 'Are we nearly there?'

Then we had swept past Old Harry, and the race was at us, powerful in the ebb, hills of water jumping, the boat pitching violently. I laughed cheerily at the standing waves. There was a sound beside me. Irina was looking at her tight white jeans. She had been sick down them. She said, 'This is horrible.' I told her she would get over it and put her to bed in the saloon, where the boat's motion was least. Then I tacked down the coast, past Swanage and Portland Bill, where the last of the tide swooshed us through the lobster buoys bobbing in the inside passage.

Once we were well into Lyme Bay, I went below for more whisky. Irina had been sick again. She said, in a blurred voice, 'This very bad.'

'It'll get better.'

'I run away with you because you are policeman,' she said. 'I think, he will protect me. I was fool. You kill me instead.'

She'll get over it, I told myself. But when we got alongside in Dartmouth, she gave me a look of hatred and walked off down the pontoon. I ran after her and took her arm. 'Get off,' she said, shaking herself loose. 'Or I call policeman. Real one.'

I let her go. I watched her, pale in the night, the slim shape of her blurring, I could not at first think why. Then I realised I was crying. I turned round and took the boat back to Poole and spent a day scrubbing the puke out of the saloon cushions, crying all the time. Everyone knew what had happened, because Cyril had told them. A manic episode, the doctor said, followed by something depressive. Translated into the hairy-chested argot of the station, this meant I was a fucking clown. Someone saw Irina pole-dancing in Eastbourne a month later. But by then I did not care, because I was on so many pills I rattled like a maraca. And someone suggested that I should leave the Police Service before I got thrown off it, which was a good idea, but not one I had the energy to carry through. And amazingly, nobody sacked me.

That time.

But here I was back in Achnabuie, and there was the *Gleaner*. I went aboard with a feeling that I was coming home.

It did not last.

Georgie was at the table, eating beans and farting. He looked up as I came in. 'Good holiday?' he said.

'Not a holiday,' I said. 'How was it at the Greenreap farms?'

'Dropped in,' he said. 'Asked around in a subtle manner. Nothing.'

'Nothing what?'

'Everywhere but Loch Mor, they're shipping nothing but salmon off of the farms. I was asking the boys, the prawn boys. They've seen nothing. So I asked Kenny Macrae on Tiree and Donald McCrum at Armadale. Salmon only, they said.'

I made myself coffee, and let the narrative roll over my head, because he had done the work, and he deserved to make his report, even if it was bloody useless. 'And then,' he said, after what felt like half an hour, 'I dropped back in on Donnie.'

'Oh,' I said, peering into the bread bin. There was a slice of Mother's Pride, not too mouldy. I stuck it in the toaster.

'He's in a state, Donnie,' said Georgie. 'He wouldn't talk to me. He kept asking where you were. Shaking. He had the fear of death on him all right, and it came off of you.'

'Me?'

'Something you said. Or maybe showed him.' The hum of an outboard came through the wheelhouse window. 'Talk of the devil,' said Georgie, and pulled the window down, and stuck his head out. 'Donnie!' he roared, in a voice of iron.

The aluminium workboat planing across the black harbour did not deviate. The man at the helm could not hear Georgie, and even if he had, he was heading straight for the *Gleaner* anyway. He came alongside and ran over the gunwale with the painter. I saw him unbutton his coat and give himself a shake, as if preparing himself for interview. Then he came in.

'Tea?' I said.

'No. Yes,' he said. 'Listen. I have to know. How do you regard me?'

'Regard you?'

'I've done my job. I've talked tae nobody. But you showed me the cockade.'

I had no idea what he was talking about. I looked at Georgie. His mouth was hanging open. 'Cockade,' he said.

Donnie was frowning, looking between us, chewing his lips. I was racking my brains. I had no idea what he was talking about. But I remembered when he had started being afraid.

I shoved my hands in the pockets of my coat, and rummaged

in the debris. My fingers found the crumpled cloth of the rosette I had picked off the dash of Johnny's Beemer. The rosette, or cockade. I held it between two fingers and tapped it on my knee and made my face grim and my eyes blank and said, 'What do you understand by this?'

His face was shining. 'That I am in shite, but I don't know what I've done.'

'Who are we?' I said.

'You're the Whiteboys.'

'No we're not,' I said. 'They burned out my tug and stole Georgie's boat though, and wrecked my partner's car, which is where I found the cockade. And we're going to have them.'

Donnie made a sound that might have been meant for a laugh. 'Oh, aye,' he said. 'You and whose army?'

'Don't tell me you're scared.'

'That is exactly what I'm telling you,' said Donnie.

'He's only a desk soldier.'

'Who is?'

'Major Davies.'

He laughed again, even worse than the first time. 'He's scared as well,' he said. 'And there's another boatload of fish heading up the Sound for his coolroom just now, so if you want to catch him, you can have him. Now if you will excuse me, I'll be getting along home.'

'Have a cup of tea.'

He shook his head. But he took one anyway, and a few HobNobs. It was cold out there on the Sound.

We talked for half an hour, inconsequential stuff; he seemed relieved to be with the good guys. Then he went out of the door. I heard the workboat's outboard start. I finished a HobNob of my own.

Beyond the windows, a green Audi rolled on to the hard behind the quay. Two men got out. One was big, the other slightly smaller. They were watching the workboat. My heart gave a mighty slam at my ribs. 'Cast off,' I said. 'Cast *off*.'

The engine was running. Georgie sprinted forward to the shelter deck, letting off the bow line and the spring. Donnie's boat was coming under our stern. I was fumbling at the stern line. One of the men put something to his shoulder and pointed it at Donnie, following him round. There was a bang. One of the wheelhouse windows blew in. Shotgun. My knees turned to custard. I went round the seaward side, crouching low behind the superstructure, and engaged full ahead. Donnie was buzzing away towards Caol Ban. The *Gleaner* spouted water under her stern. The smaller of the two men was quick. I saw him cross the burned-out tug in two jumps, stand poised to leap across at us as the *Gleaner* opened a gap of sea between her and the tug. I saw his face in a tight grin behind the curtain of hair. I saw him jump towards us, fall short, his hands clutch the rail. I heard a roar beside me and saw Georgie raise a boathook above his head and slam it down on the fingers. The fingers went. A head rose in the wake. I wound the wheel over, broadsided a lobster boat, and stuck the nose on the open sea.

Next time I looked round I saw a figure crawling up the slipway. Another figure was waiting for it. It seemed to be talking into a mobile phone. Then we were in Caol Ban and the land interposed itself. And five minutes later, we were once again on the Sound of Jura. 'Christ I gave him a skelp,' said Georgie. 'Christ I did enjoy that.'

I was looking out across the Sound. The sun was down, and a peach-coloured afterglow hung behind Islay. The sea was flat and black, catspawed with a small breeze; and empty. Empty except for Donnie's workboat, bustling away westwards towards the Sound of Islay, and a dirty black trawler coming up from the direction of Ireland. Donnie seemed to slow when he saw the trawler, and I thought the trawler altered course. Then I saw Donnie turn away from the trawler and head north.

'What's he doing?' said Georgie.

'Search me,' I said. 'Who's that trawler?'

'Don't know,' said Georgie. 'Rathlin boat, maybe. Where in the living name of hell fire is he away to?'

I reached forward and pushed buttons on the plotter. They are amazing things, plotters. This one had a flat screen. On the screen was a chart of where we were: the long yellow shore of the Mull of Kintyre astern, and ahead the teardrop of Jura. We were a little boat shape. Ahead were two triangles: one of them Donnie, moving away, and the trawler, moving on the same course. After him?

'Shee,' said Georgie, suddenly worried. And I was worried with him.

'What channel does he use?' I said.

'Six.'

I put the VHF on six, low power, and thumbed the button. 'Donnie, this is us,' I said. 'Get back here.'

'Away tae fuck!' said Donnie's voice in the ether. And try as I would, I could not make him answer again.

I moved the cursor over the screen. The plotter produced lines: our courses. Donnie's course was taking him to the top end of Jura. Georgie said, 'He never is.' I held my peace. The sky was darkening. It was a clear night, cold, with a fingernail of moon hanging to the right of the Paps. Towards that moon Donnie's workboat scuttered full chat, washed along by the middle of a big tide. And behind him, churning along at an easy twelve knots, was the loom of the black trawler, starboard light glowing green, a white cushion of water under her high axe bow.

I began to get an unpleasant feeling in my belly. 'He's never hunting him,' said Georgie.

He was, though.

The trawler was a knot faster than the workboat. They were perhaps half a mile apart. The workboat was still heading north. And everyone out there on that sheet of water knew what was waiting in the narrow neck between the northernmost tip of Jura and the little island of Scarba.

It is called the Corryvreckan. Through that gap there squeezes a lot of the water thundering north out of the Irish Sea. It is very deep. But a huge underwater pinnacle rises from the seabed in its middle. The flood rushes past the pinnacle at somewhere around six knots. This makes an eddy that sensible people call a whirlpool. It is a brute on a calm day and a monster in a gale.

And it was into this roaring gut that Donnie was heading in an aluminium workboat with a ten-horsepower outboard.

'Ach, he knows the water,' said Donnie.

But the chill would not go away.

It must have settled on Donnie too. I saw his wake silver under the pale moon. The radar signature turned away from the gulf.

The trace of the black trawler altered course to cut off his retreat.

Georgie said, 'That's not going to happen.' I found I agreed. I put the throttle on to the stop. Georgie said, 'What to do?'

'Nudge him away.'

'Good.'

The *Gleaner*'s deck was throbbing under my feet. I could see the trawler's starboard light still, half a mile away —

The light went out. He had turned it out. Now the trawler was a long black shadow sliding after the silver thread of Donnie's wake. 'He'll catch him,' said Georgie. 'Fuck no.'

The two radar traces were close now, and converging. I slammed the throttle with my hand, but it was on the stops already. The surface ahead was writhing with seams and eddies. On it, the hulking black shadow of the trawler slid forward to cover the workboat. The radar echo behind caught up the radar echo in front. They merged.

And suddenly there was no silver thread of wake, no workboat. And only one echo: the black trawler, turning north, away from the Corryvreckan. 'We'll find him,' I said.

'Mebbe he was wearing a lifejacket,' said Georgie. 'A lifeline, mebbe.'

We both knew that this was grasping at straws.

The black boat turned its navigation lights back on. The tide had pulled us past it, and this time it was his red port light we saw, hammering up for Cuan Sound and Easdale, the bastard. There was still no radar trace for Donnie. There would not be.

'There,' said Georgie. He was pointing out of the window the gun had blown out. Something wallowed in the black water, pale under the moon. An aluminium workboat. Upside down.

Maybe he had been wearing a harness with a lifeline.

But now we were in the Corryvreckan. I said, 'Keep pointing at it.' The land was sliding by. The GPS said we were doing eight knots over the ground.

A weird snoring noise drowned the engine. Up ahead, the water bunched and heaved. The pale leaf of the workboat wallowed, stuck a side out of the sea and began to slide astern. 'He's in the eddy,' said Georgie. I wound the wheel to port. The moon swung across the sky. And suddenly the wheelhouse was tilting downwards, forward. There was an enormous crash. Water piled down the deck. My breath went as an icy jet spouted in at the paneless window. I mopped it out of my eyes with my sleeve. We were spinning now, anticlockwise. I found myself wondering stupidly if whirlpools in the southern hemisphere operated the other way round. Then a more useful part of my mind banged the throttle forward and the wheel down to port, and I felt the kick of the propeller on the rudder, and the flank of Jura steadied in the window, and we began sliding backwards up the counter-eddy.

Georgie said, 'There he is,' still pointing, and there was the drowned workboat turning pale under the moon.

I took the *Gleaner* alongside it. Georgie fished out the painter with a boathook and wound it on a cleat. I kept us straight, feeling the surge and eddy batter at the rudder. Then I saw a flock of white crests above the shelter deck, and the bow went up and slammed down, and we were in pyramids of water that rolled the boat on her beam ends, port then starboard. I put the nose to the current, ferry-gliding across the flume. One final heel, a black mound of sea down the deck as we crabbed through the eddy-pits on the edge of the stream. And we were out of it, in calm black water, in a bay called Bagh Gleann nam Muc, in case you are interested.

I was not. I turned the working lights on and went on deck and looked down on the pale shape of the workboat. It had turned the right way up.

There was no lifeline.

I went into the wheelhouse and called Oban Coastguard. Then I switched off and thought of the tail of the Corryvreckan, a ten-mile torrent thundering into the dark sea to the north-northwest. The Great Race, they call it. And somewhere out there was Donnie, tumbling in the black.

He had been a crofter trying to make a few bob on the side working in a fish farm. And they had thought he had been talking to the wrong people, so they had killed him.

Georgie said, 'This is so bad.' He was shocked. So was I. We had been driving Johnny's corpse round the sea for so long that it almost seemed like a fact of life. Donnie had been a deliberate act of killing, and we had watched the whole thing.

'Nobody'll believe us if we tell them,' I said.

'Aye,' said Georgie.

I sat in the big chair by the windscreen and closed my eyes and listened to the chitter of my nerves and the snoring of the Gulf. Rotors clattered overhead. After forty-five minutes the lifeboat came alongside, brilliant orange in the working lights, and the coxswain asked efficient questions and nodded and took the boat off to search the Great Race, even if he knew and we knew it was a fool's errand.

All night the rotors clattered and the lights lashed the overfalls. But we did not see them. We pumped out the workboat and left it anchored in the bay. We slept for a little while. Then we corkscrewed across the Gulf, the tide ebbing now, the Garvellachs lying rose-pink across the dawn sea to the northeast. The nose swung. The Garvellachs came on the port bow.

It was time things started to happen to the Major.

I had a plan.

I went down into the fish hold. The Corryvreckan had shaken the ice loose, and Johnny was half out of his bin like a big black fish. I put the bigger lumps back and swept the debris into the scuppers. To tell the truth, I did not much fancy touching Johnny. The black polythene parcel had the same atmosphere as the letters Miranda's lawyers used to send me.

But I grasped the body by one of its wide parts, and hauled it squeamishly back into its bin. 'Farewell, old scout,' I said, and covered him up before he could answer.

I swept up the ice chips and slung them into the bins, wondering why I was being more polite to him in death than I had been inclined to be in life. Then I went back to the wheelhouse and conferred with Georgie, who said, 'Aye,' and went down to the hold himself.

I steered towards Seil, russet with bracken in the morning light. Far astern, a ray of sun caught a tiny yellow helicopter box-searching the whitecaps of the Great Race. I turned on my telephone. There was a missed call from the Major. When I returned it, he answered quickly. I said, 'Did I wake you up?'

'Mind your own business,' he said, colder than Johnny.

'Did you get a parcel?'

He said, 'Where are you?'

'Off the Garvellachs.'

'Get in here,' he said. 'There's a cargo waiting.'

'Yes, Major,' I said, very meek. 'About an hour, Major.'

As we closed the land, I saw a boat coming out of the Major's bay. It was a big black trawler.

'That's the boat,' said Georgie.

It was. Donnie had mentioned it. It had unloaded fish for the Major and his friends. And on the way in, it had disposed of a security risk. The men in the green Audi would have told them about it.

All right, Major, I thought. Stand by. I noted down the trawler's name and number: *Arthur Worris*, Irish flag. I trained my glasses on the bridge windows. Two faces, unshaven, looking ahead, not at us. Nobody I recognised.

We went in.

16

The day had turned grey and calm, with enough swell to rustle on the rock I had found with the *Lorne Lady*. Her wreck still lay on the beach, hauled or possibly bulldozed above the high-water mark. I vaguely wondered if the insurance assessors had been to have a look. Then I looked at the shore, and I remembered there were worse things than insurance assessors.

A big man in a black suit was walking slowly down the quay. He had a Jack Russell terrier on a lead. He was watching the *Gleaner*, the cold eyes trying to roll down the tubes of the binoculars and into my head. This was a nasty man, they were trying to tell anyone they touched. A frightening man. But that only worked if you were in a frame of mind to be frightened. What I thought as I saw those eyes was: this is where you start to get what is coming to you.

Georgie put the *Gleaner* alongside. I held up a line for the Major. The Major looked at me as if I were pavement debris, and allowed his dog to tow him away. So I jumped ashore and dropped the loop on the bollard, secure in the knowledge that he had not suddenly been converted to the doctrine of universal love. Which made what I was about to do to him much easier, not to say actively delightful.

I said, in a tone of deep respect, 'What needs doing, sir?'

He liked the 'sir'. He said over his shoulder, 'Load what's in the cold store. Then come to the house.'

He walked away. I saw the bulldog wife looking out of the picture window. The Major was a gambler, and gamblers are fundamentally idiots. I was not so sure about the wife.

The forklift was waiting outside the cold store. I opened the door and drove in. Georgie waited outside, just to make sure that nobody wanted to cool me down again. There were boxes of fish in there, five high and three across, on pallets, twelve pallets in all. The big stack of spare pallets and boxes was still piled against the wall. This was good. I shoved the forklift under the first pallet of full boxes and took them down to the harbour. Georgie trotted behind. We took the hatch covers off and got the derrick going. The boxes went down. After the sixth trip, Georgie said, as per plan, 'Rubbish.'

'Rubbish?' I shouted, extra loud. 'Okay!' And a pallet swung up out of the fish hold, piled with old cardboard boxes and net and black bags of galley debris.

I felt the discreet prickle of sweat between my shoulder blades as I trod on the GO pedal of the forklift. The rubbish teetered uneasily as I drove up the ramp from the quay. As I passed the end of the bungalow, a window opened. 'What's that?' said a woman's voice.

Once my heart had started beating again I looked up. And there was the bulldog wife, gimlet eyes drilling into the forklift's load.

'Rubbish,' I said.

'What makes you think we want your rubbish?' she said.

'There's a skip in the yard,' I said.

'For our personal use. Throw that in the sea.'

I said, 'If I throw this in the sea, it'll land up on your beach.'

'No it won't. It'll go somewhere else.'

'Your beach,' I said. 'Because I'll put it there.'

Her jowls hardened. She slammed the window. I drove to the yard as fast as the forklift would go, cold sweat flowing in sheets. That had been bloody stupid. This was not a good moment to be watched. If the Major came into the yard we were doomed. Inside at best, and dead at worst. The forklift approached the skip flat out, at half a mile an hour. Nearly there —

The kitchen door opened. The Major stood on the step, glaring. I felt a loosening of the innards. He opened his mouth to tell me what happened to people who gave his wife verbal. Then the phone rang. He gave me an extra glare and went back into the house to answer it. I turned the forklift so its load was invisible from the house, and slung the rubbish into the skip, then drove into the cold store. Here I removed the final item from the truck's forks, dragged it into a corner and covered it with a heap of the older and less desirable pallets and boxes from the pile down the side. Then I loaded up more fish boxes and drove into the outside world, the sweat drying on my body.

We finished loading by teatime. I said to Georgie, 'Hang around,' and went to knock on the kitchen door. The wife opened it, and said, 'Yes?'

'Done,' I said. 'Your husband wanted to see us.'

'Go in,' she said.

The Major was in his horrible armchair, gazing into the synthetic flames of the coal-effect fire. I said, 'Did you get my parcel?'

The colourless head swung towards me. The dull eyes

settled on me. The lipless mouth said, 'That was a very stupid thing to do.'

'I was passing a post office. I thought, why not?'

'I am very careful to send these goods to their consignees by means that combine efficacy with discretion,' he said. 'But I am not talking about your breach of security, unpardonable though it has been. I'm talking about sending me back short measure.'

I stared at him. He stared back. I said, 'What do you mean?'

'There were three kilos,' he said. 'Your very stupid parcel had two and a half. Where's the rest?'

My mind stopped running. I said, 'You could ask Tony Greely.'

'I'm asking you.' He swung his head back at the fire.

Two weeks ago, I would have been seriously worried by this question. But I knew him better now.

I said, 'The reason I didn't go into Holyhead was because I got a better price for the fish from Greely. If you'd told me I was carrying your nasty drugs I would have told you to go to hell. I had your interests in mind. Anything else is between you and Greely.'

'We'll see what my associates have to say about that,' said the Major. 'From now on, do as you are told.'

I shrugged, thinking, not long now, keep the lid on. 'By the way. You know the Loch Mor fish farm?'

'Of course,' said the Major.

'Donnie, who works there.'

'What about him?'

'He's dead.'

He turned away from the fire and trained the eyes on me. 'What happened?'

'He was run down by an Irish trawler. I got the number.'

He nodded, and conquered the shock in his face, and remembered to frown. A grey tongue came out and ran round what would have been his lips if he had had any. He said, 'That's bad,' and passed me a notebook and a pen with a hand that shook slightly. 'Write the number down. I'll look into it.' Just as if he was a genuine straight-up-and-down retired major, not an accessory after the fact. 'Now,' he said. 'That cargo you've just loaded. It's for Holyhead again. And this time do as you are told.'

'Yessir.' Fingers crossed.

He said, 'You will meet two men. William and Darren. Hand over, take what they give you, get back here. And clean the boat as you go. I have a meeting in Ireland, and you will be taking me to it. Understood?'

I shrugged. I said, 'You're the boss. One thing, though. Your friends keep trying to hurt me. Tell them to stop, would you? Or your delivery won't get made.'

'What are you talking about?'

'Two nasty Irishmen,' I said. 'Brady and McGahey. But perhaps they don't take orders from you.'

'Never heard of them,' he said. But I could see a little maggot of worry behind his eyes.

'Stop them,' I said. 'Or the stuff goes over the side.'

He said, 'Go and do what you're told.' As I left the room he was reaching for the phone.

I was right. The Major and his friend McGown were singing from different hymn sheets. Georgie and I were in the clear.

It was an airy, free sensation. It lasted an hour and a half.

We moved away from the quay as night was falling. The *Gleaner* was loaded down with black fish, pushing heavy water with her bow. But she felt somehow light and empty. It is amazing what taking a corpse out of a boat will do.

I said, 'Georgie, we're delivering cocaine to Holyhead.'

'No way.'

'It's with the fish. What do you reckon to putting it over the side?'

'Aye.'

'Fine.' And I felt loose, and liberated, and just about legal. It was a fine sensation.

As we came into open water the phone started beeping. There were messages from people who thought I should be selling their boats. There was even one from Captain Maxwell. The Captain was well past anything resembling middle age, and he was a hard man. But now his voice was firm and powerful. 'Chance,' it said. 'I hear someone's wrecked my boat. Thank you. Call.'

I frowned. I checked the voice for sarcasm. But Captain Maxwell did not do sarcasm. I rang him, hoping he would not answer.

He answered. I told him who I was.

'Gavin!' he cried. 'Marvellous to hear you!'

'Ah,' I said. 'There was —'

'Terrible thing, someone stealing my boat,' he said. 'Shocking business. Total loss, apparently. Pity.' He did not sound sorry. 'But the insurers are going to pay up. In full.'

'Excellent,' I said.

'Apparently whoever stole it piled it up in front of a retired major's holiday cottage,' he said. 'And the major is going to give them a full statement. The money's as good as in the bank.'

'Fine,' I said, frowning. 'So you've got the statement?'

'Not yet, not yet. He's away. But he'll do it as soon as he's back, apparently.' Wheezing chuckle. 'And as broker, I want you to be absolutely sure he writes it and signs it.' More laughter.

I tried to join in. I knew what I would have to do to be absolutely sure the Major wrote his report. Full cooperation would be the name of the game.

'Consider it done,' I said, and rang off, and said to Georgie, 'Maybe we won't sling that stuff over the side after all.'

'Terrible waste,' said Georgie.

The next message was from Miranda. 'I am really worried about Johnny,' she said, as if it was my fault. 'I really want you to do something about this.' I texted her back that I was not her brother's keeper, which had the merit of truth, if not kindness. Then I assumed the position, slumped in chair, feet on console, and rang Maureen in Achnabuie, asking her very nicely to bring a load of supplies down to the harbour; to which she agreed, good, kind person that she was.

At Achnabuie, Maureen came out in a punt with grocery bags lapping up against her fine knees. She handed them aboard, wrinkled her nose at the stench in the saloon, and said, 'I'll cook you a tea.'

Georgie said, 'Aye.' I attempted to protest but she told me to shut up, put a bottle of whisky on the table and hurled potatoes and steaks about the galley in a fashion that suggested she had planned this all along. Georgie put the boat on a mooring round the headland, just in case the Major's message did not get through to McGown's boys, and we gnawed away at the whisky until mellowness prevailed, at which point the steaks turned up. Maureen sat down and we all dived in, the lack of dead bodies in the hold spreading a healing balm on all. 'I'm for bed,' said Georgie, and hauled himself out of the saloon and into the bunkroom. I sat with Maureen and she told me about a couple of boats we were likely to sell, and as she talked I watched her fine cheekbones and her nice big mouth and her funny green eyes and I and the whisky thought what a beautiful woman she was.

I went on deck to check the lines. When I came back in I sat beside her, not across from her. And somehow there was nothing left in the whisky bottle, and I was telling her about Johnny, and the Major, and Holby, and McGown. And she was listening, not frowning, just nodding. And when I had finished, she said, 'There's more whisky.'

It was not sensible to start on another bottle. But I did it anyway. And she said, 'So you are making life difficult for some bad men connected to the police and some hard men in Ireland.'

I took a swig of whisky. 'That,' I said with alcoholic boldness, 'is the idea.'

'Should you be careful?' she said.

I shrugged. I noticed that she had her hand on mine. It had a sort of grounding effect. I said, 'Probably,' and felt an edge of darkness in my mind. Fear, was what it was. So I put my other hand on hers. And she put her other hand on mine. That was better. And all of a sudden we were kissing across the pile of hands.

I said, 'There's the Captain's cabin.'

She laughed and took her hands away. 'Honestly,' she said. 'You and me, having drink taken. Where would it end?'

I said, 'Are you as my employee refusing to engage in inappropriate behaviour?'

She lowered the lashes over the eyes. 'Not refusing,' she said. 'Just postponing.' And next thing I knew I was in a bunk, alone.

I went out like a match and woke in the dawn with my head in two halves. Georgie was stamping about and the engine was running. I staggered out and dropped the mooring, and away we went, pitching down the Sound into a nasty southwesterly.

The confidence was gone. Things were all tangled up, and I wanted them to stop.

But there was no stopping now. We swam or we sank. So I transferred my thoughts to Maureen, which was a soothing place for them to be. As the *Gleaner* hammered on round the Mull and headed south, I started making calls.

There were the business calls, of course: excuses to be made, lies to be told. There was even a sale, an antique Folkboat that had been peacefully rotting under a tarpaulin at Badachro until Maureen had shown a punter over it. I was now in receipt of slightly more than three hundred pounds in commission. But this was no time for gloating. I wanted to know who owned the *Arthur Worris*. I did not want to bother Maureen with it. So I called Holby in Devon, and gave him a short, edited report and the boat's number.

He rang back as we were rounding the Mull. He said, 'Got it,' sounding as pleased as a cadet with a pickpocketing collar. I began to see exactly what the Major had deprived him of. 'The boat is owned by McCool and Erris, registered in Ballycool. Directors of McCool and Erris are Doreen McGown and Erris McGown.'

I said, 'That will do nicely,' and rang off.

'Wha?' said Georgie.

'The boat that ran down Donnie belongs to a company that belongs to Mr McGown,' I said. He did not answer. I knew how he felt.

Then my phone rang, and I saw that once again Miranda wished to speak to me. Never do today what you can put off till tomorrow, I thought as usual. But if I did not pick up now, she would ring again. And if I did not answer then, she would carry on until she got her way. Furthermore, I still contained traces of whisky and the confidence induced by my evening with Maureen.

So I said, 'Hello?'

She said, 'This is getting silly.'

'What is?'

'Johnny. The reason we let you go in with him was so you could look after him.'

'No,' I said. 'It was so I could be rich enough to buy you things.'

'Don't be nasty,' she said wearily, and I could just about hear the scritch of her mind editing out things she did not want to let herself believe. 'Anyway. I've met a really nice man and he thinks there's something wrong.'

I said, 'Really?'

'He's the Chief Constable of somewhere or other. Jack Menzies. He thinks it is time to start making proper inquiries. He knows all about you and he thinks you are a very good place to start. So I should get ready to answer some questions if I were you.'

I felt a chill. Menzies was a dark-blue incorruptible, dogged and powerful. I said, 'Does he know about the full saintliness of Johnny?'

'He knows Johnny is my brother and that he gets into bad company. He thinks you might be part of the bad company.'

I sighed. I said, 'Is he with you?'

Miranda said, 'I'm in bed.'

'Exactly.'

'Pathetic,' she said. 'He'll be in touch.'

'I shall be happy to answer his questions. But before he asks them,' I said, making my voice a lot harder than it felt, 'you might like to remind him that he works for the great British public, not women he fancies.'

She clicked her tongue. She said, 'Just look out.' She rang off.

So it was out of the frying pan into the fire.

For someone.

I sat and stared out of the window at the sunset, which was picturesque but pale. High in the sky there were little clouds arranged in a delicate pattern like the ripples the tide leaves on a sandy beach. 'Looks dirty,' said Georgie.

It did. All of it.

Off we went south.

Later that night we picked up the wedding-cake lights of the Dublin ferry, then the triple green blink of Holyhead pier. Georgie cut the revs. And at 0300 we tied up in an empty slot in the Fish Dock.

I finished the lines, sat on a bollard under an orange light and waited. The rain clattered on the hood of my oilskins. Whining sounds came from the *Gleaner*, where Georgie was pulling the hatch cover off. There were headlights. A white reefer van drove on to the quay. A head in shoregoing waterproofs came out of the driver's window and looked at the name on the boat's stern. I said, 'You're late.'

He ignored me. There was no face under the hood. The van backed round until it was in line with the pallets. The driver climbed down. His mate got out of the other side. Both of them were small and thin under the waterproofs. The driver said, 'There's some stuff to get off the van.'

'What stuff?'

'Washing machines, I dunno.'

I remembered that the Major had said there was stuff to collect. This would be it, then. The driver climbed into the back of the van. Two big cardboard boxes stood under the roof light. ZANUSSI, they said in big letters.

I said, 'Get the fish off first.' I jumped down from the van and walked up the pier towards the lights on the shore.

It was a filthy night, all right. The wind was up even since we had arrived. It was in the northwest now, driving sheets of rain off the Irish Sea and into my hood; and against the windscreen of the Mercedes in the car park overlooking the harbour.

It was the same Mercedes as last time. Behind the windscreen I could see two faces, one white, the other black. The eyes watched me pass. The heads did not move. The white man lit a cigarette. I saw the glint of a heavy gold necklace. I walked on, just someone off a boat stretching his legs on a wet night with the wind off the sea. And there above the car park was a police car, parked so the view of the officer inside would include the *Gleaner*. It could have been a coincidence, of course; just as it could have been a coincidence that the officer in the car was watching the proceedings through a pair of binoculars.

The officer seemed absorbed in his surveillance. I gazed upon the *Gleaner*'s deck: the rectangular hole that was the hatch, the pallet of green boxes rising on the derrick out of the white lights of the hold and into the yellow lights of the quay. I watched the boxes go into the van, the two brown washing-machine cartons descend into the hold.

It was an industrious tableau. But I did not watch it for too long, because the rain was finding its way down my neck. I started to walk away. Then I stopped, and tapped on the window of the police car.

The policeman lowered the binoculars. He turned towards me a face that was not at all friendly. He rolled down the window and said, 'Good evening, sir?'

And I looked at him, and knew I was right, and felt something like power. I said, 'Hello again.'

'Again?' said the policeman, blank.

'We met in Swansea,' I said. 'On the quay. You're a friend of Major Davies.'

'I don't think so,' said the policeman. 'Bit late to be out, isn't it? Night like this.'

'Some of us work shifts,' I said. He was out of the car now. His torch shone in my face.

I gave him a great big smile, full of the confidence that was blooming in me like a flower. This officer was a member of the Major's private force, and I had his number. I said, 'Shall I say hello to Major Davies?' I looked at my watch. 'Goodness,' I said. 'Is that the time —'

I stopped here because something had arrived in the pit of my stomach and driven the wind right out of me, and something else had swept my legs out from under me, and down I went on to the wet tarmac, and down on my neck came something that through the fog of pain and fear around me I concluded was a boot.

'Listen,' said a voice beyond the pain. 'I do not like little toerags who take the piss. So you get on with your job and I will get on with mine, because everyone is in the same boat but I have got a uniform on. I am happy that I am working for a true British patriot.' Scrunch, went the boot, and the tarmac gouged bits out of my cheekbone. 'And if we meet again and you take the piss down you will go, and they will believe a uniform, not some clown from nowhere.'

The parts of this I liked least were the tarmac in my face and the clown word, which seemed to be in danger of entering the general vocabulary where I was concerned. But I did not resent it enough to mention it, because I knew this upstanding officer would have a baton and a can of pepper spray, and I did not at this time require a demonstration of either. Also, I was interested that the Major was a patriot. Perhaps that was how he had kept his informal liaison with the police. That, and some good wages.

'Now fuck off, and watch your manners,' he said.

The boot gave my face another grind, then left my neck. I got up and I turned my back on him and walked away, trying to walk slowly and not altogether succeeding.

By the time I got down to the quay the washing machines had gone, and the last pallet of green boxes was by the back of the van. I watched them go in. The thin man shut the door. His mate was in the cab. The window opened. A handful of beer cans bounced on to the concrete. The hand came out again with some burger boxes, a handful of disused chips and a newspaper. They were tidying up before the trip. I took hold of the wrist before he could sling it. 'I'll find you a litter bin,' I said.

'Wha?' he said.

I stuffed the rubbish in a topless oil drum on the quay and kept the paper. A gust caught the tins and sent them bouncing down the quay. The *Gleaner* farted black smoke into the lights, and Georgie made let-go gestures from inside the wheelhouse. I let go and hopped on. Another blast of engine, and the *Gleaner* churned away from the quay. I went into the wheelhouse and took off my coat and sat in one of the chairs and did a little shaking, for the stress had been considerable. 'What ate you?' said Georgie, squinting at my face.

'Trouble with the law,' I said. Outside, green flashing lights passed one by one. I wanted a drink.

'Wha?'

'A polis. I talked to him. He hit me.'

'You took the piss,' said Georgie. 'And he gave you a skelp. I'm not surprised. The mouth on you, I'm fecking astounded they've let you live this long. If you —'

'Shut up and drive,' I said. We were out of the harbour now. The *Gleaner*'s nose rose on a slope of water, then plunged down with a crash that sent a shudder through every plate of her. 'We are to pick up the Major and take him to Ireland,' I said. 'He wants the boat cleaned. You clean, I'll drive.'

'No way,' said Georgie. 'You clean, I'll drive.'

'Put her on autopilot and we'll have a drink and he can take his chances,' I said. The shaking was improving. We had got rid of the body, and probably some illegal substances. Hell, we were legal. 'Who does he think he is?'

'Aye, who?' said Georgie, reaching into a locker under the wheel and pulling out a bottle of whisky.

The sea ahead was nearly as white as it was black. Up went the nose. Down went the nose. Crash, shudder. Green water down the deck this time. Georgie handed me the whisky. 'Ye want a beer with that?' he said.

'Of course I do,' I said.

It was going to be a long night.

17

The wind kept on going up. It blew across the flood pouring through the North Channel at the top of the Irish Sea, turning the hills of water into cliffs and giving them roaring white cornices of spray. Up went the bow. Down went the bow, crash. And down went the whisky, crash, until there was nothing left in the bottle. Georgie wedged himself in his bunk and began to snore. I sat in a chair and listened to the wallop of the bow in the sea and pretended to maintain a lookout through the water streaming down the forward windows of the wheelhouse.

Another beer. Another all-round scowl into the night. Nothing out there except a little smear of blood as a white patch of foam slid under the port light. Sit down, jam can into holder. Open the newspaper the van driver had tidied out of his window.

Freeze.

'TV's Mr Fish Coke Bust,' yelled page four. And there was a picture of Tony Greely, twinkling out of the page in thigh-boots and earring, knife in one hand, fish in the other. Beside him on the demonstration table were a few onions and tomatoes, which were part of the original photograph; and a pile of white powder with a rolled-up twenty-pound note sticking out of the top, which was not. The story merely said he had been busted in possession of a quantity of controlled substances, which was code for dealable amounts. It was possible to see how the Major kept on good terms with his friends in the police.

For a moment I felt sorry for Greely. But nobody had forced him to import large amounts of black fish to sell under the most egregiously hypocritical of circumstances. And nobody had forced him to appropriate a quantity of the Major's controlled substances. He had set the knives whirling himself. Then he had marched steadily into them.

I sat wedged in my chair in that dark wheelhouse with the panel lights all around me and the tall waves marching down from the north. And suddenly I had a new and horrible thought. If I was out of the way, there would be no link between the Major's naughtinesses and Tony Greely. And the body of Johnny Bonny could be fed to the lobsters or otherwise disappeared. And the Major could sail on unmolested.

Suddenly I was very, very cold. I needed to share what I knew, and quickly.

I reached for the mobile again, and dialled Holby's number. The beeps told me there was no signal. I reached for the beer can, took a swig. It tasted flat and tinny. I went and got another from the locker and sat back in the chair, *whump.*

Something changed.

I raised my eyes from the can to the windshield. I could see the pale spearhead of the shelter deck rising on a wave. And beyond it something else. Something high and blacker than the night, with white water along the bottom of it. I tasted the air of the wheelhouse in my mouth. And as I sat there, jaw swinging, a bright red light shone into my right eye.

We were in the middle of the Irish Sea. There was nothing red out there.

Except another ship.

And there was the red light bloody on the shelter deck, and a white tower of accommodation looming over it, and I was out of the chair and on to the *Gleaner*'s wheel, so I could haul it over and not slam into the medium-sized merchant ship that had appeared out of nowhere and was some fifty yards off the *Gleaner*'s bow. But the wheel would not turn. Jammed, said my whisky-addled mind. What?

Try knocking the autopilot off, said a small, sober voice deep in my head.

I fumbled for the button. The wheel came free. I spun it hard-a-starboard. The ship's side was a cliff now, too high for me to see the red light that was bathing the *Gleaner* and the sea in a bloody glare. I pulled back on the throttle. The revs died. The nose kept turning. Too late, too late. The ship's side went up as she rolled away from us, came down again. I saw a great black cliff of metal pile down on the shelter deck. There was a great metallic crash as it came down on the *Gleaner*'s nose and pushed it deep underwater. There was a long metallic scraping; another bang, on the side this time. Two of the wheelhouse windows burst in a shower of glass. Then a wave came under, and the bow came up from the deeps, and the *Gleaner* rolled away from the ship, shedding water, then towards it again. Another bang, then another roll, this one to the first wave of the wake, a steep roll to starboard all the way on to her beam ends, a slide and a crash from the galley and the hold; black water racing down the deck and down she went, down, down, like a submarine, water pouring in at the broken windows. I thought, this is it, cold and dead in the dark, no Major to worry about, weirdly calm. Then I felt her shudder. And the bow came up. And here came Georgie stumbling across the wheelhouse, roaring and crunching glass under his feet.

And I was watching out of the port side of the wheelhouse as the bright white stern light of the ship sailed away down the Irish Sea.

'Feck,' said Georgie. 'What the feck?'

'Collision,' I said. 'Take the wheel.'

He took it. He said, 'Were you not on lookout?'

'Bad night,' I said.

'And what about the radar and the VHF?'

'Off,' I said.

He was coming to. He said, 'If we're holed, I'll fecking kill you.'

'Join the queue,' I said, still spaced right out, flashing the little red torch round the wheelhouse. There was glass everywhere. There was also my mobile phone. I picked it up. Georgie's boot had destroyed it, amphibious sim card and all. But this was no time for worrying about sim cards. This was a time to run around the boat and see how long we had left to live.

I said, 'How does she steer?'

'Perfect,' said Georgie, whistling in the dark.

I clattered down into the hold.

I expected to find water, sloshing. There did not seem to be any. There was ice across the deck, and one of the washing machines had jumped out of the bin in which sloppy Georgie had stowed it instead of lashing it down, and was sliding around in its box. The collision seemed to have burned up all the alcohol in my head. I was stone-cold twenty-twenty sober. All that remained was a powerful headache and a tendency to shake, though that could have been the terror.

It sounded dreadful down here. There was the roar of the engine, the hammer of the waves, and the strange wail of the hull through the sea. That was old. But there was something new, too: a nasty creaking. It came from the port bow. It was the port bow that had hit the ship. There would be damage. I went to the watertight door at the forward end of the hold. It opened easily. No wall of water roared through and washed me away. This was positive.

Up went the bow.

A short alleyway stretched ahead of me, with a watertight door on each side. The port-hand door frame was a steel oval. It had a buckled look, and the door did not seem to fit it any more.

Down went the bow.

I wedged myself in the alleyway, suddenly weightless. Water crashed two thicknesses of metal away, and my weight returned as the bow came down. A jet of water squirted between door and frame. A lot of water. But not a ship-sinking amount, as long as the pumps worked and the doors held. I stood there and gawped at it through my instant hangover. There was a whining in my head. The water sloshing on the alleyway deck sank away. Not tinnitus. The sound of the pumps. Better.

I reversed out of the alleyway, dogging the watertight door behind me. A washing-machine box slid past me on a bed of ice chips and slammed into the bulkhead. The box had burst. I pulled a strop from the rack on the side, made an end fast and waited for the roll. The washing machine trundled back across the deck. As it slammed into the side I dodged it, got the strop round it and a turn on a stringer on the side, and put on some half-hitches. Genius, I said to myself, so perhaps the whisky had not left me after all. Whistling, I took a broom and began chasing ice chips across the bucking plates.

We were slightly holed in a gale and a bent major had good reason to wish us dead. But at least we were not playing undertakers any more. I swept on, weightless one moment, three Gs the next. And as I swept I whistled.

It is famously unlucky to whistle at sea.

The last chip of ice had gone. The hold was neat as an operating theatre in the lights, though the washing machines lowered the tone. The one that had jumped out of its bin had battered the other two. Polyurethane foam packing was visible through a couple of gaping tears in the cardboard cartons. The Major would not like this. I did my zero-to-three-G dance across the deck to the tool locker and pulled out some duck tape and danced back to the boxes to tidy up.

The biggest rip was the shape of two sides of a square. The edge of a foam block showed inside. And something that was not foam. Something brownish, with a putty-like consistency. The headache was making me stupid. I poked the brown stuff with my gloved finger. The finger left a dent. I prodded it again.

Then my heart gave me a giant bump in the chest.

I blinked. Perhaps it would go away.

It did not.

The horrible stuff just sat there, peering coyly round the edge of the rip in the cardboard. I walked across to the toolbox, not dancing now, off balance, staggering to the horrible writhe and corkscrew of the deck. I pulled a filleting knife off the rack and carried it back to the box. Very gently, I eased the razor-sharp blade down the join in the carton until the whole side of it peeled away. And I stood and looked at it and felt ill.

There was a little wall of bricks of the stuff that looked like putty. Wires ran from a box on top of the wall to a plug-like object stuffed into the topmost brick. Taped to the top of the box was a mobile phone plugged into a hands-free kit whose wire ran into the box.

I had used stuff like that to destroy command bunkers in Bosnia. The puttyish stuff was an explosive: C4, more than likely, because you could play football with a lump of C4 in perfect safety, or eat it, or bump it into a boat's hold and let it jump out of its bin and rattle round on a rink of crushed ice in a gale, and it would not blow up. The only way it would blow up is if you stuck a detonator into it and applied a current to the detonator. And one way of doing this while maintaining a safe distance was to attach a switch to a battery, and connect the switch to a mobile phone.

No phone, no bang; no bang, no bloody great hole in the side of the boat.

I took the filleting knife and cut the mobile free from the top of the box. I unplugged the wire from the hands-fee slot. I thought: Major, you bastard, you were wanting to do something to make sure that neither I nor Georgie lived to tell anyone how Tony Greely had come by his cocaine, or who his friends were, or how he made his money. But you have had no luck. I disconnected the battery and very gently pulled out the detonator. Then I fetched a bucket and put out my hand to pull the C4 bricks off the machine.

And stopped. This was really quite a professional bomb. The Major was a professional, of course. But he had been in the Logistics Corps. Was he this kind of professional?

If that washing machine had not developed a hole in the carton, we would have found out, one way or another. As it was, it would be wise to think about this carefully. There was no rush now.

So I dropped the mobile into my pocket and went up to the wheelhouse.

'What?' said Georgie.

I told him about the leak, but not the washing machine. He scowled out of the window. The wind was dropping, and the dawn was making a cold grey line along the horizon, and the Mull of Kintyre was blinking in the northeast. He said, 'I'll weld her up.'

Halfway down the tide, the *Gleaner* nosed between two headlands at the north end of Gigha, dropped a kedge over the stern, pushed gently at the white sand and took the ground. Georgie had been replacing broken wheelhouse windows with plywood. Now he slid a ladder over the side and went to shake his head at the bow. There were a cracked weld and a couple of plates stove at the waterline. 'Could have been worse,' he said.

It certainly could. Someone could have made a mobile phone call, for a start.

I went below and started to clean up for the Major. When I had finished, I took the bomb phone out of my pocket and turned it on. There were no missed calls. As far as the Major was concerned, we were still alive. I thought I would call Holby. But his number had been on the sim card that Georgie had crushed under his mighty boot last night.

I was on my own.

'Good,' said Georgie, coming back smug after the turn of the tide. We hoisted his gas bottles up, and put the kedge cable on a winch, and hauled out into deep water as soon as she floated. The bow compartment stayed dry. 'Aye,' said Georgie. 'I can weld, me. I'm a good welder. Welding's one of the things I can do. Me and welding, we're made for each other.'

'Yes,' I said. 'Now will we go in to Achnabuie for a moment? I need to borrow your phone.'

I called the Gavin Chance Marine number. Maureen answered. I said, 'Is there a spare phone?'

'There is. Where's yours?'

'Broken.'

'Where are you?'

I told her.

We headed north. It was raining. As we passed Achnabuie a white plastic fishing boat buzzed out from the shore; and there was Maureen, grinning, holding a Spar bag. 'Phone,' she shouted, running parallel, wind snatching at the red tangle of her hair. 'Mine, but they're forwarding your calls to it. And something to eat, and something to wash it down.'

She came close. I snagged the bag. She blew me a kiss and sheered off, and the last I saw of her she was away up the Sound, spewing white wake from her outboard. I was sorry to see her go.

There were steaks in the bag, and whisky, and a phone with a charger. 'Heck of a woman,' said Georgie. 'Bad taste in men.'

'What does that mean?'

'She fancies you,' said Georgie glumly. 'Stupid cow.' And on we went.

I called the Major. 'What the hell happened to you?' he said.

'Telephone broken,' I said. 'Stress of weather.' I searched his voice for indications that he had found Johnny's corpse in his cold store, and that he knew we were riding a bomb up the Sound of Jura. But he was cold, and dry, and neutral as ever.

'So how are you calling?'

'My secretary brought me a new one.'

'Secretary,' he said, as if I did not deserve one. 'Get here. We'll call at Loch Mor, load and proceed to Ireland.' He rang off.

We took the tide up the Sound of Luing. As the headland outside the Major's bay came in sight, the phone rang, number withheld. I answered it.

'Who's that?' said a voice. It sounded surprised.

'Gavin Chance Marine.'

'That's right,' said the voice, a man's voice, soft and warm. 'I couldn't get you on the other number, Gavin. We've met, have we not? Erris McGown here, by the way.'

Something was happening to my head. I found I was actually flattered to be addressed by this cold-eyed little brute. Whose men had murdered Johnny. Who had personally tossed me over the side after his card game on *Velma*. Which should certainly have killed me, the way a boat registered in his name had killed Donnie. Why should I feel this desire to please the bastard? Struggling out from under the ether, I said, 'In the Solent.'

'That's right,' he said, as warmly as if I had revealed to him the innermost secrets of Creation. 'You've been doing great work since then, Gavin, great work, we're very pleased, all that business in the Solent, just to keep you on your toes, you know? Oh, and I hear you're coming across this way with Major Davies?'

And some black fish, and a bomb in a washing machine. Not the Major's bomb. McGown's bomb, I was sure now. I considered telling him no, we were not coming. But I wanted to go. He had done enough damage. We were coming all right.

'So I hear,' I said.

He laughed. He had tried to kill me, and his bomb was in the *Gleaner's* hold. But he left me with the impression I had said something really funny. 'I tell you what. Change of plan. When you're over, come up to the house, let's have a jar. And we have some boats here that might interest you. We could have a return match, maybe.'

'Ah.' What the hell was he on about?

'Mind how you go, now,' he said. And the phone went dead.

'Who was that?' said Georgie.

I told him. 'The Major's been passing our number round his little organisation.'

'Right,' said Georgie. 'So I hope he tells those two boys of his to get over to where I can cut their heads off.'

'I'm sure he will,' I said, hoping the opposite. Then we were rounding the headland and there was the bay, with the quay, and the Major on its end, no dog this time, but a small overnight case on the ground by his feet. He looked grim. Had he found Johnny in the freezer?

We went alongside. He stepped aboard. He said, 'We will proceed to Loch Mor,' like a real major. No mention of Johnny or fridges.

Water churned white against the rudder. The bulldog lady waved from the bungalow's picture window and the Major gave her a faint tilt of the head. My rock slid by to starboard, a smooth patch in the water.

I said, 'What happened to the boat?'

'Which boat?' said the Major, cold grey eyes on me.

'The yacht.'

'*Lorne Lady*? The insurer arranged for collection, which was duly executed.'

'You didn't put in a word, then?'

'I saw no need.'

Bastard. He stumped below into the hold. I followed him. I said, 'I hope everything is up to standard, Major.'

The cold eyes landed on me. 'You do,' he said. The eyes went on. They rested on the washing-machine boxes. 'What are they?' he said.

I could have told him that they were an unexploded bomb. But there seemed no point. Either he knew, in which case he would not have been so cool. Or he did not know, in which case I was not going to tell him. 'Washing machines,' I said. 'They came off the van in Holyhead.'

The Major nodded, as if he had known all along. 'That's what it was,' he said. 'They're for Ireland.' And I knew I had been right.

It looked as if the Major's friends were getting tired of him.

He continued his inspection. He found grease on a pipe in the accommodation, or maybe he had brought it with him. I did not care.

We went south, familiar as the M1 to a lorry driver now, and hammered through the Sound of Islay against the tide, and picked up the Loch Mor channel. The Major stayed in the wheelhouse. A trawler was coming out. I kept as far away as the channel would let me. Its lights were out, understandably, because it would have been unloading by-catch. The Major turned his head away from it, just in case. Georgie went to work on deck and let me take the boat in. He seemed not to like being in confined spaces with the Major, and I could see his point.

We were passing the second buoy when the lights tore a white globe in the black drizzle, and the cold-store door made a paler square, and a loaded forklift doddered down the concrete apron on to the quay. Georgie had the hatch cover off and the derrick ready. There were two figures waiting on the quay, big men in oilskins that shone in the lights as the *Gleaner* surged alongside.

'Too fast,' said the Major. 'You're going too fast.'

I was tired of his nonsense, so I gave the boat a little too much right wheel. The nose hit one of the tyre fenders on the quay, hard. There was a large and complicated crash. The Major staggered, and his face turned at me, and for the first time ever it had an expression on it, and the expression was about fifty-fifty anger and fear. And I realised with extreme pleasure that the Major did not at all like getting about on the sea.

I straightened up and gave her some port helm and a burst ahead to wind the stern in. And there we were, tied up, with the quay stretching away from the wheelhouse, and the fork-lift already here with the second load, and the business end of the derrick coming down into the lights to connect with the pallet of green boxes. I waited for Georgie to lumber into the lights. Georgie did not come. So I picked up the loudhailer mike and thumbed the button and said, 'Move it.'

The two men in oilskins stood there looking bulky but indefinite. 'Go and help,' said the Major.

I went.

The rain was falling cold and steady as I stepped on to the quay. There was something familiar about the men. I said, 'What's your problem?'

'No problem,' said the big one.

'Then take your hands out of your pockets and get those boxes on the derrick.'

The head moved. The light shone into the hood. And I found that I was looking at a face that was indeed familiar. I had seen it looking down on us from the lockside at Milford, and on the quay at Achnabuie; the face of the saloon-car-sized Dinny Brady, who with his only slightly smaller colleague Kevin McGahey had murdered Johnny and stolen Georgie's boat and blown out the windows of the *Gleaner* with a shotgun blast meant for Donnie. They were both there, both looking at me. I looked back. I smiled at them, to hide how scared I was of them. I said, 'You do it like this,' and showed them how to put the catches in the latches.

Brady said, 'I am not a fecking docker.'

'Nor am I,' I said.

He gave me a chilly look and laughed. It was a laugh that made me want to run away. Perhaps I would have if I had not caught a movement in the dark behind them. So I said,

'Like this,' took hold of the derrick controller and pressed the green button. Up went the pallet of boxes into the air. Brady and McGahey watched it go, mouths open. The forklift rolled down the quay and left another pile of boxes as they stood and gawped. And I gawped too, but not at them.

The figure in the dark was moving closer. It was a big, hulking figure. It came down the quay behind Brady, two steps, change feet; taking a runup. In its right hand was something long and narrow. The thing in its hand went back and swung round, gleaming silver in the lights. The wheelhouse loudhailer made an incoherent squawk. Brady started to look round. Which was just as well for him, because if he had not, the ground-down edge of the head of the four-foot adjustable spanner in Georgie's hand would have taken his head off at the shoulders. As it was he was able to half-duck, and instead of decapitating him, the ground edge sheared through the hood on the side of his head, and he went down screaming, and Georgie turned his attention to McGahey.

An ordinary person might have been surprised. McGahey was not an ordinary person. He was a nasty soldier in the army of Erris McGown. So his hand went into his pocket, and I knew he would have a gun in there. Scared I certainly was. But I was encouraged by Georgie, and I had a joystick in my hand, and I twitched it, and the half-ton of green boxes hanging in the air came across and smashed McGahey on the upper arm, and there was a loud, nasty snap that could have been the pallet breaking but was more likely to be the bone, and then he was face down in a puddle on the concrete, screaming into the blood that was running out of the side of his mate's head.

'Georgie,' I said, in a voice that definitely wobbled. 'We are supposed to be loading fish.'

'Those are the neds who stole my boat,' said Georgie. 'And

they killed your partner. And they shot my boat up. I'm not taking that from any man.'

'When you have finished?' said a big metal voice from the wheelhouse loudhailer.

This was a touching display of concern by a military man for the troops on the ground. McGahey moaned. He said, 'We wasn't shooting at you.'

'Who, then?'

'Donnie.'

Georgie kicked him in the face. Then he rinsed the blood and bits of head off his spanner and lumbered back onto the *Gleaner*'s deck and into the hold. And we started to load fish.

While the first pallet was in the air, the forklift trundled down the quay again. The driver looked at the bodies and screwed up his face. It was a weatherbeaten Islay face, and it looked scared. I went down on my knees by McGahey, and pulled out my knife and cut the oilskins away. He was wearing a fleece. I cut that away too. There was something heavy in the fleece pocket. It felt like a gun. The right arm had developed an extra elbow, and he screamed when I touched it. I helped him up and on to the *Gleaner*. The fleece stayed where it was in the puddle on the quay. I picked it up and looked in the pocket. The light gleamed on dark metal: a .22 pistol, as used by target shooters and executioners. I was careful not to touch it. I wrapped it up again and said in a low voice to the forklift driver, 'Put that coat in a bag and get it to the police. Call them now.'

He nodded, terrified. The eyes flicked at the boat.

'There's a lot of people going down,' I said. 'You want to be on the right side, eh?'

'Side?' he said. But he understood, and drove back into the night. He was a long time collecting this last load. But he came, and said, 'Fine.'

I walked on and helped Georgie with the casualties. The screaming was horrible. 'What is this, an ambulance?' said the Major.

'Maybe you would like them in hospital in Campbeltown,' I said. 'We could get them evacuated by chopper. And they could explain who they are and what they are doing, and then Georgie can have his turn. It will make a nice story. The nationals might even pick it up.'

'Talking about picking stuff up,' said Georgie. 'I found this.' He tossed something red and grey on to the console. I looked at it and looked away quickly. It seemed to be an ear.

'Put it on ice,' said the Major.

'Put it on ice yourself,' said Georgie. 'Gavin, do the lines.'

I did the lines and the hatch cover. The violence seemed to have done Georgie good. When I went back to the wheelhouse he was at the wheel, beer in hand, and the Major was staring stonily out of the window. When I shut the door he said, 'Chance, please tell your colleague to stop drinking.'

'It's his boat,' I said, taking a beer of my own. There was only the light from the chart plotter and the faint glow of the instruments. But it seemed to me that the Major was looking a little haggard.

I was beginning to feel that I had been right about the sea not being the Major's comfort zone. I finished the beer and went to look at the patients.

I attended plenty of car crashes when I was a policeman. Even so, Brady's head was a stomach-turner. He was greyish white on the bunk pillow, except where he was the colour of raw meat. It looked to me as if the doctors were going to have trouble finding anything to sew the ear back on to.

McGahey was awake, but not at all cheerful. I said, 'Do you want to go to a hospital?'

He told me to fuck off and promised to kill me as soon as he could use his right arm again. I believed him. So it was a relief to go back to the wheelhouse and shut the door and watch the nose hurdle the swells coming out of the black northwest. Except that the Major was hogging my chair, so I had to sit wedged against the console.

'So it's Ballycool, is it?' said Georgie, as the Mull light crawled past the remaining non-plywood windows.

'What did you think?' said the Major. There was something in his voice that filled me with a sudden joy. I pulled down a flashlight, told Georgie to shut his eyes a minute, and shone it on the face. The cold, slightly greenish-grey face.

I said, 'Did you eat yet, Georgie?'

'You know fine I didn't.'

'You want a steak?' I said. 'We've got a couple of beauties here. Size of your hand, and the fat on them, well, the pan'll be swimming in grease. So I'll cut in a load of onions. Wonderful stuff, beef grease. You can roll it round your mouth like wine. Damn near drink it. And there's a load of nice white bread to soak it up with. Waste not, want not.'

'Aye,' said Georgie. He might not be the quickest thing on God's earth, but his dislike of the Major was pumping up his IQ. 'And leave the galley door open so I can smell it frying.'

So I went into the galley, and lit the gas, and pretty soon I had a fine grey smoke rolling into the wheelhouse. And the next thing, there was a slam of the door and the Major was on deck heaving his tea at the fish.

'Couldn't happen to a nicer guy,' said Georgie. 'So what's this about?'

I told him. He lay slumped in his chair, gazing steadily out of the windscreen. It was dark out there. The Oa was falling astern, and Rathlin light was a white loom on the horizon. Then he said, 'So you're going to see this McGown?'

'That's right.'

Georgie stared ahead, silent and unmoving. Then he said, 'Any chance of air support?'

'I think we're on our own. When his boys shot out the windows they were aiming at Donnie, not us. And if he'd wanted to blow us up with his washing machines, he would have done it on the way up from Holyhead.' I had been thinking about this. 'He wants to give me a beating, all right. But I think it's the Major he's getting tired of.'

'Wha?'

'I think the Major's broke and getting broker. As far as McGown's concerned, he's a security risk.'

'So up he goes.'

'That was the plan,' I said.

'Aye.' Pause. 'Look,' he said. There were lights out there: a green and a red, with a white on top. Someone coming straight at us, fast.

'Alter course,' I said.

He altered course. The lights altered course too. I switched on the AIS. The little triangle was converging on our boat shape. When I put the cursor on it, the black letters on the screen told me what I thought they would. I put out my hand and pulled back the throttle. The radio said, '*Sirius Gleaner*, I am boarding you for inspection.'

'Come along,' I said. 'And welcome.'

'Stand by,' said the VHF, sounding surprised.

We stood by. The *Gleaner* rolled and pitched, a horrible corkscrew that sent the horizon reeling across the wheelhouse windows. There was a bang as the door opened. The Major lurched in, a big, dark shape that stank of vomit. He said, 'What is it?'

'Fisheries Protection,' I said. 'They're boarding to inspect.'

'Oh.' He stood slumped against the bulkhead, hoping to die.

'So you've got two choices,' I said. 'You can say goodbye to your glittering career, if you've still got one. Or you can show them some ID and get something ready to tell them.'

No answer. The wheelhouse door opened and closed, and he was outside again. 'Feck,' said Georgie. 'I thought he was going to boke on the upholstery.'

I did not point out that he was on the brink of losing his boat and going to jail. I stood and watched.

A brilliant white light bloomed on the Fisheries Protection boat. The wheelhouse filled with with black stripes of shadow. Outside, the Major stood slumped against the rail. A black RIB with four men in it was corkscrewing across the sea towards us. They came alongside and hooked on and stepped over the rail, timing it neatly with the roll. I leaned by the broken window of the wheelhouse. I did not care what happened to the Major. But I did care what happened to me. And, I found, to Georgie. And in a different way to McGown.

So I watched.

The Major stood by the rail. The four men out of the Zodiac were talking to him. He fumbled in an inner pocket. I saw him take something out. I saw him show the thing to the man in charge. I saw the man nod, speak into a radio, pause; checking up, no doubt, on whether this was a genuine spook on a fishing boat halfway between Scotland and Ireland at 4 a.m. Eventually the man nodded, a respectful nod. I saw the Major's head go over the side. He was vomiting again.

'Right in the Zodiac,' said Georgie, in tones of quiet joy.

The men climbed back over the side and snarled off. The searchlight went out.

'Things are looking up,' said Georgie.

We proceeded in the direction of Ballycool.

18

It is not a long way across the North Channel. We went in on the plotter, ignoring the lights that flashed at us under the dark loom of the land. It was six o'clock when we slid under the green blink on the end of Ballycool quay. The Major was asleep, having sicked up most of his strength into the sea. Georgie was in the wheelhouse dressed in rigger's boots and dirty grey pyjamas with khaki stripes. I went on to the quay to do the lines.

Ballycool was a nice little harbour for a postcard. There was the quay, with a picturesque straggle of fishing boats. There was a little fleet of elegant wooden dayboats nodding on a group of moorings. And there was a big enclosed sheet of water, grey in the predawn, shut off from the Irish Sea by a bar that left a narrow entrance between itself and the pierhead. A delightful place to bring the family on holiday. A less delightful place if you took into consideration the fact that it was the home port of Erris McGown, who would certainly want me dead.

I had his number on my phone. He answered after the second ring, crisp and bright as if he had been in the office for hours. I said, 'We're alongside.'

He said, 'I saw you,' as if the fact had brought him great pleasure. 'That's me with the light on.' The grey streak on the eastern horizon was brightening. A yellow square of window shone from a big bungalow across the bay.

I said, 'We've got two of your men on board. They need medical attention. And we have the Major.'

'Dear me,' he said. 'I'll send an ambulance down, so.' The voice level and easy, no curiosity. 'We'll take the fish off tomorrow.' A pause. 'What happened to the lads?'

'They had an accident,' I said. 'One of them's got a broken arm. The other one's lost an ear.'

'Heavens,' said McGown mildly.

'Dangerous things, fishing boats,' I said.

He laughed. 'You're the boy, Gavin,' he said. 'The little gathering tonight, eight o'clock onwards, see you then? The Major'll be there.'

As usual, he managed to give the impression that only my presence would save the occasion from failure. But I was developing an immunity. I said, 'See you then.'

'And tomorrow,' he said, 'I'm going sailing. You'll come too. Well, now.' He rang off.

It sounded as if the reprieve was to continue at least till we had had our sail. I pulled the bomb phone out of my pocket. There were no missed calls. I yawned. I was tired, as usual.

There was a howling in the distance, and the ambulance turned on to the quay. A couple of paramedics jumped down and climbed aboard. It seemed to me that they were avoiding my eye. I pointed to the bunkroom where the casualties were. I sat in the skipper's chair and watched as they brought McGahey out, hugging his arm now, too agonised to glare. Once he was parked in the ambulance they hauled Brady on to the wheelhouse deck and examined the wreck of his head under a bright light. I averted my eyes, and gazed upon the bungalow of Erris McGown glowing like a plastic Parthenon in the morning sun.

'Who did this?' said the paramedic, looking up from the bloody mess.

'You know how it is, on a fishing boat.' I said.

'I'd like to shake hands with the boat that did it,' said the smaller of the two.

I gave him my hand. He grinned at me. 'There's an ear too,' I said. 'It's on ice. Do you want it?'

'Dunno,' said the paramedic. 'We'll ask him, shall we. Ear?' he said quietly to Brady.

No reply.

'Ear?' said the paramedic, only a very little louder. 'No? Only I remember when we went to the Castleimpney bomb there was Mary Moore calling for her legs that you had blown off for her, Mr Brady. Maybe you just don't have as close a relationship with your body parts as Mary did.'

No reply.

'So give the ear to the gulls,' said the paramedic. He rolled Brady on to the stretcher, and his mate picked up the other end, and they wheeled him up the brow and on to the quay.

And I watched them go, and thought about the Castleimpney bomb.

It had been in the papers a few years back. Some citizens had been watching a parade. There had been a group of bad people gripped with nostalgia for the good old days, and keeping their hand in with a little protection and intimidation, and perhaps competing for turf with the employers of Dinny Brady. The bad people had been sitting on a pile of bales as the floats rolled by. And the bales had blown up and the bad people had blown up with them, and a round dozen innocent parade-goers had had bits blown off them, including Mary Moore, the Castleimpney Dairy Queen, in her white muslin dress with her hair the colour of butter. Mary Moore had been twelve years old, and she had lost both her legs.

I watched McGown's residence and wondered exactly what part he had played in the Castleimpney horror. And my thoughts drifted from him to the mobile phone and all that C4 going to waste in the hold.

But I was really too tired for thoughts of any kind at all. So I went and lay down on the less bloody of the two bunks in the murderers' cabin, and closed my eyes.

I should have gone to sleep straight away. I did not. Things kept me awake. There was the nasty flat smell of blood. There was that horrible ear, and Tony Greely in the nick, and the Johnny's jellied eyes, and Miranda jabbing her finger at me, and in the background an accusing chorus of people whose boats I was meant to be selling or whose deposits I was meant to be passing on.

And in the foreground, a twelve-year-old girl in a white muslin dress with a skirt wet and red, weeping for her poor lost legs.

I began to have a pretty good idea what I had to do.

The racket between my ears faded. I went to sleep.

Georgie woke me by dropping all the saucepans in the galley into a galvanised bucket. I crawled into the wheelhouse. The clock said six. Georgie said, 'Let's take the fish off and get out of this place.'

'We don't land the fish until tomorrow.'

'It's my boat.'

I said, 'It's no use to you if you're dead.' My head was full of fog. I groped for the kettle, lit the gas and slammed it on. 'We leave tomorrow morning,' I said. 'McGown wants me to play with him.'

'Oh, aye,' said Georgie.

'And you want him off your back.'

'Oh, aye,' said Georgie.

'So you'll just have to trust me. Sod it,' I said, for I had poured boiling water over my hand.

'Trust you?' said Georgie. He opened his mouth to tell me never, no way. Through the gap between his teeth I could just about hear his mind's gears clashing. 'The way I see it you're a right chancer,' he said. 'Like your name. Get it? Chance, Chancer. Almost the same. I bet nobody ever —'

'Never,' I said, wearily. At some point in all my relationships someone invariably raised the remarkable appropriateness of my surname to my style of conducting business. 'Now I am going to take a shower and find a pub and walk over to his horrible bloody bungalow and see what happens.'

'Huh,' said Georgie. 'I'll stay on the boat.'

I made myself clean, and put myself into a blue shirt and a pair of black corduroy trousers that were part of what Maureen had supplied me with, bless her heart. Then I pulled on a tweed coat. Georgie was reading a copy of the *Daily Sport* in the skipper's chair. I said, 'Come up on the quay.'

Up on the quay we went. There was a flat expanse of concrete next to the *Gleaner*. To seaward there was a windproof screen, and a hut with a bar counter, and a couple of tables and chairs between it and the little lighthouse on the end of the quay. It was getting dark: the sky in the west was gory red, and catspaws of breeze ran over the grey harbour. A man was moving the chairs into the bar hut. I said, 'Do you want a drink, Georgie?'

The crate man looked up. His Irish eyes were not smiling. 'It's private,' he said.

'What is?'

'This is.'

'But I am a friend of Mr McGown.'

He said, 'I will believe this when Mr McGown tells me, no offence.'

I said, 'Offence taken.' Nasty little Napoleon, I thought. Then an idea struck me. 'When will he be coming?'

'He has his lunch here, weather permitting.' said the man. 'Now piss off, I have to close up, no offence.'

This time I just smiled at him, while the wheels of my brain whizzed round. As we walked away, I said to Georgie, 'So he can take his lunch next to some nice fish. Can you get in on the quay by half twelve?'

'I can get it on the quay right now.'

I tried to keep the smile going. I said, 'It needs to go on starting at noon, no earlier.'

He opened his mouth. Whatever he saw in my face made him shut it again. He nodded. 'Drink?' I said.

'No way,' he said. 'This is bandit country. I'm staying on the boat.'

Myself, I did want a drink. Just one. One drink would help.

There were times when drink did not help; such as during most of my life, actually. But it had been useful in getting me out of jobs I was tired of.

Take the Police Service.

After the Irina trip, my roof sort of caved in. I began doing a lot of research in public houses, detecting big numbers of pints and large whiskies. Oddly, this did not adversely affect my career, because I was meeting the bad guys on their own level, and they were just drunk enough to tell me things that I was just sober enough to remember.

One day I was waiting for a source in the Harbour Hotel in Sandbanks, which is the part of Poole that footballers and their estate agents have made very expensive. The Harbour was built in the thirties and recently redecorated to suit the footballers' wives. I was at a table in the back of the room, drinking a bottle of California sauvignon. I was on the third glass when a voice said, 'It's Gavin, innit?'

I raised my eyes towards the voice. All I could see was blonde hair with sun through it, and a face, backlit. I screwed up my eyes and made out a tanned woman about my age, heavily made up by experts, wearing a white trouser suit and red shoes with four-inch silver heels. I said, 'Good morning.'

'And he hasn't got a bloody clue,' said the voice. 'It's me. Samantha.'

'Ah, Samantha,' I said, still without the faintest idea.

'Samantha Stead,' she said. 'Was. Samantha Donner now. We went out together.'

And through the wine and the make-up and the toughening effect of a lot of years of sun and Sandbanks, I dimly discerned Samantha Stead, the beautiful blonde girl with whom I had fornicated in my Dad's Westerly Centaur; daughter of Ricky Stead, the fruit-machines-and-violence king. I was pleased to see her, and I told her so. 'You started this, did you know that?' I said.

'Started what?' she said.

'My glittering career.'

She glanced at her watch. Her face looked animated, as if unexpected things did not happen to her very often and she had taken to making the best of them. 'You mean I changed your life?'

'Yes.'

'So come and explain.'

I started to tell her I had a meeting. Then I pulled out my phone and cancelled my source. And I went to her nice sunny table on the terrace, and upgraded to Sancerre. And I told her.

When I had finished, she looked at me with her mouth

slightly open. There were lines at the corners now, but time had done less to her than it had to me. When I had finished, she lit a cigarette, and said, 'So your wife pissed off with this restaurant bloke.'

'Yes.'

'And you didn't do nothing about it.'

'What would I do?'

The blue eyes narrowed, as if she could not believe what she was hearing. She said, 'Kill him?'

I said, 'In the army you only kill foreigners. In the police you don't kill anyone at all.'

'Pafetic,' she said. Then she sighed. 'But if it hadn't been for me you wouldn't have gone off into the army and that.

'Maybe not.'

'You need looking after, you do,' she said. A horn tooted in the car park. 'That'll be Dad,' she said. She gathered up her gold sunglasses and gold lighter and swept her Bensons into her gold handbag. 'Come along.'

I went along, full of wine and somewhat dazed, following her as she teetered through the tables. 'Wait a minute,' I said. 'He doesn't like me.'

'He's gone senile,' she said. 'You'll be fine. Hello, Dad!'

A liver-spotted dogfish face was contemplating us from the driver's window of a black Mercedes. 'Who's that?' it said.

'Friend.'

'Looks like a tosser.'

'Shut up and drive. Where d'you want to go, Gaz?'

I gave him the coordinates of a street corner I often used, equidistant between the nick and a half-decent pub. The old man took off with a screech of tyres. As he hurtled through Sandbanks, his daughter told him in a high, aggrieved voice of my troubles with Tony Greely, and how it was all his fault. I sat in a winey daze, marvelling at her flow of speech.

The old man took a short cut that turned into a dead end. 'They keep moving the fucking streets,' he said, reversing. He turned round, giving me a blast of white false teeth and terrible breath. 'So he's a restronteur, this pillock, izzee,' he said. 'Healy's.'

'Greely's.'

'What I said,' said Ricky Stead. And drove me to my destination, where Samantha took my mobile number and waved a handful of gold rings out of the window as the Merc screamed off through a red light.

And I went off to the Sun and Stars and changed to Guinness and thought no more of it. Until the following day, when I got a text message that said: ALL SQUARE NOW – SAM. And while I was debating what this might mean, the phone rang. 'Chance?' said the voice of Iris Murchison, my boss. 'Get up here, will you?'

'I'm just —'

'Now,' said Murchison.

I went, crunching a whole tube of Extra Strongs on the way.

She was waiting in her office. Bare desk, one millimetre of lip showing all the way round her letterbox mouth. Bad sign. She said, 'I want you to explain something.'

'Explain what?'

'At dinner time today there was a queue at Healy's Fish Bar in Firs Road. In the queue was PC Hadland. A male entered the fish shop premises and shouted, "This one's to show you not to fuck with Inspector Gavin Chance." Then the male instructed proprietor and clientele to stand back and threw a bucket of cold water into the fryer, causing an explosion and collateral fire.'

I felt the alcohol drain from my head.

The lips vanished entirely. 'PC Hadland was carrying a voice recorder, and her notebook. She used both of them. Healy's Fish Bar is burned out. Chance, I can't understand how anyone can get it so wrong so often. I now have two choices.'

I think I nodded, mildly curious. Perhaps I was in shock. In a vague, abstract way I wanted to murder cretinous demented Ricky Stead. But I knew I had only myself to blame for him. And all the rest of it, really.

'I can arrest you and charge you with conspiracy, arson, and the rest of it,' said Murchison. 'Or you can resign now, on personal grounds. Your ex-wife will probably be keen that you take the second option. That might be because she feels sorry for you. Or it might be that she does not wish to embarrass someone she is seeing.'

I nodded. I was probably going to cry again. I said, 'I'll be off, then.'

'And pray it doesn't make the papers.'

It did, though. It went all the way through the police force and into the *Daily Mail*. But by that time I was far to the north in Achnabuie, hammering woolly-board on to battens to make the tugboat I had bought on eBay a home fit to live in.

I had got it wrong then, and most of the other times. Now, as I walked down Ballycool quay on my way to Erris McGown's card party, I decided I was going to get it right.

But first I went to the pub. It was a grisly object with an oak-pattern vinyl bar. I drank a pint of Guinness, which was a very good pint. Then I had a short argument with myself, lost, and ordered a double Teacher's, because Irish whiskey tastes of petrol, and another pint and a steak. Rendered confident by this and another large Teachers, I tried to fall into conversation with three locals and the scatterbrained barmaid. The locals kicked my nudges about McGown straight into touch. The barmaid gave me her mother's recipe for sloe gin and a bit of an essay on what the English Conservative Party was up to. She managed not to mention McGown at all, and it struck me that perhaps she was not scatterbrained at all.

The conversation sputtered and died. The clock on the wall said five to eight. I said goodnight to my new friends and walked out into the road. The whisky was running strongly in me. Oh, yes. I was going to get it right.

A big black Range Rover swished past, then two BMWs. I could smell bladder-wrack rotting on the beach. The tarmac led round the edge of the sea, in which plenty of stars were dancing. Finally it ran past the portentous gateposts of McGown's Parthenon. I turned in at the gate and walked between massed ranks of hydrangeas towards the house. The drive made a double curve and became a sheet of tarmac. Half a dozen cars stood outside the front door, and lights showed through chinks in the curtains. The smell of bladder-wrack had given way to the smell of turf smoke. The whisky was dying in me, but by no means gone. It produced a sentimental joy. Some people in this place had kindly asked me round in the mellowness of their hearts, because I had brought fish to them across the sea. My mind rambled to the *Gleaner*'s hold and chanced on the washing machines. And suddenly the whisky was in full flight, and I was freezing cold and very frightened, but it was too late to run away because I was on the doorstep and the door was open and a man the size of an industrial boiler was checking me out.

And I was walking in.

There were eight men in the front room, no women. McGown came forward and gave me a happy smile and a bonecrusher handshake before I could flatten my palm. He introduced me round, but my eyes were watering from the handshake, so there was a blur instead of people, and I did not catch any of the names except the Major's. In fact the only thing I really heard McGown say was, 'Drink?'

I said, 'Whisky. Scotch.' Someone gave me a glass. Then everyone ignored me, so I drank the first slug, a big one, before I realised what I was doing. Someone gave me another and I drank that, too, and someone else turned up the brightness in the room, and I was not nervous any more, not even a tiny bit. I let my eyes rove. The people were glossy and thickset, not very interesting. There was a sideboard with trophies for golf and sailing, and a row of photographs. No paintings; it was not that kind of house. I rested my eyes on the photographs. More glossy people, some on boats. And a family group.

A great big whisky gong banged in my head. I gazed at the family group long and hard. I was about to take a step towards it when McGown was alongside me, saying something about cards.

'Cards?' I said.

'You'll play.'

The photograph slid out of my mind. 'I am boracic,' I said. 'Not a bean. Alas,' and felt pleased to be off the hook, because cards is about the only vice I have not got.

'I'll stake you,' he said. He stuffed something into the pocket of my trousers. 'You can owe it to me.'

I put my hand after it. It felt like money, a wad of it. I said, 'I could leave now.'

'No you couldn't,' he said. And all the charm was gone, and I knew he was telling nothing but the truth, and he was the man with the power, and I was getting it wrong.

'Fine,' I said. 'What are we playing?'

'Poker.'

'I don't know the rules.'

'You'll learn,' he said. And then there was another glass in my hand and we were shuffling into a room with a round green baize table with a shaded light and ashtrays.

I sat down between a big man who was in building and

a big man who was in fish. The Major was across the table. His eyes settled on me for a moment. He wrinkled his nose faintly, as at a fart in church, and swivelled the eyes away to rest on McGown. His face took on a whipped look. 'Right,' said McGown. 'Nothing elaborate, just five-card stud. Cut to deal.'

He cut. Someone dealt. I had not been telling the whole truth when I had said that I did not know the rules. We had played poker in the army, and at the nick on long, boring nights. But in the army it had been for undesirable parts of the ration packs, and in the police for Rich Tea biscuits. Johnny would have liked it here, in the sickly stink of big money. Personally, I was scared stiff.

But someone was hauling the wad of fifties out of my pocket, and shovelling them to the industrial boiler, who exchanged them for plastic chips. And I was shocked to discover that the someone was me. So I had some more whisky and looked at my hole card.

A king looked back. Another king arrived, face up. I shoved out five hundred quid. Everyone folded. I raked in the antes. 'Steady,' said McGown, with an authority I greatly resented, because he had no right to it, no damn right at all, I thought, draining the most recent whisky.

Steady, I told myself. Steady, steady. McGown had said steady, the jerk. This was me saying it. I would take this sort of talk from myself. No-one else, though.

Card in front of me. I took a look at it. Nine of diamonds. Steady. Shove out a hundred. Just like that. All the others were doing it, big hands in the light, fat spiders with hair on their legs. Another card, nine of clubs, whoopee. Face straight. Actually, face seemed to be somewhat numb. More whisky might restore sensation.

I had some. My fellow sportsmen were glowering at me

under the fringe on the lampshade. There was a hill of money in the middle of the green baize, and we had only just started. And I did not have any money. I had McGown's money. What was I doing here?

Playing poker. Brace up. The chips started at a hundred pounds a go, though. Which could make you nervous. Think of them as Rich Tea biscuits. Better. Swig of whisky.

'Card,' said the man who was dealing. Flat Newry accent. Eyes like holes burned in a sheet.

'Thanks, sarge,' I said. 'Don't mind if I do.'

Frozen silence. It occurred to me in a faraway, unimportant part of my brain that it might have been wiser not to give this gathering any clues about my past in law enforcement. So I banged my glass on the table for more whisky, and tried to work out what the hell my cards were, and raised everyone a grand. And the incident (I told myself) passed away. Unlike the pot, which amounted to fifteen thousand quid, and which I won, full house, nines and threes.

Goodness, this is going well, I thought, peering at the first hole card of the next deal. Hello, hello, I thought, and winked at it, because I thought it was a jack and some jacks have one eye. Then I saw that actually it was a queen, and looked up and saw they were watching me, and I realised that I was supposed to be keeping a poker face. So I said, 'Cards,' and got a queen and a ten and a three, bet a thousand pounds a card, and got raised five hundred on each of the last two. And when I got the last hole card, I observed that it was a ten.

This probably meant something, but I could not immediately work out what. People were betting. I watched their faces.

McGown looked as if he was cheerful, until you noticed the eyes. The eyes were unpleasantly watchful, the way a webcam is watchful. But there was sweat on the forehead. An electric worm would be moving in his belly. Eyes or no eyes, McGown was emotionally involved.

The Major was sweating too. There was a glass of tap water by his hand, and his big nostril twitched at a waft of smoke from the cigar of the farmerish man on his right. His eyes were clammy as ever, resting on me. But he kept pressing his invisible lips together, and there was a faint shine where the grey stubble ceased on his temples, and a movement in his neck as he swallowed. I was watching a couple of randomness junkies getting their dose.

'Call,' said McGown.

'Call,' said the Major.

And suddenly the world came clear, the way it does when you are standing on top of a mountain made of whisky. I could see for miles and miles. I could see that I was under a strong obligation to give these toxic robots and their nasty beefy friends the hiding of their lives. But I was not necessarily going to do it with two pairs. So I said, 'Call.'

And down went the cards. And as it turned out I had done it. Across came another mountain of Rich Tea biscuits. And I thought: this is the capital with which I will wreck you, lads. And the perfect vision continued as on we played and on. The Major lost and lost, and his mouth went as thin as Iris Murchison's, and his eyes strayed towards McGown as if McGown was the man who would save him. Twice he wrote cheques and McGown gave him chips; about fifty thousand quid's worth. The Major went greyer and greyer. But McGown paid him no attention. McGown had troubles of his own.

Because the one doing all the winning was me.

At one in the morning I surveyed the faces around me, barely visible over the alp of chips in front of me. And for the tenth time, I called for more whisky.

Error.

I knew as the first swallow went down that I might as well have asked for a Mickey Finn. The twenty-twenty vision blurred and doubled. I grew several extra fingers of the largest size, with which I dropped Rich Tea biscuits and fumbled cards and spilt whisky on my trousers. I had the vague notion that the eyes around the table had homed in on me. I decided to prove them wrong, and blundered through the next dozen hands like a bull in a skittle alley. The hill of biscuits became a mound, then a tump. Then there was none of it left.

'So that's you,' said McGown.

'Clown,' said the Major.

It would be nice to say that this sobered me up. But nothing was going to do that, except eight hours' sleep or possibly a stomach pump. So it made me drunker.

I said, 'I need to make a call.'

'Call away,' said McGown, not bothering to hide the scorn.

I lurched into the living room. The fire was low, the air cold. I dialled Georgie. He took a long time to answer. I said what I had to say. He said, 'Wha?'

I said it again.

He said, 'You're drunk.'

'Not at all. If it doesn't work, I'll make it up. I've already done it once.'

'That was lucky.'

I did not answer. I did not want to use that word. I said, 'Trust me.'

'I don't.'

'You should.' That was the best I could do. I thought: so this is the end. Hang on, though, said the voice of reason. The only thing we have lost so far is five grand of McGown's money. It would not be right to throw real money after false —

'All right,' said Georgie, and the voice of reason fled.

I said, '*What*?'

'Do what you have to do,' said Georgie. 'I used to think you were a wanker. I still do. But you're not a bad guy for a wanker. Do it.' Having uttered this oddly concise string of thoughts, he rang off. And I went back into the card room.

The fug of smoke and drink acted like a bugle on a warhorse. I said, 'Lend me fifty grand. You can have Georgie's house as security.'

Faces turned. They looked scornful. The drunk was going to bet the farm. McGown said, 'We'll take it off you. And then we'll go after your friend Georgie.'

This was encouraging, since it showed he was at least considering the idea. 'You can try,' I said.

He shoved across fifty thousand. I was feeling so much better that I nearly asked for more whisky. No, I thought. Afterwards.

The first couple of hands I folded. I could see they still thought I was fumbling drunk. The third hand, my hole card, was the three of clubs. I peered at it, screwing up my face. Then the face-up cards started to arrive. I could see that my fellow sportsmen were tired; it was four in the morning, and they did not have my sleep-deprivation training. The next round produced a nine of hearts and another three. The beefy men folded. I stayed in; a pair was better than nothing. McGown was showing a king, and he had not folded, so maybe he had something up his sleeve. I had the sense that this needed getting over with, but that was the whisky again. There were two more cards to go. So now I did call for more whisky, and took an ostentatious swig that was actually the merest sip, and along came the next card. Which was another three for me, and a king for McGown, which made a pair, and the Major stayed in too, so maybe he had two pairs in there somewhere. McGown was showing the highest cards. He looked at me with the friendly smile under the glass-lens eyes and said, 'Raise you ten grand.'

'And another ten,' said the Major.

'And another,' said a voice I recognised as my own.

Last cards. This was it: all there was, really. I said, 'All in,' and pushed the remains of my borrowed roll out in front of me, every last biscuit of it.

The Major and McGown followed suit. 'All right,' I said.

'Full house, kings and nines,' said McGown.

'I'm out,' said the Major. I could practically smell the pleasure coming off him. Losing was such luxury when you were a born winner.

I turned over my last card. I had the impression of a low, dark card, insignificant. And insignificant it was, by itself; about as insignificant as you can get; the three of spades.

But if you put it with some other threes, it added up.

I said, 'Four threes. Cash her up, please, vicar,' and stood up, knocking my chair over.

They all stared at me with their smoke-bleared eyes. Mouths opened. 'Clown,' said the Major.

McGown was the first to recover. 'Back from the dead, eh?' he said, with a smile like a slit trench. 'Well, we'll have a chance at a little revenge tomorrow.'

'No more cards,' I said. 'Not ever.'

'No, no, I don't mean cards,' said McGown. 'We're sailing, right? With the tide like this you'll not get off the quay till noon anyway. The fish truck comes at two. Shall we say eight, and lunch on the quay after?' He pushed a block-of-flats-sized stack of notes across the table to me.

'Eight it is,' I said, 'Gosh, is that the time? I must run.'

'Clown,' said the Major. But it was a pathetic attempt at

self-assertion, stingless now. I only smiled. I pushed McGown's loan money back at him across the table, and wandered forth with some two hundred thousand pounds in notes stuffed up my jumper.

It was a fine, cool, clear night, with a snappy little breeze that whipped at my face. I should have felt triumphant. Actually I felt drunk, and tired, and as if I was carrying the best part of two hundred thousand pounds through enemy territory to a boat with a big bomb on it, and my night's work was not yet over. So I started to run. And as I stumbled along the beach the big black cars swished past, their drivers fuming behind their smoked glass. And at last I arrived in the tangle of sheds at the root of the quay.

There I paused in the shadows, holding on to my nine-months-gone bellyful of banknotes. The masts of the fishing boats bristled black against the stars. Nothing moved. So I took a deep breath and stepped out of the shadow and walked down the quay in a cloud of whisky, ears pricked for footsteps. No footsteps came. I reached the *Gleaner* and jumped down on the deck. It was slightly tilted, aground. I hammered on the window.

Stirrings from within. 'Who's there?' said the sleep-thickened voice of Georgie.

I identified myself. A key turned. The door opened. A torch shone in my eyes. I went in. 'Yeuch, the whisky on you,' said Georgie.

I did not answer. Instead I pulled my jersey out of my trousers and let the bundles of fifties thunder on to the deck. There was a bigger thump as Georgie went on his knees after them. 'Christ,' he said.

'Take twenty grand for interest,' I said. He was making noises like someone singing to a baby. I probably would have been making the same noises if I had not had work to do.

But I had. And the principal sound in my head was my teeth chattering.

'Night!' said Georgie, practically chortling.

'Night,' I said. But I did not go to bed. I walked down into the hold, took a few deep breaths, and spent an hour doing what I had to do there. Then I took a final swig of whisky from Maureen's bottle and went to my bunk.

And two hours later, there was Georgie, looking nervous, carrying a cup of Nescafé. 'How are you doing?' he said.

I closed my eyes to stop my eyeballs rolling down my face. My hands stank of fish. 'Never better,' I said.

'There's a man on the quay says he wants you to go yachting.'

'Yes.' I got my feet out of bed. The coffee tasted like sugared rat's bile, and the cabin walls rotated with a nasty droning noise.

Georgie looked at me, frowning. 'You want some whisky in that?' he said.

My gorge rose. I shook my head. My brain slopped around behind my eyes. I said, 'How about a fried-egg sandwich?'

'Coming up,' said Georgie.

I washed in washing-up liquid and pulled on my jeans and a couple of jerseys and stumbled on deck. McGown was standing on the quay, wearing red oilskins that looked as if someone had ironed them. I said, 'Ten minutes,' and went round to the other side of the wheelhouse where he could not see me.

The tide was coming in. I stood and watched it and hung on to the rail so the whisky would not spin me over the side. It was a good harbour, this Ballycool. Even this close to low tide there was a sheet of water out in the middle, with a sandbar, drying now, pointing at a yellow buoy. The yellow buoy was not altogether in safe water, I noted; though as I watched, two sheets of water slapped together over the bar and the buoy began to rock restlessly, trying to float. A man in a RIB was towing a couple of the elegant dayboats in from the moorings towards a jetty that stretched off the quay into deep water. It occurred to me that they might have something to do with the morning's entertainment. I walked into the wheelhouse and pulled my oilskin coat off its hook. I said, 'Can you work the cargo on your own?'

'Sure,' said Georgie, still somewhat awestruck.

'Don't start till half eleven,' I said.

'Sure,' he said again. I could see McGown gazing into the wheelhouse, blank-eyed now that nobody was looking. I hoped he could not read lips.

'And keep an eye on us,' I said.

'Never fear,' said Georgie.

But I feared. Oh, I feared all right.

I took a deep breath and went up the steps to the quay.

19

McGown was standing between the industrial boiler and a skinny man with reddish hair and a bad complexion. He led me to the bar at the seaward end of the quay. 'Declan, two double espressos.'

'Milk for me.'

'He means macciato, Declan,' said McGown to the whippety man. 'Whiskey?'

'No, thank you,' I said.

McGown winked his cold eye and pulled a bit of paper out of the pocket of his bandbox-fresh Henri Lloyds. The coffee arrived. I took a sip. Probably he would say something soon.

'You had the best of the breeze on the Solent,' he said, and even in the muddy hollow that passed for my head I felt a small tweak of triumph. He was a vain little tosser, and a bad loser. 'So we'll have a little race today, if you don't mind. I'd like my revenge.'

I said, 'Revenge?'

'You walked off with a lot of money last night,' he said. 'I'll sail you double or quits.'

I said, 'Whatever's in the bag, fine.' As soon as it was out of my mouth I regretted it. I was not a gambler. That was enough money to get me clear of all the unpleasantnesses that hemmed me in and start me on a new life. But his hand was out to seal the bet. 'We have these boats,' he said. 'Ballycool one-designs, we call them. Built by the white settlers above at Ballycool House. It's a lunatic asylum now. Always was, really. Anyway they're nice little boats. You can choose yours. Fair's fair.'

The face was smiling. The eyes were not. 'So come on now,' said this nasty little killer. 'Sail me a race and give me a chance.'

The thoughts drove the whisky to the corners of my mind. On the one hand, financial security and a life expectancy of about four hours. On the other, broke again, and a life expectancy of . . . well, there was no telling, really. Better the devil you don't know than the devil you do; the ancient motto of the Chances. So I gripped his hand, and squeezed it hard before he was entirely ready, and said, 'Lead me to it.'

'That's the way,' he said. 'Declan, lunch on the quay as planned.'

'I told you, I have to leave with the tide,' I said.

He smiled. 'I changed my mind about asking you,' he said. 'That's lunch for me, not you. Declan will hold the stakes.'

What a nice guy, I thought. I jumped down on to *Gleaner*'s wheelhouse and into the bunkroom and took out the plastic shopping bag with the money in it, and tossed it on to the quay and scrambled up after it.

McGown looked into the bag, shuffled a sheaf of notes, checking. 'Declan, mind it,' he said.

I took the handles and tied them together in a tight knot. Declan scuttled over and took possession. And I followed McGown down to the boats, my brain slapping the inside of my skull with every step. 'Well,' said McGown, hands on hips, feet planted. 'You can choose your boat. Only this one's mine.' He batted the shroud of the boat on his right. It was a beautiful wooden blade of a thing, with a deck of perfect grey teak, a hull enamelled ice-cream white, and spars with the honey-dipped look of fifteen coats of varnish lovingly applied.

'So I'll take this one,' I said, batting the shroud of the other, which had a painted canvas deck, rusty galvanised shrouds, and very little varnish.

McGown laughed, at his joke, not mine. 'Well, now,' he said, and again I could sense that electric worm of excitement he had been feeling at the poker table. 'You'll need this.' He pushed a sheet of paper at me. It was headed 'Ballycool S.C.' It was a chart of the harbour, with a course drawn on it in green felt-tip. I checked it against the harbour. There was a start, which appeared to be between a trawler and a north cardinal just off the jetty. Then there was a beat up to the yellow at the end of the sandbar at the far side of the harbour, and a reach up to a red can at the entrance, and back to the yellow, and a run back to the start line.

I looked out over the harbour. The tide was running hard. The bar was covered, and flaws of breeze were making brief zigzag flurries on the slaty water.

'Lovely day for a sail,' said McGown. 'Shall we say nine o'clock? Paddy will give us a ten-minute gun and a gun for the minute and the start.' Paddy seemed to be the industrial boiler. Presumably the start gun was in his shoulder holster. I lurched into the boat and started to find my way round.

It was not a complicated object, which was just as well, since I was about to match-race it singlehanded for a purse of nearly two hundred grand. The thought of the money just about flattened me. But this was no time for being flattened. This was a time for discovering which was the main halyard, and hauling up the mainsail – a mainsail of a certain age, the leech with more stretch in it than was wholly desirable, the luff baggier than was perfect. McGown's mainsail, on the other hand, rode into the sky with the crisp rumple of new cloth. He was in a boat he knew, on water he knew, with nice new gear —

Concentrate. Focus. Never mind the whisky, or the money, or the competition. Put your mind into the boat and sail it. I hauled, sweated, made fast with fingers that definitely shook.

It was not a complicated rig. There was a row of reefing points, pennants at the clew, hooks at the tack, all in order. There was a kicking strap. The jib was on a roller. My heart sank. There was a chute in the foredeck. And underneath the chute, lurking like a nasty DayGlo python ready to strangle me, was the spinnaker.

Practice needed.

Well, I had a whole twenty-five minutes for that.

I checked the lead of the lines and observed that one of the spinnaker sheets was inside a shroud, which was either Irish insouciance or a delicate form of sabotage. When I had everything running as it should, I unrolled the jib, hauled it aback and let go the bow line. The nose peeled off the quay. The mainsail drew. I let go the stern line. The boat slid out into the harbour. McGown was fiddling with his mainsheet. He looked over his shoulder; no expression. I glimpsed the Major standing like a mummy on the quay. Then a puff hit, and I moved my weight up to the side-deck, hearing the wake roar, feeling the tug of weather helm on the tiller. I let out three inches of mainsheet. The weather helm moderated. I commenced sea trials.

Your Ballycool one-design was heavy by modern standards, with long overhangs at bow and stern. I watched the compass. It settled on 225°, and the rig slotted into into that magic groove between luffing and stalling, and I felt a lift of the heart as the boat slid forward with a smooth acceleration. The counter kissed the sea, lengthening the waterline, and the broken numbers of the log went from 6.0 to 6.3 and stayed there. Then I eased the tiller towards the downhill side of the boat and tacked.

She came round smoothly. The jib eased across the forward face of the mast, and I sheeted it in a second before it started to pull, and we were back in the groove again, sliding swiftly ahead, in silence except for the rush of water and the clatter of the leech. The compass steadied on 135°. Over my shoulder I could see McGown talking to someone on the quay. My watch said twenty minutes to the start. I began to feel vaguely sanguine. There were worse boats than this one.

I eased sheets and reached down towards the inside of the harbour. Again she found a groove; and again as she dunked the run of her counter there was that little surge of extra speed.

I was liking this boat. The money and the whisky had faded into the background. I was sliding through cold water balanced on a fine hard edge of breeze, and it was beautiful.

The shore was coming up. I had no chart and no sounder. It would not be sensible to go aground. So I put the bow back on the quay, the best part of a mile off now. It was time to try the kite.

I laid the boat in front of the wind, crossed myself in my mind, prepared the spinnaker pole and hauled on the halyard. Up came the sail out of the chute. I steered with my knee while I dealt with the sheets. And there I was, tearing down the breeze in the finest style, watching the quay come up, the spinnaker a taut red balloon against the blue-and-white sky.

A hulking figure walked to the end of the jetty, glanced at its wrist, raised a handgun. A puff of smoke, then the bang.

Ten minutes. Suddenly my heart was beating at high speed. I bent to pick up the spinnaker sheet. As I reached down, a flaw in the wind got the wrong side of the mainsail, and the boom slammed across, gybed all standing, and the boat swerved up to windward, broaching, and suddenly I was standing on the lee coaming and water was pouring over the downhill side as the wind beat the spinnaker down into the sea, and my heart tried to jump out of my chest, because we were going to fill and sink before the race had even started.

So I did the only thing I could. I let go the halyard, and it rushed away into the mast, and suddenly the boat was upright and the spinnaker was wallowing on the water. I got hold of it and hauled it in and stuffed it under the foredeck. Then I went down to the line, behind which the immaculately-trimmed sails of McGown's boat were nodding demurely along. I concentrated on working the pump so as not to show my damn silly whisky-hangover face. I was racing for two hundred grand on a course with a downwind leg, and now I had no spinnaker.

The pump sucked air. I sheeted in the jib and headed for the area behind the line. I was close enough to McGown to see his face now. He was looking at me with a little smile. His lips moved, and his hand went up and down. *Wanker.* And there he sat, sail rattling, hovering at the pin end, in control.

I was close to him now; close enough to see the wave-reflections in the perfect white paint of his boat, the little square murderer's hand resting on the coaming, stroking the varnish as if he loved it. Perhaps it was the only thing he did love . . .

I found I was having to stop myself grinning. I was going to have to mess with him. And now I knew how it had to be done.

I was on the port tack. He was the right-of-way boat. He sat there and watched me as I reached down on him, waiting for me to haul the tiller into my stomach and duck under his stern. On the jetty, Paddy was looking at his watch. Ninety seconds to the start gun. I said, 'Get out of the way.'

He crinkled his eyes at me. They said that all he had to do was sit where he was, on the starboard tack at the end of the line, and he would be the right-of-way boat, and he could set off at a stately pace with me trailing in his wake, and any time I started to make a move he could frustrate it. These were the rules of match racing.

This morning I was not too bothered by the rules. But I did not want to give anything away yet. So I waited until my boat's nose was half a boat's length from his side, and crash-tacked, from a reach to a reach, and saw his mouth open and shut, and the reflex caress of his hand on his beautiful varnish. And I knew I was right.

The minute gun went when I was down at the far end of the line. I checked my watch, ran out of the area, gybed after thirty seconds and came back for the left-hand end. A puff of wind whipped across. My boat heeled its counter into the sea, and the numbers went up, 6.3, 6.5, and the wake hissed down the side. Up at the other end of the line McGown still hung, sails rattling. With ten seconds to go I was fifty yards short of the line. But I saw McGown's sails harden up, his boat head for the line, and I thought: good, he's freaked, he'll be over early and he'll have to come back and start again.

Which was stupid of me, because it did not take into consideration who Paddy the industrial boiler worked for.

My watch said there were ten seconds to go. The gun went off. It went at the precise moment McGown's nose touched the line. It was a perfect start for a dirty little murdering cheat.

But he had been so busy hugging the pin end that he had no speed up, and these were heavy boats that took time to get going. Whereas I was trucking along nicely. So I kept going, and crossed five seconds after him. And there we were on converging courses, him with right of way. The wind was roaring in my left ear, and the lee chainplates were tearing a white plume out of the sea. For a moment I was almost enjoying myself.

Only for a moment, though. For the two boats were coming together fast. McGown was heeled steeply towards me, steaming along, his beautiful sails with the curve of a gull's wing. When I peered under the jib I saw his rudder-post. The bearing between me and him was not changing. Which meant my boat was on a collision course with his boat.

His elegant and beautifully painted boat, which he loved.

I settled myself firmly on the side-deck and stormed on. The bearing remained unchanged. I saw him look under the boom. He would be calculating that I would hit him in way of the rudder-post: so he would expect me to duck under his stern, or to tack now. Either way, it would put him ahead of me and in a position to interfere with the supply of wind to my sails.

I pressed on. I saw him look again. I shouted, 'You were early over the line.'

He shouted something dismissive. I said, 'I'm coming through. Give me water.'

I saw him laugh. I saw the laugh freeze on his face as my boat's bow ploughed towards him. Then he shoved the tiller down to leeward, and the boat came round, and he was sailing away from me, on port now, losing ground, properly fouled.

I said, 'One good turn deserves another,' and sailed on for the mark. I was drawing away from him, but my confidence had waned somewhat. The bungalows of Ballycool gazed with blank windows from the low green land, watching the big man in the town take a beating from a chancer. Certainly McGown did not want to bend his beautiful boat. But his honour was at stake now. And soon we would be round the buoy and on the reaching leg, and he would have a spinnaker, and he would catch me.

There was a nasty itching sensation on the back of my neck where the skull met the spinal column. The spot through which someone had put a bullet into Johnny Bonny's head.

Sail the boat.

The buoy came abeam, canted in the tide. Leave it well astern. Bear away. Ease sheets to show more sail to the wind. The log said six knots through the water, but I was only making four over the ground. The sea rushed past, but the land merely crawled. And I heard a rustle astern, and looked round, and saw McGown round the buoy, the spinnaker rise in a ribbon and *whap* open as he sheeted it in. The white moustache under his boat's bow thickened. My stomach sank. I turned away, and concentrated on sailing for the next mark.

It sat far up by the harbour mouth, that mark, a little red crumb against the green jut of the land. And I crept towards it. The breeze was up, and the slender hull of the boat made a big bow wave, then a trough, and a stern wave from the back end. And I began to feel a jet of hope. Boats like these have a maximum speed, because they are unable to sail over their own bow wave, the way you are unable to lift yourself up by your bootstraps. And as far as I could see I was sailing just about flat out: hull speed, you call it. Spinnaker or no spinnaker, McGown's hull speed was the same as mine.

So on I flew, clattering through the chop kicked up by the breeze. And on he came, a fraction faster than me, because he had the power of the spinnaker to get through the chop, catching me. But slowly; very slowly. And all the time the crumb of red metal inside the point grew bigger.

Sail the boat. Jib, mainsheet, kicker, the flaws of wind snaking across the water from the land. And here at last was the buoy, the tide eddying at its base. And there was the white bow of McGown's boat crawling towards me under the green tower of the spinnaker. Inshore of me. Coming up fast. And I realised that the bastard knew the harbour, and he had found a stripe of slacker tide.

I had a bad feeling that this was falling apart. The buoy came abeam. I rounded. The counter missed the rust-blistered paint by a couple of inches. Then there was a crack and a shopping-bag rustle, and McGown was round too. But when I looked back I saw that he was busy changing the pole on his spinnaker, and I was out in the tide again, moving, and the gap was widening.

But not for long. We flew down the tide, the breeze well up now, heeled thirty degrees. I should have put in a reef, but that would have lost me half a minute, which would have put him past me. So up came that big green spinnaker, dipping and swaying like a pigeon's breast, and then he was right on my tail, and my main came back at me as he ate the wind out of it; but he was windward boat, so I had right of way. I eased the tiller away from me and went across his bows, and I saw that white bow just forward of my shroud, heard the spinnaker rustle and flap as he luffed. Then there was a rending noise, and a streak of light shot from the foot of his spinnaker to the peak. And suddenly that fat, stately sail was Christmas decorations fluttering in the wind.

'Bad luck, old man,' I said, and gave him a big smug fake smile.

Which was a foolish lapse of concentration. Because as he was pulling down the rags of the sail and unrolling his jib, and I was moving out of his wind-shadow, the biggest gust of the day came bouncing across the water. I still had my sails trimmed in after the big luff. The wind slammed into them. And over I went, a green waterfall pouring over the lee coaming. And by the time I had let off the sheets and retrimmed and started pumping, there was McGown's nose level with my stern, going like a train, and I was windward boat, and the next mark was coming up, the yellow buoy.

I took a quick look at the quay. The *Gleaner* had lost her list. She was afloat. There was a green pile of boxes on the quay.

The yellow buoy was close now. An hour ago I had watched the two sheets of tide join over the bar whose end it marked. A ten-foot tide, say. Maybe three feet of rise since I had watched the bar cover.

I looked over my shoulder. There was McGown, perched up on his side deck. I was pleased to see that he looked tired. I did not feel so great myself, but I was going to make him feel worse.

I pretended to fumble the jib, keeping inside, heading for the buoy. The sail backed and flapped, and the boat lost way, and I bore away to fill it, so I was heading below the buoy. I heard the roar of his bow wave, and saw him come up just by my left hand, thinking he could power past me to windward. I heard him shout, 'Mast abeam!' which meant I was not allowed to shove the tiller away and push him out of my ear.

But I shouted, 'Balls! Water!' and I escorted that tiller round in a smooth curve, and I heard him yell, and there was a big, fine crash and a grinding, and then he was off and away up the wind, and there was the buoy flashing under my lee, and no sign of McGown.

Until I turned round. And there he was, with a good big yellow splintery gouge out of his beautiful white hull and his sails clattering and his face pale with rage, aground on the bar.

I stood looking over the stern in the quiet you get as you turn on to a run. 'Bad luck,' I said.

McGown looked at me with a face that had become entirely calm. He pointed his finger at me, and said,'You die.' I was sure he meant it.

Then I had my phone out, and I was calling Georgie, and the *Gleaner* was coming off the quay, a big, blackened, reeking slab of salvation. I said into the phone, 'Pick me up by the green fishing boat.'

'Aye,' he said.

Down I ran, everything quiet and peaceful; which is the way it feels when you are sailing at the same speed as the wind, or drifting through life. It is only when you start to go against the drift that you realise the power of what you are up against.

When I sailed over the finishing line, nobody fired a gun. But there was the *Gleaner*, better than any gun, and I put the helm up and went alongside her downwind side, let all the sheets go, scrambled up on to her deck and went into the wheelhouse. 'Had ye a nice time?' said Georgie scornfully.

'Great,' I said. 'Now we should leave.'

'Without your money?' he said.

'Never mind the money.' I was excessively nervous now. 'Go.'

He knocked the throttle forward. The yacht rocked in the propwash, sails flopping. McGown came down the harbour on a dead run, standing at the after end of the cockpit steering with his knees. He looked at us as he passed. The eyes were cold and hooded. I blew him a kiss. He did not blow one back.

'We've got a passenger,' said Georgie through the wheelhouse window. And on to the deck walked the Major, looking tired, with black bags under his eyes.

He said, 'Clown.'

I was getting tired of this. I said, 'It is more usual to be grateful to your host.'

He said, 'I will choose who I am grateful to.'

'You know what I think?' I said. 'I think you lost a lot of money last night. And I think you couldn't afford it. And I think that you are having a bit of a sulk, and taking it out on the first person you see.'

The face got paler, the eyebags darker. 'Who do you think you're talking to?' he said.

'An ordinary thief,' I said. 'I may not have been the world's greatest policeman, but I didn't pretend to be Her Majesty's liaison man with Her Majesty's Police Service while I nicked Her Majesty's cocaine and conspired with Her Majesty's enemies. Now watch your manners, and if you're going to puke, puke over the side.'

He opened his mouth. He shut it again. What he did next I neither know nor care, because I had the binoculars out and I was watching the quay.

The sun had come out. There were umbrellas over the tables at McGown's private continental café on the pierhead, for God's sake, divided by a canvas windbreak from the pile of Greenreap boxes we had landed. McGown was at the bar; someone was handing him a pint of Guinness. He looked straight at me with that look of his, and my flesh crawled, though he would hardly have been able to see me. Then he went and sat down at one of the tables. The industrial boiler went and sat down with him. And a man with his arm in a sling, and another man with his head wrapped in bandages. The whole nasty lot of them were there on the quay, drinking away, watching the *Gleaner* ploughing out of the harbour against the tide. As if they had assembled to watch something special.

'Aren't you going to wave?' I said to the Major.

'Why would I do that?'

'To say goodbye?'

He did not answer. Or wave.

The figures on the quay were shrinking now. A green buoy went past to port. Far ahead in the open sea, the east cardinal showed: safe water out there. I began to feel heavy twinges of apprehension. We were sailing away from some very nasty people, and they were letting us go. Certainly they had nearly two hundred thousand of my pounds, and they were the kind of people to whom money was very important. But it was less important than the enforcement of their dumb, savage notion of justice.

They were shrinking now. As far as they were concerned we would be halfway up the sea to the horizon, our figures on the deck tiny, faces invisible. But I had McGown in my glasses. I saw him take a delicate sip of his pint. I saw him pick up a mobile phone from the table in front of him. He did not put it to his ear. He held it up, and he pointed it at us like someone pointing a remote at a TV. And he dialled a number. And then I suppose he must have pressed the little green button, but I was too far away to see.

Besides, something else happened.

The end of the quay disappeared in a sudden blinding flash of light. And a split second later there was an enormous noise, a noise that drove in my eardrums till I thought they were going to meet in the middle of my head. The shockwave slammed me away from the *Gleaner*'s rail and into the wheelhouse, and when I picked myself up I saw that the air above the quay was full of gulls, and under the gulls there billowed a heavy plume of black smoke, and in among the black smoke a lot of tiny things like leaves that caught the sun as they fluttered in the air, and for all I knew they were the angelic portions of McGown and his crew, except that I strongly suspected that

McGown and his men did not have any angelic portions, and that these were in fact fifty-pound notes. Notes that were in a manner of speaking my property, not that I was going to hang around to claim them.

After a while the wind took away the smoke, and all that remained was the end of the quay, scoured clean by blast and fire, and some things on which the gulls dived hungrily.

I heard a whimpering noise. I looked round. It was the Major. The explosion had blown him halfway through the wheelhouse window, and he was streaming blood and shivering with pain and shock. I was not feeling so good myself, and I had been ready for it.

'Hats off, nice one, Gavin,' said Georgie, wiping blood off his forehead.

I nodded. But I felt sick, and ill, and not in the mood for praise, even from a connoisseur like Georgie. I said, 'We'll go back to Scotland, then.'

I went into the wheelhouse. I pointed the *Gleaner*'s nose to miss the cardinal by quarter of a mile and hit the autopilot. The Major was on his hands and knees. He looked up at me, two white eyes in a faceful of blood. He crawled up the wall until he was leaning against it. He said, 'I'm hurt.'

I went into the galley and got some water and a dishcloth and said, 'Wipe your face.'

He wiped it. He was whimpering. I like to think I am a nice person, but somehow it was not a sound I minded hearing. I took a closer look at the cuts on his face. A couple were deep, but none was squirting. 'You'll live,' I said. I should have been feeling relieved, I suppose. I wasn't, though.

Because I was wondering if I actually was a nice person. I had killed people. I had sailed my ex-brother-in-law's corpse around for weeks without telling his sister he was dead. And I was really regretting that two hundred grand.

Look on the bright side, I told myself. The bright side was not being dead.

I went out in the breeze and made some phone calls. Then I sat in the chair and listened to the Major sniffling and watched the blue shadow of the Mull of Kintyre rise steadily out of the sea. Not dead, I thought. Only wishing I was. But that would be the whisky.

The Major said something. The voice was meant to be his chilly Welsh monotone, but it wobbled to a halt. He tried again. 'What was that?'

'It is like this,' I said. 'We had some washing machines in the hold.'

'Yes,' said the Major.

'Did you know anything about them?'

'They're mine,' said the Major.

'So why are we carrying them round the sea?'

'You misunderstand,' said the Major, recapturing his old chill. 'Mr McGown asked me to have them picked up from Holyhead, for transport to Ireland. But when we got them to Ireland he said he didn't need them any more. So he gave them to me.'

'So you could bring them home and give them to Mrs Davies, was it?' I said. 'Or perhaps sell them on eBay, because you've lost every penny you ever had playing cards with the enemy.'

'I don't have to listen to this,' said the Major.

'Yes you do,' I said. 'Or jump overboard, I don't care. So these washing machines. One of them was a bomb.'

'It was *what*?' said the Major.

'An IED. Improvised explosive device. C4 explosive, detonator, triggered by a mobile phone. Your pal McGown thought you were getting unreliable. Which you were. And perhaps that you knew too much about him. Which you probably did. He was going to blow us up on the way over. But then he decided he wanted to give me a beating, so he decided to save it for our trip home.'

There was a nice corkscrew roll to the boat, but that was not all that was making the Major look sick. 'I tell you what it is,' I said. 'These McGown-type people are not great ones for forgiving and forgetting. They don't know whether they're living in the twenty-first century or the twelfth, doesn't matter what side they say they're on. And you don't want to leave any loose ends with them, not if you want to sleep at night ever again in your life. So I took the explosives out of the washing machine and put them in a fish box, and Georgie put the fish box on the quay and put the other boxes on top and we stacked them next to where they were having lunch. So when McGown dialled up to say goodbye, he dialled himself.'

The Major leaned against the bulkhead as if he was in the queue for the intensive care unit. I saw him work it through in his head. 'He wanted to dissolve your partnership,' I said. 'And he did. So all's well that ends well. Eh?'

'The body,' said Georgie.

'Ah, yes,' I said. 'The body.'

The Major rolled his eyes round. 'What body?' he croaked.

'The body of Johnny Bonneville-Clark,' I said. 'Another of your creditors. With a bullet in the back of his head. It's in your cold store.'

The eyes closed.

'The police have the gun that shot him, covered in McGahey's prints,' I said. 'McGahey worked for McGown, who was a known associate of yours. And you have a really good motive. Because Johnny won a lot of money off you. And he came and took your boat. And you could have got very cross.'

The Major's eyes opened again. They were not cold any more. They were weak and desperate. He said, 'What will it take for you to forget about this?'

'It's not only this,' I said. 'I mean, there you are, a police liaison officer. Buy you have used the police as a private army. And you have stolen drugs from a big bust and destroyed careers and given aid and comfort to the enemy, and all because you like a little flutter.'

The eyes were on me. 'Clown,' he said, but the conviction was gone.

'No doubt,' I said. 'But what would you do to you if you were me?'

Silence.

'You would turn me in,' I said. 'Full majesty of the law. Well, I'm not going to do that.'

I saw a little colour come back into the face. All right, Major, I thought. This is what it feels like. 'So I made some calls just now, and I'm letting Tony Greely do it instead. He will have told a friend of yours called Holby a lot of things that have cheered him up. And Holby will have talked to Chief Constable Jack Menzies, who is a friend of a friend. And he will have let Greely out of prison and sent some people round to your cold store. And Holby will have talked to your wife. Very cross, I expect she will have been. Hoi!' For the Major was heading for the door, perhaps planning to fling himself over the side, and Georgie had jumped at his neck, and his head had slammed into the bulkhead.

'You are going nowhere,' I said. 'Two main reasons. One, this Holby would like to hear a true explanation from you as to what happened in the Weinstein bust in Liverpool the other year. And two, there are some papers you need to sign. A memo for Georgie Strother, acknowledging his one hundred per cent beneficial interest in the *Sirius Gleaner*, blah blah. I'm a broker. I'll write it. You sign it. And one for me, saying that there was as far as you could see no negligence in my handling of the *Lorne Lady* prior to her hitting an unmarked stone in your bay.'

I wrote the papers. He signed them.

'Excellent,' I said. 'Home for tea, eh?'

And home we went; to the Major's home, anyway. There was scene-of-crime tape everywhere, and blue lights making corpse-flares on white bungalow cement, and a van to carry away the large quantity of class A drugs found in the same cold store as the body. The Major came on deck to watch. It was hard to see his face. I did not really want to look. He was going to be drummed out of his job, and then he was going to spend a long, long time locked up with people who would not like him much.

We went alongside the quay. He stepped onto the concrete like an old, old man. A policeman walked out of the dark and said, 'Major Horace Davies?' The arrest rigmarole followed. They led him away.

I could see a curtain twitched back in the bungalow. There was a police car parked outside. Its light shone blue in the tears on the cheeks of Mrs Davies, peering round the curtain.

Mrs Davies was in for a long sentence too. But she was going to find it hard to find anyone to share hers with.

Someone was saying something to me. 'I beg your pardon?' I said.

'We will require a statement from you,' said the policeman on the deck. He took our names and addresses. I gave him Achnabuie. 'Away,' growled Georgie from the wheelhouse.

A churn of white water under the stern. Lines off. The nose seeking the bay. We rounded the point, and the blue flashes vanished behind the loom of the land. Through the dark Sound of Jura we slid, in long dark jumps from emerald flash to ruby blink; and a couple of hours later we were clattering down the channel at Achnabuie. 'Thanks for my boat,' said Georgie as we came alongside the quay. 'I hope I never see you again.'

Then I was standing on the quay in my oilskins, and the black loom of the *Gleaner* was sliding away down the channel so Georgie could drink himself horizontal at the pub in Craighouse. I had a pickup truck, in whose cab I would sleep. And when I woke up, I would no doubt make a plan.

My telephone rang. I looked at the screen. It was Miranda. I decided that I would start confronting issues tomorrow, and turned the phone off.

A voice said, 'Gavin?'

I jumped about a foot, but landed well. I said, 'Maureen?'

'Aye.' A hand took mine, a firm hand, dry. She pulled me through the dark. She said, 'You've nowhere to stay. You'd better come home.' She kissed my cheek. She was chewing gum. Her breath smelled of spearmint.

I went.

I knew Maureen's place pretty well. It was a little stone doll's house in a square of garden. The garden had dahlias in autumn and daffodils in spring and midges in summer. Tonight it was mostly full of rain.

She pushed open the door and said, 'I'll put the kettle on. Did you eat yet?'

'No,' I said. 'But I'm fine.' Rain rattled against the window. It was a filthy night. It would get worse.

'Ach, what's wrong with you?' she said. She crouched at the fire, blew life into the peat, her well-shaped back to me. 'Are you sick?'

'No,' I said. I liked Maureen. I fancied Maureen. But I was

not going to take anything from her, because I was genuinely worried that she would poison me.

She turned round. Fine eyes, narrowed, realising something was wrong. That mighty hair. A kind and good-looking woman. Frowning, though. 'So what's the problem?'

I said, 'You are.' The eyes softened, and a smile began. 'No,' I said. 'A real problem. You know when you lent me your phone? Erris McGown rang. I thought he had got the number from the Major. But he hadn't. He thought he was ringing you. I thought he was sounding surprised because I was alive. But he was surprised because it wasn't you.'

'What the hell are you talking about?' she said. She was shaking her head.

'Your brother.'

'Who?'

'I have just been at Ballycool,' I said. 'I was playing poker with a man called McGown. There is a family group on his living-room wall. And you're in it.'

There was a silence then. Finally, she said, 'So what is it?'

'He tried to kill me.'

She nodded. She said, 'Of course he did. And?'

'He killed himself instead.'

Her head went down. She said, 'He's not my brother.'

'No?' I did not believe her. I was tired, tired, tired.

'He's my husband. Was.'

I scrutinised her face. She did not look like someone who had just been widowed.

'He was a religious man,' she said. 'The kind of religious man who sets bombs and kills children. But not the kind that divorces.'

'Why didn't you tell me?'

'You didn't ask.'

I looked into her eyes: her green, slanted, unreadable Celtic bloody eyes. I saw nothing I could understand. She said, 'Do you want a drink?' I spread my hands. 'Because I'm having one.'

I watched her carefully, and she knew it. She took two clean glasses out of the cupboard, and broke the seal of a new bottle of Te Bheag, and put three fingers in each glass, and let me choose, and drank first. Convinced that this was not a deep-laid poison plot, I followed suit. And the liquid fire sank, and the spirits rose.

I said, 'You told your husband about me.'

'It wasn't like that. I . . . accidentally introduced him to Johnny.'

'Accidentally?'

'Johnny was here. Erris came in one day. To pay me maintenance, if you want to know. They started talking about cards. Erris asked him to a game. That's where he met Davies.'

I stared at her. I had not been the only person holed up in Achnabuie. I said, 'Thanks.'

'Sorry.' She shook her head. 'I thought you were as much of an idiot as your friend Johnny.'

'You were right,' I said, and took some more whisky.

'I was wrong,' she said. 'You're an okay guy. You do stupid things when you drink, that's all. But by the time I put that together it was too late. And I was desperate, really.' She shook her head. 'Have you any idea what it is like to be married to a man like Erris in a land with no divorce? I mean, there's another way out of a marriage for a man like that.' She paused, to let that sink in. 'But if it means anything to you, I saved your bloody life.'

'Yes?' I said, feeling the forty-proof contrariness grow in me.

'When they set your boat on fire,' she said. 'You mebbe thought you were being hellish discreet. There was a man with a rifle on your head all the time, and I told him not to fire because you were a coward and you'd take being burned out as a warning.'

This stopped me. Contrariness or no contrariness, I had to admit this could be true. And there I had been thinking it was my splendid outdoorsmanship that had got me away.

Her mouth had turned down at the corners in a way I had never seen before. She began to play with a packet of spearmint Extra. I said, 'And you put the white rosette on the tug.'

'Stupid thing,' she said. 'Erris told me to.'

'And you just did it.'

'He had a bit of a hold over me,' she said, still with that mouth. 'It's not a great living, working for Gavin Chance Marine. I needed the maintenance.'

I lowered my head. There was a lot of truth in that. I said, 'And you told him Donnie was here.'

'He said he just wanted to talk to him. Listen,' she said. 'I looked after you.' The eyes narrowed again. 'I began to believe you'd get rid of him for me. And you did. So thank you for that.'

I shrugged. I did not know what to believe. 'But no more maintenance,' I said.

'But no more husband,' she said, too fierce for my liking. 'It's worth it.'

'Is that a proposition?'

She gave me a smile. It was a kind smile, but there was too much pity in it for my personal taste. She said, 'My kind of guy is one who can tie his own shoelaces.'

'Yes,' I said. 'Well.'

'But do you want to stay the night?' She kept her eyes on mine. 'There's a spare bedroom.'

I said. 'I shall be making other arrangements.' I stood up. 'Thank you for everything you have done.'

'Aye, well,' she said. 'I resign. You'd best take the computer. And the bottle.'

'Thank you,' I said. 'I shall.'

So an hour and a half later Gavin Chance Marine, its records, goodwill, business plan and proprietor were rolling down the A83 towards Rest-and-be-Thankful, with the rain hammering on its windscreen and about twice the legal limit of alcohol in its blood. It had been a big day for agreements. I had secured an agreement from Maureen that nobody would learn from her about the circumstances of the death of the lunch party on the end of Ballycool Quay. Tony Greely had secured himself immunity from prosecution by agreeing to tell all about the Major; though it seemed unlikely that his business would survive. Holby had agreed that the murder of Johnny Bonneville-Clark would be attributed to what we were going to call Irish post-paramilitaries. Both these things would be sad for Miranda. But she had her Chief Constable. She would survive.

I pulled the cork out of the bottle and took a mighty swig. You are a bastard, Chance, I thought. But sod Miranda. Sod the Bonneville-Clarks, and the Major, and all fish cooks and policemen and personal assistants and bastards who were scraping the seas clean and poisoning their fellow humans and pretending they were doing politics when they were doing nasty bullying greed. Sod the lot of them.

I was partially drunk. But I was still alive, and still Gavin, who was unquestionably in free fall between a frying pan and a fire, but for the time being weightless, which was the important thing.

The phone rang. A young voice said, 'Gavin Chance Marine? Sorry to ring so late. I've got a boat I'd like to sell.'

'Send me an email,' I said. 'We'll sell her next week, or maybe the week after.'

'Really?'

'Really.'

The phone went down. I applied the boot. The pickup's needle Parkinsoned its way up to sixty, and the white line unrolled. Gavin Chance Marine hammered south, towards next week, and maybe the week after.

Author's Note

Many people have been involved in the writing of this book. I should like to thank the friends with whom I have sailed the waters of the west coast of Scotland for the past twenty years; they know who they are. I should also like to thank the people who live there, for their unfailing hospitality and kindness.

And I want to thank Terry Smallwood and Mike Kerr for their enthusiasm and support; Richenda Todd for her skill and vicelike grip on reality; Glenn Storhaug for his extraordinary grasp of the way words should look on a page; and Maggie Young, who has been deciphering the hieroglyphics since the Pharaohs ruled Egypt.

Finally, I should like to thank the birds, fish and marine mammals of the West Coast for being there, and to apologise to them in the name of the human race for the rough shake they are getting at the hands of a greed-crazed few. They know who they are too. But they don't care. Yet.